Finding Mikayla

Samantha Christy

*A*thena Books Publishing Group, LLC.
Saint Augustine, FL 32092

ISBN-13: 978-1502538031
ISBN-10: 1502538032

This one is for Ryan, may you always remember how much I love you.

Books by Samantha Christy

Be My Reason
Abstract Love
Finding Mikayla

Finding Mikayla

Samantha Christy

Prologue

Dear Jeff,

Nothing is different here since I last wrote to you. Things never change. Not anymore. That is the one reality I can count on now, other than the sun rising and setting every day. After eleven months, I've all but given up hope that we will ever get back to what we used to be. Sometimes I can't even bring myself to write about what put me here in the first place. It all seems so unreal.

Yet, I continue to write my letters to you, even if I'm the only one that will ever read them. I haven't seen you in what feels like forever, but I can still remember your strong eyes and the curves of your face. I don't need a picture to remind me of you—I can't afford myself that luxury when nobody else has the option.

In medical school, they taught us to be tough; to be the type of person others can count on in a crisis. I know that is what you would expect of me, too. I try every day not to let you down. I won't let this defeat me. I won't lose faith . . .

I'll write more later. I'm needed now.

Chapter One

"What do we have?" I ask, pulling an elastic band from my wrist to secure my long hair in a ponytail. I run over to help pull the stretcher through the front doors of the base medical clinic. I have to shield my eyes from the setting sun to get a clear look at our new patient.

"Male," Bill says. "I'd say mid-twenties. He's bad off, Doc. He ran his pickup truck straight into our rig when we came around a blind corner. He probably didn't even see us coming."

Bill tries to explain to me in detail what happened as he and Evan lift the man onto the bed in the examination area.

I quickly check his vitals. "Has he regained consciousness at all since the accident?" I ask them, flashing my pen light into the stranger's eyes.

"No," Bill answers. "But he never stopped breathing and he doesn't seem to be bleeding, other than the cuts on his arm. Must have hit his head or something, poor guy."

"Evan, can you please track down one of the nurses for me. Try the mess hall, or maybe the—"

"No need. I'm here," interrupts Holly, coming up behind me. "I heard the truck driving over here and I figured something might be wrong." I nod at her, knowing that if a crowd isn't already

3

gathering out front, it will be soon. Our few working vehicles never waste the gas to come back as far as the clinic unless there's an emergency. And word travels fast around Camp Brady.

"We can take it from here, guys. Thanks for your help," I say.

"No problem. Just let Colonel Andrews know when the guy wakes up," Evan tells me.

"Yup," I respond, "I know the procedures."

I quickly explain to Holly what I know about our patient as we check him over for injuries. I run my hands through his unruly dark-as-night hair to check for head trauma. Then I re-check his eyes, confirming that his pupils are reactive and responsive to light. Holly and I remove his clothing and do a visual inspection of his body.

"Whoa!" she says. "Kay, I know I'm a nurse and all, and that I should be used to this by now, working on all the ripped bodies of army guys for so long, but . . . wow. Can I call dibbs?"

I roll my eyes at her. "Hol, I'm not sure Tom would appreciate that much. Can we please just concentrate on the patient right now?"

"That's exactly what I'm doing. Anyway, Tom and I have an arrangement." Her eyes continue to peruse his body like a cat that has found a mouse and is eager to eat it alive. I have to admit he is nice looking, in a sexy-rugged-unconscious kind of way. He's tall, probably at least six feet. He's got muscles, but not the kind of bulging ones the soldiers around the base have. No, his look like they are from a good hard day's work, not from pumping iron for hours at the gym when there's nothing better to do around here.

Our tall, dark stranger does not appear to have much more than a few bumps and bruises. "See here," I say, pointing out a line of contusions running down his chest, "he was wearing a seat belt."

"Huh," Holly ponders. "Old habits die hard I guess."

"Good thing," I say, "it probably saved his life." I continue palpating his chest area and move on to his extremities when I see a tattoo on his left arm. "He's army." I show her the tattoo that is similar to a Caduceus except it depicts two snakes around an army knife on top of a red cross. "This is a combat medic tattoo," I tell her.

Holly's eyes snap up to meet mine. "Gorgeous *and* humane, what a combination. The colonel will surely want him to stay with his medical training. God knows you could use the help."

"We all could, Hol." I bend down to check his eyes for the third time, knowing that evidence of head trauma doesn't always present itself immediately. His pupils are still equal and reactive and I notice, now that it's not so hectic, that he has incredible sapphire-blue eyes. Not that I tell Holly, she doesn't need another reason to make her swoon over the mysterious stranger.

I love Holly Becker. She is my best friend. She is also one hell of a nurse, even learning more advanced procedures than the others, but she's kind of a wild child, a wandering soul. Her on-again-off-again boyfriend Tom, bless his heart, puts up with her because she is nice, compassionate and very beautiful. Unlike my nothing-special straight brown hair, she has glorious spirals of golden-blonde locks. She is tall and voluptuous, while I'm of average height and lack her curves. The only thing I've got on her are my deep emerald-green eyes, and maybe my trademark freckles that extend from cheek to cheek spanning my nose. I hated the freckles as a child, but once boys discovered me and thought they were attractive, I learned to embrace them.

Holly and I didn't even know each other until I came to Camp Brady, but we became friends almost instantly. We were bound not only by medicine, but the unfortunate reality that our loved ones might never return home. I watch in a trance as she cleans the abrasions on his arm.

Think, Mikayla! What's wrong with him?

His vitals are normal, he's breathing on his own, and he has no obvious injuries. It's times like this I wish a more experienced physician were around. There is only so much I can do with my limited training. After I run every test possible under the conditions, Holly and I simply make him comfortable and set up an IV to keep him hydrated. "It's a waiting game," I tell her. "If he doesn't regain consciousness within a few days, there's no telling what will happen."

She only nods. Holly knows the drill. She was once an army nurse; it's how she met her husband, Carter, a soldier and part of the 7th Infantry Brigade stationed over in Afghanistan, who are now all among the missing.

The front door of the clinic opens and Major Burnell walks in. "Hey, Dr. Kay, I hear you have a new patient."

"Hi, John," I say, knowing he prefers civilians call him by his given name. "We do, but he's still unconscious so there's not much to tell at this point. Oh, except that it appears he's a combat medic based on the tattoo on his arm."

"Really?" His eyes light up. "The colonel will be pleased if that's the case." He looks around the room. "Did he come in with any belongings? Any ID?"

"No, I don't think so," I say, "but you can check with Bill and Evan. They were the ones who brought him in."

"Alright, thanks Dr. Kay." He gives me a more-than-friendly rub of the shoulders before he turns to leave. "Don't work too hard. Maybe I'll see you at The Oasis later?" he asks, referring to the local bar and general nighttime gathering place.

"Maybe. It all depends on our new patient here," I tell him, glad to have a new excuse not to join him.

When he walks out, Holly asks, "He's still at it, huh? You'd think after almost a year of your repeated rejections he'd give up already."

I shrug my shoulders. "You can't really fault him given the high ratio of men to women around here. I don't know, maybe if it were under different circumstances, I might even date him. If he weren't so creepy, that is."

She sees my frown. "Kay, maybe you should then, or if not him, *someone*. It's been almost a year."

"I know that, Holly," I say, using her full name so that she knows I'm serious, "but I'm not ready to give up hope yet. I don't fault you or anyone else who has, but please, just respect my decision."

She walks around the bed to pull me into a hug. "Okay. And I do know how you feel. I just want you to find some sliver of happiness in this God-forsaken place." I nod my head at her and continue to embrace her while I stare down at the unconscious man lying on the bed.

The past twenty-four hours were spent with all the medical staff covering a shift—something we have to do on any occasion when one of our eight-hundred or so residents must be monitored continuously. Nancy, our oldest and most experienced nurse, took the first overnight shift. Holly and Jamie split the day shift. Jamie is a registered nurse who used to be a charge nurse at a large hospital in Tampa. She's only thirty years old but sharp as a tack. The problem with her is that she's just smart enough to think she's a know-it-all but not trained enough to actually be one. She's all too quick to point out my own limited training that ended during my second year of residency. Needless to say, we aren't BFFs.

Dr. Jacobs is the senior physician here. However, he is almost useless when it comes to practicing emergency medicine considering he's a psychiatrist who did his residency over forty years ago. He's more of the administrative head of the clinic. All eyes still look to me when it comes to urgent medical issues. At twenty-seven, it's a heavy burden to bear, but what choice do I have?

This evening, I take over for Holly who reports no change in our patient's status. I sit by the tall stranger's bed and read a book by the dim light of the setting sun shining through the window behind me. After a while, I get bored and decide to read to him. I'm a few chapters into an old Stephen King novel—not my favorite genre but pickings are slim—when he finally stirs.

"Uhh . . ." he mumbles. I quickly toss the book aside and check his vitals. He struggles to open his eyes and then under heavy lids, he looks up at me, confused and frightened.

"It's okay," I tell him, grabbing his hand to calm him. "You're going to be okay. Can you speak?" He mumbles a few incoherent words as he stares at me. This is a positive sign, but I still won't be able to assess brain function unless he can speak to me. I pull away to take my seat again, but he won't let go of my hand. He's scared—that's another positive sign. If he were severely brain damaged, he wouldn't be scared. Fear is something you only experience if you have most of your wits about you.

So I sit and hold his hand. I hold it for what seems like hours until his falls away, going limp as he slips back into unconsciousness. When I'm no longer holding it, I'm aware of the loss I feel at its absence. Of how our hands fit together like pieces of a puzzle. Of how nice it felt to have a man's hand in mine after all this time.

Holly comes to relieve me in the morning, but I send her away. "He was in and out of consciousness all night so I'm going to stay with him. Can you go by the daycare for me and check on Katie and Cole to make sure their stomach bugs are gone? And then go see if Mr. Jones is doing okay without his blood pressure meds?"

"I'm on it, boss. I'll come back later to let you have a nap." She picks up a small medical bag and heads back out the door.

The dark-haired stranger's hand keeps feeling frantically around the bed every so often when he comes to. Once I realized that he was searching for my hand, I just decided to leave it on the edge of the bed. From time to time, he will open his eyes and stare at me. Sometimes he will mumble, but so far I've been unable to understand anything.

Almost forty-eight hours after they brought him in, he fully wakes up. "Uhh . . ." he tries to speak again. He motions to his mouth with the hand that does not currently have mine in a vice grip. I know he wants a drink. His throat must be incredibly dry and scratchy after two days without taking fluids by mouth. I grab my bottle of water that is sitting on his side table.

"Have a drink, but not too much at first." He takes the bottle with a trembling hand so I help guide it to his lips. Water spills out the sides of his mouth as he's drinking like it's the last water he'll ever taste. "Whoa, hold on. Go slowly," I say, gently easing the bottle back down. "You gave us quite a scare. Can you talk? Can you tell me your name?"

"Mmm . . ." he mumbles. He takes another drink and clears his throat. "M-Mitch," he says with a low, shaky voice.

"Okay, Mitch, I'm going to check your vitals." He watches me as I take his pulse, which is understandably higher than it was before. His blood pressure and respirations are within normal range.

He breaks his stare and looks around the room at his unfamiliar surroundings. "Where . . . ?"

"You're at Camp Brady," I inform him. He looks confused so I ask him some standard questions. "Mitch, can you tell me your last name?"

"Matheson," he says.

"What about the date. Can you tell me what that is?"

He thinks about my question as his eyes shift from one side of the room to the other. "Um . . . March something?"

I look up at the makeshift calendar on the wall that has been turned to March for a couple of days now. "That's right. It's March the third. You were brought in two days ago. Do you remember anything about your accident?"

He stares at me, still confused. "I know you," he says.

"Yes. I'm the doctor who has been tending to you these past few days. You've been in and out of consciousness since you were brought in."

He looks me up and down and takes in his surroundings again. "Where are your fatigues? Is this a civilian hospital?"

"No, this is Camp Brady," I repeat, knowing he's probably still fuzzy about the details. "It's an army base, but I'm a civilian. Everyone calls me Dr. Kay, but my given name is Mikayla."

"Camp Brady?" He shakes his head. I can see that he is still clearly confused.

"Yes, Camp Brady. Just outside of Ocala, Florida, remember? You were driving your pickup truck just thirty miles or so from here when you had your accident."

"Florida?" he asks, as his body stiffens and his eyes go wide with terror. "How . . . uh, why . . .?" He looks around at the table and the floor like he's trying to locate something. "Um, can I have my cell phone?" he asks in a gravelly voice that's probably still scratchy from his dry throat. "I'd like to call a friend of mine. Maybe Kevin can explain this."

Cell phone? He's asking for a cell phone? I realize in this moment that he has a memory deficit. It's not all that uncommon to have some memory loss after an accident, but it's usually a loss of the actual event itself, or the hours and maybe days leading up to the event. He said, correctly, that it was March so I can only assume he's lost an entire year.

"Mitch, can you please tell me what year it is?" I ask him.

He looks at me like I'm asking a stupid question. When he rattles off the year, my eyes close and my chin falls to my chest as I absorb the reality of what he's revealed. Two years. He's lost two whole years. I raise my head and look around hoping Dr. Jacobs will magically appear. He is a psychiatrist. He may know what to do in this situation. But I see that the clinic is empty and Mitch and I are the only two people around.

"Uh, Mikayla is it?" Mitch asks. "You just went completely pale. Is something wrong with me?"

I try to think back to my psych rotation. Can I damage his remaining mental faculties if I tell him?

"Mikayla . . . Dr. Kay, whatever it is, just tell me," he begs.

"Mitch, first tell me the last thing you remember."

I sit in stunned silence as he tells me that he remembers flying out of a hot zone with a couple of wounded soldiers. He tells me that one of them, a young man who was only twenty years old, ended up dying from wounds sustained when a car bomb exploded, taking most of his leg off. He talks about a couple of men in his unit that he went out drinking with to toast the young fallen soldier. He tells me every detail, like it was only yesterday, and I didn't even realize that sometime during his story, he grabbed my hand and is now holding it tight to his side.

"So, you're a flight medic?" I ask.

He nods his head. "Yeah, a Sergeant." He looks around again. "How did I get to an army base in Florida? Can I please call Kevin?" Then he looks down at the ground and closes his eyes as a frown crosses his face. "Kevin is my CO, but I guess if I'm in the states I should probably call my dad."

He reaches up to grab his chest, pinching at the hospital gown between his pectorals, something I noticed a few times when he would come to. "Are you having chest pain?" I ask.

"No, why?"

"Because you keep grabbing at your chest," I say.

He looks down at himself with his own questioning glance as if his hand has a mind of its own. "No, no chest pain. I don't know why I did that." He looks back at me. "Can you please get me a phone?" He's starting to get irritated with me so I make a decision. Based on his strong vitals and the fact that he's a medic and probably would understand traumatic memory loss, I decide to tell him.

"Mitch." I take in a deep breath and blow it out. "It seems you are experiencing a gap in your memory. It may be from the accident, but without the proper equipment, I can't be sure if you have any swelling in your brain."

"Gap in my memory? What do you mean no proper equipment? Didn't you do a CT scan?"

"I'm sorry, no. We don't have a CT scanner here, but even if we did, it wouldn't work."

"Why not?" he asks, clearly in a desperate state of confusion.

"Mitch, I'm just going to come out and say it." I squeeze his hand tight, the hand that has encompassed mine throughout our entire conversation. "You've lost two years of your memory." When I tell him what year it is, he looks at me in utter disbelief so I quickly say, "Most traumatic memory loss is temporary and does return in time. Since you remembered my face from a few days ago, I'd say you have retrograde amnesia that was caused by you slamming your pickup truck into another vehicle at a high speed, causing your brain to keep moving while your skull was held back thanks to your seatbelt. It's a condition called DAI, diffuse axonal injury, and it's common in auto accidents. However, if that's what it is, you are very lucky as most people never wake up afterwards, about ninety percent if I remember correctly."

"Two years?" he asks, still trying to absorb the reality of what has happened to him. His hand is holding mine as if he will slip away if he lets go. His bright blue eyes stare into mine begging for answers.

I pray what I'm about to tell him won't send his body spiraling into a state of shock. "Mitch, there's more."

He senses my hesitation and must realize that what I'm going to tell him is even worse than the two-year memory loss he is experiencing. He says, "You can tell me. I'm a combat medic. I'm trained to handle stressful situations. I won't freak out on you. I'm fine. Just tell me, Mikayla."

Why is it that I love the way he calls me Mikayla? The way my name rolls over his tongue is sensual and sends a twinge of . . . something running through me. I close my eyes briefly and then I tell him. "It happened about a year ago, on March 31st to be exact,

Easter Sunday. As best we can tell, there was a solar flare, one so large that it caused an EMP, an electromagnetic pulse, that took out anything with a semiconductor or microchip, which was virtually everything electronic."

He looks around the clinic and realizes what he missed before. There are no overhead fluorescent lights on, no humming of medical machines or beeping of monitors. He looks down at his IV insertion site and then glances up at the IV bag that is infusing on a gravity drip. He notices that the room is devoid of technology, resembling what you might see in an early nineteenth century clinic, not the advanced medical clinic he was expecting.

"Oh, my God," he says with a pale face as he realizes the truth of the words I've just spoken.

Chapter Two

I feel like I've explained everything until I'm blue in the face, but Mitch keeps asking questions. I'm trying to be patient. I can only imagine what it must be like to lose two years of your life only to wake up in a different world. It must seem like a dream. I remember when for the first few weeks, even though I lived through it, I still thought I would wake up one day and realize none of it was real.

"So, how many people are out there? How many other communities like this exist?" Mitch asks.

"We're still not sure. It's taken a long time to get the small amount of information that we have. We know there are other places because we've reached them by short-wave radio. Most are small, like we are, but nobody will reveal their location for security reasons. And if the government predictions were right, the general population will have been reduced by seventy to ninety percent after an event such as this. We are lucky, we only lost thirty percent, and that was pretty early on. Most of our casualties were insulin-dependent diabetics, heart patients, people on dialysis, and others with medical conditions that required drugs or equipment that we didn't have."

"How do you get supplies?" he asks. "Surely the army didn't stockpile enough for this kind of event."

"We have a team that goes out every other week or so. Once the obvious places like grocery stores, box warehouses and gas stations were cleaned out, they moved on to housing developments. They were out scouting supplies when they found you. Or, more accurately, when you ran into them."

"Did they give you any of my belongings?" he asks.

I shake my head, knowing how difficult it must be not to have a sliver of information about your past. "I'm sorry, no. When they get back over in the area, they've promised to look for anything you might have had. But it will be quite some time before they cover that area again, and they can't waste any fuel just to look for your things."

He doesn't even put up an argument. Being in the army, he must realize everyone has a task and can't deviate from their orders. He continues to question me about our camp. "What about food and water?" he asks.

"Water was never an issue. The camp actually backs up to Silver Springs, a nature preserve with numerous artesian wells that supply water from the aquifer. As for food, we're lucky enough to be here in central Florida where the land is nearly perfect for farming and ranching. We managed to bring in locals early on who wanted security in exchange for their expertise and resources."

"You have farms here on the base?" He looks surprised.

"Yes, some are where the old shooting ranges resided, but most are on land extending to the far, previously unused, corners of the base's acreage. When you are well enough to leave, I'll give you a tour if you would like."

Ignoring my offer he asks, "How do you handle security? Surely there are outsiders that want what you have in here. From what I've heard so far, you are doing pretty well."

I belatedly realize that it's not my place to divulge this kind of information. But the ease and odd familiarity of him has made me want to keep talking. I shake my head. "I've probably said too much as it is. Colonel Andrews will be by shortly to talk to you. I'm sure he will ask you to stay since your medical training will come in handy. That is, if you decide you want to be here," I say. I want him to stay. Of course I want him to stay, but as I look into his eyes, I start to question if my desires are purely medical, or if I have other reasons for wanting him here.

$$\sim \ \sim \ \sim$$

"Kay, are you even listening to a word I've said?"

I look over to see Holly glowering at me. "Uh . . . sorry," I say, reaching over to shuffle some papers that didn't need shuffling.

She looks over to where I was staring and sees the colonel talking with Mitch. She raises an eyebrow at me. "What's so interesting in there? Are you worried that Mitch won't stay on?"

"Of course I am," I say. "From a purely medical standpoint. He would be a great addition to our team."

"Uh huh . . . and not too hard on the eyes either," she says, smirking at me.

I ignore her comment. "I wonder what it would be like to wake up and realize that two years of your life were gone . . . erased . . . forgotten. I didn't see a wedding ring, but that doesn't mean he's not married. Some men don't wear one. A lot can happen over the course of two years."

"Mmm hmm." Holly smiles over at me.

"What?" I snap at her.

"It's just that of all the things to wonder about—how he survived, where he got a truck, why he was alone—you chose to wonder if he's married."

I roll my eyes at her as Colonel Andrews comes out of Mitch's room.

"Dr. Parker," he addresses me, always being more formal than anyone else, "Sergeant Matheson will be staying on."

"Really?" I say, with maybe a little too much enthusiasm.

I feel a wave of relief surge through my body. I try to convince myself that the sole reason is that he can help us provide better medical care to the masses.

"Well, I had to promise him a trip outside the gates," he says. "He wants to see it for himself. It must be difficult not remembering any of it. But even as sketchy as his memory may be, he seems to remember his medical training like it was yesterday. As soon as you see fit, discharge him and show him the ropes. Get him acquainted with the community and take him to the PX to get his allotted provisions. Have him report to me after he decides where to hang his hat. I trust you can help him with all of that?"

"Of course, Colonel," I say.

When he walks out the door, Holly turns to me smiling. "Get him acquainted with the community? Show him the ropes? Well, Kay, what an interesting job for the town doctor." She winks at me.

"Give it a rest, Hol."

"Mikayla?" Mitch calls from his room.

"Mikayla?" Holly whispers to me with raised eyebrows. I ignore her stare and go in to see what Mitch needs.

"So, you've decided to stay?" I ask.

"Where else would I go?" he says. "Anyway, I kind of like the scenery."

I furrow my brow at him. "But you haven't even seen the place yet."

He just stares at me until I understand the meaning behind his statement. Then I blush, searching my mind for something . . . anything to say. "Uh, what can I do for you before I head out?" I ask.

"Head out?" he asks, and I think I see the hint of a scowl.

"Yes, I have plans." I check his vitals again as long as I'm standing here. "Girls' Night."

He laughs. "You still do that? Even after . . . everything?"

"Yes. We have to maintain some semblance of normalcy around here. We have an operational PX, organized activities and sports, even a night club. You'll see when I show you around."

"And when might that be? I'm feeling much better, pretty good in fact," he says, looking up at me with hopeful eyes.

"We'll see, Mitch. You were unconscious for two days. Let's give it a day or so before you go running any marathons, okay?"

"But it's boring here," he whines. I can't help but think of my boyfriend, Jeff, who would do the very same thing on his days off from the hospital. That man could not sit still even if I had stapled his ass to a chair. I get the feeling Mitch is one of those guys, always moving, continuously on the go, forever needing to keep his hands busy. Lying here in a hospital bed is probably torture for him. Just one more reason he will be an asset to the base.

"I hear Nancy loves to play Gin Rummy. Do you play?" I tease him.

"Gin Rummy? And . . . Nancy? Don't get me wrong, she's great and all, but what would I have to do to get *you* to stay? Maybe you could read to me some more."

I look at him, surprised. "You remember that?"

He nods his head. "It was very soothing—the sound of your voice. It's the first thing I remember from after the accident." He looks up at me with those sapphire eyes, begging me to give in to him.

Dammit, I don't want to miss a night with the girls. It is one of the things that helps keep my sanity intact in this insane world. I try to think of a way to accommodate him.

"I have an idea that might satisfy us both," I tell him. "I could move Girls' Night here."

"Huh?" He looks at me like I'm crazy, and I giggle when I realize that he has no idea what a post-apocalyptic Girls' Night entails. It's certainly not limo rides and bar-hopping.

"Sure, I don't see why not," I say. "We just play poker and stuff. You are the only patient here so we wouldn't be bothering anyone else. And Nancy would probably love me for it, she hates working nights. Me—I can sleep anywhere. It's something I learned to do pretty quickly when I was a resident."

His eyes light up. "You play poker?" he asks.

"You know this is an army base, right?"

He laughs at me and the deep rumbly sound coming from him is doing strange things to my body. "Yes, but I've just never played with a bunch of girls before. This should be fun," he says.

"Oh, no," I tell him. "You can watch from here. Girls only, that's the rule. Or no deal."

He takes a minute as he contemplates whether or not to argue with me. "Fine." He frowns. "But will you still read to me after?"

"Are your eyes broken?" I ask him. "Or did you simply forget how to read?"

"Are you really making jokes about my memory loss, Mikayla?" He looks hurt and suddenly I feel terrible about my comment.

"Oh, God, Mitch. I'm so sorry, I didn't mean—"

He cuts me off with his laughter and huge face-splitting smile that just makes those damn sapphires sparkle. "You are way too easy . . . I'm kidding, Mikayla."

I shake my head at him. I've forgotten what it's like to have any man other than my good friend, Austin, joke around with me. "You'll pay for that one, Matheson. Maybe I'll torture you by reading *Little Women* or *Pride and Prejudice* later."

"Anything is fine with me as long as I get to hear your voice," he says.

My insides quiver at his statement. Then I'm startled by Dr. Jacobs' voice behind me. "Dr. Kay, can I speak with you for a minute?" I turn around to see him standing in the doorway.

"Duty calls," I say to Mitch. "I'll check back on you later."

"I look forward to it." He smiles at me as I leave the room. And I realize that the only reason I know that is because I turned around to look.

"Dr. Jacobs, what can I do for you?"

He tells me about his examination of Mitch earlier in the day. He concurs with my diagnosis of DAI. He warns me that with a lack of familiar people and possessions to spark his memories that it may take longer than normal to regain his memory. "How's his behavior been?" he asks.

"Normal, I guess. He's a nice guy, ready to get up and wanting to lend a hand here at the clinic."

"That's good. That's a good sign," he says. "No depression that you've seen over his memory loss?"

"Not that I can tell. In fact, he's been a bit flirty. He seems to fancy me."

Dr. Jacobs nods his head. "That's not at all unusual in these cases. You were there when he was in and out of consciousness, and you were the first person he saw when he woke up so you are the only familiar person to him. It's natural for him to grasp onto that."

Neither of us can come up with any reason to keep him in the clinic after tonight since he's showing no signs of serious brain injury, but we agree to keep a close eye on him over the next few weeks.

After my meeting with Dr. Jacobs, I emerge to find Amanda in the front room. Amanda is a nursing assistant. She is wonderful and has been very helpful around the clinic, even taking on some of the more complicated nursing procedures when needed. She is holding her one-year-old daughter, Rachel, who is just about my favorite person in the world.

"Kaykay!" She toddles over to me with outstretched arms.

I pick her up and plant a kiss on her full, rosy lips. "Hey, baby girl. You are so pretty today." I take in her stick-straight auburn hair and brown eyes that make her the mirror image of her mom.

"Want, want." She pulls at one of the many hair ties that I keep around my wrist—a habit I got into in med school to always be able to pull my hair back at a moment's notice. I give her one which keeps her busy for a few minutes while I talk to Amanda.

"Are we still on for tonight?" she asks.

"Of course," I say, "but can we change our location? I'd like to move it here so I can keep an eye on Mitch. That is if you don't think the others will mind."

She arches an eyebrow at me and gives me that look that only a friend can give that says a thousand words without ever speaking.

"Good God," I say with an eye roll for emphasis. "You've been talking to Holly, haven't you?"

"Well, she is our roommate, Kay," she reminds me.

"Holly is somewhat delusional when it comes to men. You should know that by now." I shake my head at her. Amanda puts a gentle hand on my arm. She understands me.

Holly and I, along with Amanda and her daughter share a little three-bedroom apartment. Pam, my other good friend who works over at the daycare, used to live with us as well, with her two-year-old son, but she moved out to live with her boyfriend.

I have categorized the women around base in one of two ways. The *haves* and the *have-nots*. The *haves* are those that have moved on and accepted the fact that their significant others may never return from overseas. Of my friends, this includes Holly and Pam. Amanda and I, on the other hand, belong to the *have-nots*. She is twenty-two years old with a small child—someone you might expect to move on quickly, but she hasn't. In fact, she will tell you that she's absolutely sure that her husband will find his way back to them. Although I belong to the latter group, I'm not sure I share Amanda's unwavering optimism about our men ever returning. I mean, if they are as bad off as we are, surely they have fewer resources than we have here. Still, I know if there was any way Jeff could return to me, he would.

"I'm sure everyone will be fine with moving it here. I'll leave a note for Holly at home and track down Pam and the others." She goes to leave and looks around for Rachel, who seems to have found her way into Mitch's room where he is sitting on the floor with her, putting her hair into a ponytail.

Amanda and I look at them and then at each other before we crack up into a fit of giggles. She says to me, "He's a keeper . . . for someone anyway." I nod my head in agreement, mildly aware, but trying to deny the little twinge of jealously that is working its way through my body at the thought of who that someone might be.

We walk into the room and Rachel looks up at us with her adorable little cherub-like face. Her hair is now nicely secured in a ponytail that looks like it's been done by a tried-and-true mom, not a combat medic. It makes me wonder what he's been missing these past few years. Does he have a daughter? Surely not one old enough to have the length of hair to require a ponytail. He only lost two years. That's not enough time to have had a pregnancy and child that he doesn't remember. Step-daughter maybe? I run through scenarios in my head of how this manly-man would know how to interact with and do the hair of a one-year-old.

He sees us staring at him in awe and wonder and says, "Nieces. Lots of them." I release the breath I was holding and look over at Amanda who is shaking her head and smirking at me. Then I look back to Mitch and see him frowning. I can only imagine that he's wondering about the fate of his nieces, and the rest of his family, much like we all are. That is something we all have in common with him even though we haven't lost time like he has.

His smile returns when Rachel squeals, "Mish, Mish!" as she climbs into his lap.

Amanda's jaw drops. "Wow, she never warms up to anyone this easily. You must have incredible uncle skills."

He smiles and continues to play with Rachel. Seeing him play with the toddler reminds me of the conversations Jeff and I would have. I wanted kids—want kids—but he always said it would be better to wait until I was done with my residency to get married and start a family. I look at Rachel and see the love and joy she brings to Amanda's life and I wonder why anyone would want to wait to experience that. People did it all the time, had kids during residency. But we were so completely focused on our careers. Now, I wish I had a child. I wish I had a small piece of Jeff to remind me that life can still be filled with happiness. Rachel knows no other world, yet she is as happy and carefree as any child I had ever come across in the past. This isn't the first time in the last year that I've regretted not having a child, but it's the first time that I've had this desperate feeling of wanting and emptiness. I just wonder which of the two people on the floor could fill it.

Chapter Three

When the girls start showing up, I run home to get my stuff while they set up for the poker game on folding tables out in the main room of the clinic. Back at my apartment, I grab my poker backpack from my bedroom and look around to see what else I can add to it. We haven't played in a few weeks so surely there is something I can find. On my way out the door, I pick up a copy of an old Nora Roberts book I've read a dozen times and stick it under my arm.

Everyone is ready to play by the time I get back. Pam, Amanda and Holly are here. The four of us are the core players. We never miss a game. There are some other girls that show up when they can, and we usually end up with anywhere between our core group of four up to about eight players. Tonight, Nancy's daughter, Susan, and Pam's friend and fellow daycare worker, Michelle, have joined us. I smile, knowing that there's sure to be new additions to the pot.

Michelle has two young boys and is one of the lucky few who has an intact family. Her husband was home and living on base with her at the time of the blackout. I ask her, "Did your husband get babysitting duty?"

"Yup," she says, spreading out her stash that has some of the others going bug-eyed.

We set an oil lamp on the table in the room that is quickly darkening due to the setting sun. I glance over in Mitch's direction and see that he's been given a lamp of his own and is reading a book in the low, glimmering flicker of light. He looks up and catches me watching him. I see a smile creep up his face, and he tips his chin up at me before I quickly look away.

Thirty minutes later, I've won a couple of hands, and have just been dealt another decent hand. But I know how badly some of the other girls want to win this round so I fold almost immediately.

"Kay?" Holly looks at me like I'm crazy. "Don't you even want to draw a card?"

I shake my head at her. "Nope. My cards suck," I lie. "I'm not going to waste anything else on this hand. What the hell would I do with three condoms anyway?"

Simultaneously, we all look over to see Mitch choking on a drink of water he just took while standing in the doorway to his room, trying to silently watch us. "Uh . . ." He looks at me in confusion as he takes a closer look at the poker table. "Just what kind of poker are you playing anyway?"

The girls and I look at the table then at each other, and when it hits us, we all laugh. And by laugh, I'm talking big belly-laugh, like hope-your-bladder-is-empty laugh. When the laughter dies down, we look back at Mitch and it starts all over again. I watch his eyes peruse the table and gaze from seat to seat to take in what we have placed before us. There are piles of tampons, a razor, a few travel-sized bottles of conditioner, some shaving cream, condoms, cigarettes, books, and some partially used makeup and deodorant.

When I stop laughing enough to speak, I say to him, "I told you, girls only."

When he manages to wipe the surprised look off his face and turn around to march back into his room, the table falls into another fit of laughter. I suddenly realize how good it feels to be happy, even if it's just for this moment, even though it's a fleeting feeling. I haven't laughed this hard in . . . well, since before *it* happened. I look back into Mitch's room and see him trying to read again, but the large smile on his face tells me that he's doing anything but. He looks up and, dammit, he catches me watching him again which does nothing to stifle his silly grin. I roll my eyes at him and go back to playing poker. Holly kicks me under the table and gives me a knowing smirk. I shoot her my 'WTF' look to wipe it clean off her face.

Mitch wisely stays put in his room for the next few hours. Then, the front door opens and in walks Austin. I smile at him as he walks up and greets all the women at the table. He comes over behind me, puts his hands on my shoulders, and reaches down to kiss my cheek. I almost instinctively look over at Mitch to see him eyeing Austin with a solicitous stare, and I don't exactly know why, but I wiggle out of Austin's grasp as I feign an itch on my leg.

Austin is most definitely my best guy friend. He too, is missing someone overseas. His wife, Shannon, is an army nurse who was deployed for the first time just weeks before everything happened. Austin and I have established somewhat of a sibling relationship, and although he is three years my junior, he has taken on the role of big brother and protector—and given that he's about twice my size that's not hard for him to do. I'm actually surprised it has taken him three days to get over here. The rumor mill usually spreads quickly around this camp. I'm guessing he hasn't talked to Holly.

"Where's the fresh meat?" he asks me, knowing good and well that Mitch is in the next room listening and watching everything that is going on out here.

I stand up and walk towards Mitch's room. "Come on, I'll introduce you."

Mitch puts down the book he was pretending to read when we walk in. I have to press my lips together to keep myself from giggling when Mitch visibly puffs out his chest as Austin follows me through the door. Mitch looks like one of those birds I remember seeing on some nature channel that makes itself bigger to become more attractive to the opposite sex, or stave off the enemy, I forget which. He might as well give up. Even as tall and built as Mitch is, there aren't many men that are as big and buff as Austin's six-foot-six, two-hundred-fifty-pound frame of pure muscle. I have to say that sometimes he comes in handy as my personal bodyguard. No man in his right mind would cross him in order to get to me. Of course, by now, everyone here knows that Austin is really a softy-at-heart. Everyone but Mitch, that is.

"Sergeant Austin Begley, meet Sergeant Mitch Matheson," I say.

Austin steps over to the bed. Mitch sits up as tall as he possibly can and extends a hand to him.

"Nice to meet you, Mitch," Austin says, shaking Mitch's hand. I have to hold in my giggle when this big lug grimaces at Mitch's grip. "I thought I'd better come rescue you when I heard the Tupperware party was moved to the clinic. I wouldn't want you to grow a vagina or anything." The two of them laugh when I swat Austin in the back of the head.

They start talking army so I bow out. "Okay then, I'll just leave you two to your testosterone and go back to my game." Austin dismisses me with his hand like he can't be bothered to acknowledge me properly. See—brother. Mitch, however, follows me with his eyes as I walk all the way back to the table. I know this because Holly doesn't hesitate to tell me as soon as I sit down next to her.

"He can't take his eyes off you, you know," she says.

"It's nothing. Florence Nightingale syndrome, Hol," I whisper to keep our conversation private. "You should know that as well as anyone. You've probably had hundreds of patients fall for you." With her incredible looks and her compassionate bedside manner I'm surprised Holly's real name isn't Florence.

"Just hundreds? What, have I lost my touch?" she teases.

An hour later, the troops disband and Austin walks some of the girls home. Not that they need an escort around here. But it's nice to know chivalry isn't dead along with the rest of the world.

"Are you going to show me your winnings?" Mitch says from the doorway of his room.

"Only if you get back into bed. You are still my patient until tomorrow." I point at his bed through the flickering light of his oil lamp. "In fact, you are still my patient until I can confidently say you haven't sustained any lasting injuries, and who knows how long that will take." I silently wonder how long I can get away with finding excuses to take his vitals and shine my pen light into those alluring eyes.

"Yes ma'am," he says as he salutes me.

"Oh, God." I roll my eyes. "Don't ever call me ma'am unless you really want to turn me off." Then, realizing what I said, my eyes go wide and I think I turn two shades of red. I'm glad he, more than likely, can't see my embarrassment in the relative darkness. "And Colonel Andrews will court-martial you if you joke around about saluting," I tease.

"Duly noted . . . Mikayla."

My name rolls off his tongue like an ice-cream cone melts over your fingers on a hot day. I contemplate for about two seconds asking him to call me Dr. Kay like everyone else. But I don't, and that sends a tiny splinter of guilt right into my heart.

I pour the contents of my bag onto his hospital bed, spilling out my winnings as well as the stash I brought with me. I did pretty well tonight. I'm up about twenty cigarettes. I also got a small sample bottle of perfume, a new razor, and a couple of books I haven't yet read. I quickly gather up all the tampons and push them back into my bag.

"Cigarettes? You don't smoke, do you? I mean you smell so good."

I try not to notice that my skin prickles a little at his comment. "No, I don't smoke, but a lot of soldiers do, and cigarettes are like gold around here. They will trade just about anything for them. Well, except liquor, that's pretty much like gold, too."

"So, how do you decide who gets what around camp?"

"Our basic needs are all free and taken care of. Food, water, shelter, basic clothing, and medication if we have it, are all provided. But the so-called luxury items are all 'for sale' at the PX. The scouts that go on supply runs bring back not only necessities, but they find lots of other stuff that makes life seem a little more normal. Each resident is allotted a certain number of credits per week to spend at the PX. You'll see when I give you the grand tour tomorrow—if you're up for it."

He snaps his eyes away from my stash and up to mine. "Hell, yes! I hate sitting in this damn bed. I'm useless here, and if I have to stay much longer I'll go plain crazy. Then Dr. Jacobs would *really* have to help me." We laugh and I get that he already understands that Dr. Jacobs is more of a figure head than anything else around here.

"So," he says, looking at me expectantly, "is it going to be . . . what was it, *Little Women*?"

I thought he was kidding, but it looks like he really wants me to read to him. I bet, and lost, the Nora Roberts book I was going to read so I pick up the same old Stephen King novel that I swear weighs as much as little Rachel and I sit down in the chair next to the bed.

Not fifteen minutes later, I realize that Mitch is asleep. He must still be getting over his injuries. I hope there isn't anything I've missed, but without the proper equipment, I just can't be sure. I stare at him in the dancing light of the lamp and notice things that I didn't before. Or maybe I notice things that I didn't want to before. He has very distinct cheekbones, a square jaw and a narrow face that boasts an incredibly sexy almost-beard that is evidence of his lack of shaving for a week or so. He has long, dark eyelashes that most women would kill for and his complexion is flawless. I look down at his hands, resting comfortably at his sides and suddenly I feel empty not holding one in mine as I sit next to him.

I shake my head as if the motion of it will remove the unbefitting thoughts from my mind. I turn the lamp down to the lowest flame and get out a piece of paper to pen a new letter.

Dear Jeff,

A combat medic showed up a few days ago. In some strange way, he makes me feel closer to you. Unfortunately, he has retrograde amnesia and there is absolutely nothing I can do for him. I'm sure you would know of some spectacular new-fangled theory that we could try on him. I'll bet not even the apocalypse can hold you back from advancing the face of medicine.

I think that's why you would hate it here. Everything is calm, laid back . . . slow. Holly hates it here. She is an army nurse who did two tours, so like you, she was always on the go. I think you'd like her. She'd try to suck all the knowledge out of your head.

We played poker tonight. It's hard to believe that I never used to take the time for such trivial activities, yet now these are the things I look forward to the most. I hope you have found something to enhance your life and keep you busy until you can make your way back to me.

Until next time. All my love,

Kay

Chapter Four

I wake up in an unfamiliar bed. I look around the room and realize I'm still in the clinic. But I don't remember ever walking into the other patient room. I wipe the sleep from my eyes and get out of bed only to see Mitch standing in the doorway, fully dressed in the same clothes that he was wearing the day he was brought in. We laundered them of course, and as my eyes wander over him, I take in the dark jeans that fit his body so well along with the snug blue t-shirt that brings out the blue in his eyes even from across the room. He runs a hand through his unruly dark hair and says, "It's about time. I've been waiting for you to wake up."

I look around the room again. "How did I get here? The last I remember, I was dozing off in your room."

"I woke up and saw you asleep in the chair. It couldn't have been very comfortable so I carried you in here."

"Carried me in here? Mitch, you shouldn't be doing things like that right now." As I say the words, I also feel the slight disappointment of not being able to remember his hands picking me up and carrying me across the clinic. I try to push the thought from my mind, just as I try to un-remember the dream that is flashing back to me right now about a dark-haired stranger. Jeff— he is the man I dream about. He is the brilliant surgeon that has taught me so much. I don't dream about anything or anyone else. Not ever—or at least not in the 455 days since I've seen him. There are plenty of men around base. Attractive men. Available men. Why is this *one* man affecting me in ways that I don't understand?

"Are you kidding? You're as light as a feather," he says. "I wasn't about to let you sleep in that chair all night. You would have awakened with a very sore neck." He looks down at his wrist as if a watch were on it. "Now, how long do I have to wait to blow this popsicle stand?"

I laugh. I imagine that after four days here, he wants to get going, especially since he has no idea what awaits him outside those doors.

"Shower first," I say.

"Okay, but I draw the line at washing your feet."

A blush comes over me as he raises a suggestive eyebrow. "Were you always like this," I ask, "or has your accident caused you to turn into a wiseass?"

"I like to think of it as charm. And yes, it's one of my endearing qualities."

"One of them?" I ask. I mentally smack my forehead because I really don't want him to run down a list for me.

He shakes his head at me with a smug smile. "A shower would be nice, Mikayla. Thank you."

I go into his room to strip the bed sheets only to see he's already done it for me. Amanda's words from yesterday echo through my head. *He's a keeper.*

I gather up my backpack and walk out into the main area where he is waiting for me. "Shower first, then food. After that, we'll spend the day getting you acquainted with the base. You'll have to tell me if you get too tired. I don't want you overdoing it on your first day."

"Don't worry about me. I'm tougher than I look." He gives me a wink. "Anyway, if I do collapse, I'm in good hands, right?"

Jamie comes through the front door for her shift. She eyes Mitch all dressed in his street clothes and it's more than obvious what she's thinking when her jaw drops slightly as she takes him in from head to toe. "You're leaving?" she asks, with a look of disappointment. "Do you think that's a good idea?"

"Mitch has been cleared by both Dr. Jacobs and me. We'll keep a close eye on him for a while just to make sure."

"Oh." She looks directly at Mitch. "Can I show you around after my shift?" she asks, practically batting her eyelashes at him.

I roll my eyes at her. Must she try to garner the attention of *every* man in camp?

"Thanks for the offer," he says to her. He turns to look at me and he continues, "But Colonel Andrews assigned Mikayla here to give me the grand tour."

"Mikayla?" she says, my name laced with disgust.

"I know everyone around here calls her Dr. Kay, but I think Mikayla has a nice ring to it, don't you?" he asks her.

"Whatever." She walks straight past us and into the office.

I shout after her. "Jamie, don't forget that Mr. Skala is coming in this morning for his checkup!"

I turn back to Mitch. "Pneumonia," I say. "We don't see a lot in the way of colds and flu anymore, but every once in a while someone will pick up a nasty bug. At least there's no shortage of antibiotics. The army stockpiled plenty of those." I walk towards the door. "But we'll wait on the clinic orientation until you start work. Today, we find you a place to live and tour the base."

When we emerge from the clinic and Mitch gets his first look at our little community, he stops in his tracks and puts a hand on my arm.

"What is it?" I ask, feeling the slight burning of my flesh where he's touching me.

He shakes his head as he looks around and takes everything in. "I don't know," he says. "I guess I expected to walk into something from the Wild West. You know, with dust balls, tall weeds, and dilapidated buildings. But whatever I thought, it wasn't this."

I try to see it through Mitch's eyes. I guess it would seem strange to some that we have appealing grounds adorned with flowers and freshly cut green grass. I explain, "Some of the older ladies have taken it upon themselves to beautify the grounds. They even found one of those old lawn clippers to keep the grass cut. And you'll probably see them out here watering the landscaping every day that it doesn't rain."

Mitch cocks his head in wonder so I add, "It's nice for people to have a hobby, you know, to keep their mind off everything. We're trying to make things as normal as possible around here. Seeing the beautiful flowers is just part of that. It reminds you to stop and smell the roses even after all that's happened."

"Do you have any?" he asks.

"What, flowers?"

"No . . . hobbies. Do you have a hobby, Mikayla?"

A smile plays on my lips when I think about how I spend much of my free time. "Not so much a hobby. I guess it's more like a passion." I point over in the direction of the barracks. "Behind the barracks there are horse stables. Early on, we realized that we would need transportation, so in addition to all the bikes we could find, we took in local farmers who would bring their horses. I had never ridden before. But the first time I looked a horse in the eye, I knew I had found a kindred spirit. I go out as often as I can."

Mitch looks at me with fascination, so I ask, "What?"

"My granddad had a farm just east of Sacramento where I grew up," he says. "He had a half-dozen horses. I was practically raised along with those horses."

"Oh, so you know how to ride—that will simplify things when we take a tour of the grounds."

His eyes light up. "That will be great!" he says. "It's been forever since I've ridden." He reaches up to grasp the material of the shirt over his chest like I've seen him do so many times in the past few days. "At least I think it has." He looks to the ground as he obviously mourns the years that he has lost.

We stand in front of the clinic as I point out the general location of everything around camp. To our left is the old commissary, which isn't in use anymore, and the PX, which is our version of Walmart. Beyond those are the chapel, the old bank, and the old post office. To our right, down a winding road is the housing development. I explain, "Some people still live there, but not many because it's a hike back to the main camp."

"Does everyone live in the barracks?" he asks.

"Most do. Some of us have gotten together to live in the apartments over there between the barracks and the daycare center." I point them out over the top of the community center. "The good news about the barracks is that you don't have to use your own lantern or flashlight. The barracks have been allotted community lanterns. Of course the downside is that everyone sleeps in bunks in very close quarters."

"Where do you live?" he asks.

"I room with Holly, Amanda and Rachel in a three-bedroom apartment. We pool our resources and it works for us." We start walking down the sidewalk across from the medical center. "The only other downside to the apartments is the latrine situation. The barracks have community latrines. However, it's about a hundred-yard walk from the apartments. You can make your own latrine behind the apartment building, but then you are responsible for it."

"Who takes care of the community latrines?" he asks.

I laugh because there's a story behind the answer to his question. "That would be Lieutenant Camden."

Mitch furrows a brow at me when he asks, "You have an officer on latrine duty?"

I nod my head and tell him the story as we walk over to the community center. "Jerry's wife was in labor with twins when the base lost all electricity. He was so distraught over her difficult labor that he got some enlisted men to help him get out the generator and some other medical equipment from a Faraday cage." I tell him that the base had two Faraday cages specifically for events such as this. "A Faraday cage is a hardened room that protects electronics from things like solar flares, EMPs and nuclear attacks."

"I know what a Faraday cage is, Mikayla." He rolls his eyes at me so I elbow him in the ribs.

He doubles over in pain so I quickly run my hands along his rib cage to check for injuries as I apologize to him. "Mitch, I'm so sorry. Are you okay?" When my eyes meet his and see them dancing with laughter, I punch his arm—right over his sexy medic tattoo.

"You are so easy," he says, laughing, as I start to walk away in a huff. He pulls me back by my hand and says, "So, he got assigned to latrine duty for breaking the rules? My guess is that the first pulse was followed sometime later by a second one that took out any equipment you had pulled from the cage."

I notice a twinge race up my arm and I realize it's because he hasn't released my hand yet. When I look at our entwined hands, he follows my gaze. He pulls his hand away then gives me a shrug and a smile.

"Yes, Lt. Camden broke the rules by getting the equipment out too soon. But he is one of the happiest men around camp. He never complains about having, as he says, 'the crappiest job on base.' He's got two healthy boys, so it was all worth it."

We are almost to the community center, the main hub of camp, when he asks, "You said you had two Faraday cages. What about the second?"

I shake my head. "It's just a generator and some minor medical equipment. We only use it in case of emergencies at the clinic. We used it for you the day you came here, to run an EKG. We can also run a ventilator and a nebulizer, and run lights and fans, of course, but that's about it."

I give him a tour of the community center which, thankfully, has lots of activities to keep the masses busy. There are some pool and Ping-Pong tables, shuffleboard, a gym, even two bowling lanes—which we set up by hand. At the far end of the center is The Oasis—the base bar and grill that has simply become a nightly hangout for the adults.

Mitch eyes the empty bowling lanes and looks at me inquisitively. "Oh no," I say. "We need to get you settled first. Plus, you have nothing to wager yet." I grin at him.

"Do I have to have some kind of makeup or tampons for you to play me?" He winks.

My face heats up. "No, but when you have a roll of toilet paper, come find me."

He laughs. Then, realizing what I just said, his eyes go wide as the actuality of our situation hits him. I walk him over to the far doors of the community center so that we will emerge on the opposite side. He once again holds the door for me. I take him through the barracks, and then the dining hall next to them. To the left of those is the old Burger King and coffee shop. Towards the front of the base is the gas station, where we hand pump gas into the few working vehicles that are still in operation. Across from that is a large outdoor recreation area with a baseball and soccer field.

"So, Sgt. Matheson," I say, "where would you like to call home?"

He looks around at the camp, turning his body in each direction as he takes it all in. I'm watching him as he absorbs the reality of what happened almost a year ago. I wonder how long it will take before he demands that off-base trip to see the outside world. Civilians aren't allowed past the main gates unless there are extreme circumstances, but he is army. I've only been out once since I arrived the very day of the event, and that was to help save a trapped woman who would have died without immediate medical attention. It wasn't until then, almost six months ago, that I fully realized the scope of the situation. I also realized how nice we have it here. Our little community is somewhat of a post-apocalyptic utopia. As I watch Mitch view each facet of our camp, I hope he comes to see it that way, too. A part of me wonders if he will leave once his memory returns. Surely he was searching for someone, being that he was on the road alone.

All of a sudden I find myself wishing, just a little, that he never recovers his memory. And the guilt I feel over that floods through me like a tsunami.

"Are there any apartments left?" he asks, pulling me back from my thoughts.

I hesitate to even tell him. I shouldn't say the words, but somehow they come out anyway. "You can ask Austin about rooming with him. His roommate recently moved in with my friend, Pam, leaving Austin alone in his apartment."

The apartment that is directly across the hall from mine.

Chapter Five

Mitch and I head over to the barracks for a shower. I brought clean clothes in my backpack, but he hasn't been issued any yet—that comes later. I look at him guiltily and say, "I hope you don't mind putting those same clothes back on. We did wash them for you so they are fresh."

He cocks his head to the side and replies, "I did two tours in the sand pit, Mikayla. I think I can handle it."

I smile at him. "Right . . . sorry," I say, with a wrinkle of my nose that leaves him staring at my face.

The sun is bright this morning as he examines me and I wonder momentarily if yesterday's eyeliner is smudged down my cheek. In our hurry to leave the clinic, I didn't even look in the mirror. Ordinarily, I don't wear makeup. But, yesterday when I went home to grab my overnight bag and poker supplies, I was compelled to put some on. I was sprucing up for Girls' Night. Or at least that's what I tried to convince myself I was doing. I think back over the past year and can probably count on one hand the number of times that I bothered with my appearance. It was usually because the community was having an organized affair such as a dance, or when the girls and I got together to give makeovers out of sheer boredom.

I quickly run a finger under my eyes to wipe up any stray liner when Mitch says, "You have the most unique pattern of freckles spanning your nose. It really does flatter your face."

Heat creeps up from my neck as a blush warms over me. *What is wrong with me?* John doles out compliments to me left and right without my body betraying me like this. "Uh . . ." I'm flustered as we enter the barracks. I point him in the direction of the men's showers. "You can wash me over there."

Mitch snickers at me as my mind replays what just came out of my mouth. "I mean, you can wash up over there." I turn in the direction of the ladies' showers and walk away, but what I really want to do is dig a hole in the ground and stick my head into it.

I stand under the tepid stream of water, that only gets slightly warmed making its way through the long maze of pipes from the aquifer, and I try to wash away the embarrassment. I grab my small personal shampoo bottle and measure out a dime-sized portion of the fruity liquid to wash my hair in lieu of using the community soap that smells of lye. After my shower, I decide to forgo the makeup that is packed in my bag. Who am I trying to impress, anyway? The only person I care about looking good for is thousands of miles away.

I run my fingers through my still-wet hair in an attempt to give my stick-straight locks a slight lift. My reflection shrugs back at me as I decide this is as good as it's gonna get. I quickly dress and go out to the common area to find Mitch surrounded by some of the kids who are heading off to school this morning. He is doing a magic trick with a rock, pulling it from the ears of the children, causing fits of laughter and giggles to come from the youngsters. I take in his dark, dampened hair as he brushes a chunk of it away when it falls into his eyes. He catches me watching him and sends the kids on their way for their morning lessons.

"Are you hungry?" I ask, picking my pack up off the floor.

Mitch takes the bag out of my hands and flips it onto his shoulder. It's the exact same thing that Austin has done for me numerous times, but somehow this small gesture coming from Mitch chips away at my heart.

"I could eat." He opens the door for me. "Lead the way, doctor."

Waiting in line for breakfast, I introduce Mitch to an endless number of people who are all very curious about the new addition to our camp. I notice the women stand a little straighter and try to fix their hair as we approach. Some of the men shake their heads and sneer at him due to the simple fact that the male-to-female ratio went up yet again. The men in camp already outnumber the women by about three to one.

We make our way through the buffet line and take our trays over to join Pam and Craig. I set my tray down and say, "Mitch, you remember Pam from last night? This is her boyfriend, Craig."

Mitch shakes Craig's hand. "Mitch Matheson. Nice to meet you, Craig."

"Craig Nolan. You, too, man. You army?" Craig asks, nodding his head at Mitch's tattoo.

"Yup, you?"

"No, I work the crops. You been out that way yet?" Craig asks, but Mitch is busy looking around and taking in the hard stares of some of the soldiers at nearby tables. I notice that John is among the rude culprits.

Pam grabs Mitch's arm and points her thumb at the onlookers. "Hey, don't worry about them. They are just mad that you lowered their chances around here. With your good looks, the ladies will be cat-fighting."

"Hey!" Craig sulks at Pam, causing the three of us to laugh.

"Just sayin'," Pam replies. Then she looks at me. "Oh, God, has Jamie seen him yet?"

I nod and Mitch looks at me with a smirk and says, "You mean the one with the batty eyelashes and the big . . . teeth?" He looks at Craig and they bump fists as Pam and I roll our eyes.

Over breakfast, Craig explains to Mitch about the large buried propane tanks that are used only for cooking and sterilizing equipment. Pam enlightens him about the youth population here since she works at the daycare. There are about fifty kids under the age of eighteen. Most are on the younger side, going to daycare or the community school that we set up a few months after the blackout.

Mitch says, "I thought there would be more kids here. Weren't there a lot of families stationed here before?"

"There were," Pam replies, "but since the outage occurred on Easter, which also coincided with the local school's spring break, many families—or should I say women and their kids—had gone off base to visit family for the holiday since their men were deployed."

Craig adds, "That's why there were just ten officers on base at the time. There was a skeleton staff for the holiday."

I feel a hand on my shoulder, but before I can turn around to see who it belongs to, I see Mitch's eyes burning a hole into it.

"Hey, Dr. Kay," I hear John say, as he rubs a possessive thumb on my neck. I lower my shoulder and lean away from him, grabbing the piece of toast from Pam's tray. Mitch locks eyes with me and tries to stifle a grin as I introduce them.

"Major John Burnell, meet Sergeant Mitch Matheson. Sgt. Matheson will be staying on and helping in the medical clinic."

Mitch stands and address John with, "Hello, sir."

"Matheson," John says dryly. "You're the head injury, eh?"

"Well, sir, I prefer to think of myself as *the combat medic*," Mitch retorts.

I feel Pam kick my leg under the table.

"Well then, let's just hope the accident didn't scramble your brains so much that you can't pull your weight around here," John says.

"No, sir. My brains, along with the rest of me, seem to be working perfectly fine."

John ignores him and turns to me. "I'll see you later, Dr. Kay?" he asks, like we have plans to meet or something.

"Sir, the colonel has burdened the good doctor with showing me the ropes this week, so I believe she has a full schedule." He turns to me and adds, "Isn't that right, Mikayla?"

I can practically *hear* Pam and Craig straining to hold in their laughter.

"Is that so?" John bites the inside of his cheek as his eyes shoot daggers at Mitch. "Well then, I guess I'll see you at the softball game," he says to me before walking away.

Our foursome watches him walk out the front door of the mess hall, and then Pam and Craig simultaneously blow out a breath and fall into a fit of laughter. "Shit, man," Craig says to Mitch, "I think you just made him enemy number one."

Mitch turns to me with an apology. "I'm sorry about that, but he was sending venomous stares at me all throughout breakfast. And when I saw the way you reacted to his hand on you . . ." Regret washes over him as he lowers his head. "I'm sorry. I didn't mean to turn that into a pissing match."

"It's okay," I reassure him with a quick nudge of my elbow. "He's been hitting on me for months, but he can't take a hint."

"Yeah, you just did Kay a huge favor," Pam says. "But I'm afraid you landed yourself on John's shit list in the process."

Craig stands up with his tray. "Well, the corn ain't gonna husk itself," he drawls. "Maybe we can meet up for a beer sometime this week," he says to Mitch.

Mitch's eyes go wide. "Beer?" he asks, looking excitedly between the three of us.

"I may have a few lying around if you're interested," Craig says.

"Hell yes!" Mitch replies. "I may not remember much, but I'll never forget how good a beer tastes."

"I hope you feel the same way after drinking a can of warm suds, my friend," Craig says, laughing as he turns to go to work.

After saying goodbye to Pam and taking Mitch through the routine of breakfast clean-up, we head over to the PX with his order for supplies from Colonel Andrews.

On our way over I explain to Mitch, "Don runs the PX. He's a civilian who managed the commissary before. He has a rough exterior, but don't let him fool you, he's a great guy. Just don't piss him off like you did John."

"Well, that depends," he says. "Is he going to hit on you, too?"

I laugh at him. "I hope not. He's my grandpa's age. And I'm pretty sure he's gay."

I silently wonder why Mitch feels the need to piss off everyone that might hit on me. Well, he doesn't have to worry. Other than John, who is a stubborn ass, the men here pretty much leave me alone. They all know that I'm not available. They all know I don't date and that I don't plan on dating.

"It would behoove you to make fast friends with Don," I say.

"Why is that?" he asks.

"Because he can get you things. If he likes you, he will hold stuff back from the masses for you. But if you get on his bad side, he'll only sell you the sloppy seconds."

"Is that so?" Mitch looks thoughtful as he holds the door for me and we walk through into the PX.

Don must hear us come in because he emerges from the back room to greet us. "Well, if it isn't the lovely Dr. Parker." He pulls me into a hug. "I didn't expect to see you on a Wednesday. To what do I owe the pleasure, Kay?"

I motion to Mitch. "Don Jorgensen, meet Mitch Matheson, our newest resident."

As they shake hands, Don says, "Ahh, yes, the mysterious newcomer."

"It's a pleasure to meet you, sir." Mitch pats their clasped hands with his free one and I chuckle to myself wondering what he is up to.

"Hmmm," Don mumbles. "Polite and easy on the eyes, too. Call me Don, son."

"Okay, Don. I have an order here from the colonel to get some supplies. Can you help me out with this?"

Don takes the slip of paper from Mitch. "Sure thing, right this way. I think I have a new male resident pack all ready to go." He leads us to the large customer service counter that he ducks behind to retrieve a large backpack. He opens it up and inventories the contents out loud as he places each item on the counter. "One lamp. A quart of lamp oil. A toothbrush and small tube of paste." He looks up at Mitch. "Sorry, son, it's that nasty baking soda kind. You can use your credits to buy the minty stuff if you want to."

"It's not a problem, Don. I'm just happy to have any at all."

Don turns to me, nodding his head. "I like this one," he says with a wink. Then he continues listing the contents of the backpack. "One standard issue comb. One new razor. One generic bottle of shampoo. A stick of deodorant. Some bedding and a pillow. And, finally, one roll of toilet paper." He holds up the toilet paper and says to Mitch, "You can probably trade this for something really nice. The ladies go crazy for toilet paper."

"I'll keep that in mind, Don. Thanks." He flashes Don an award-winning smile that makes me press my lips tightly together to suppress my giggle. He sure knows how to charm this guy.

Don points Mitch towards the clothing section of the store and tells him, "You can pick out a week's worth of clothing. That equals seven shirts and four trousers or short pants. Seven pairs of socks and underwear and one extra pair of shoes if you already got you a pair. I'll leave you kids to it. Just let me know when you are ready to check out."

We thank him and head over to pick out his clothing. Mitch asks, "Is there anything in particular I need to wear to work in the clinic? I haven't seen you in scrubs, so I assume street clothes are the norm."

I nod my head. "Whatever you want to wear will be fine."

His eyes peruse the shelves of clothing. "Will you help me pick, Mikayla?"

"Okay, what do you normally like to wear?"

"I'm not picky. T-shirts mostly. Jeans. Maybe some cargo shorts or something. Whatever fits decently will be fine. I wear a large shirt, size 34/34 pants, and my shoe size is eleven."

As he rattles through the numbers, I find myself staring at the very pieces of clothing on his body that he is describing. When I realize what I'm doing I shake my head and turn around quickly to do some shopping.

While Mitch browses the shirts, I pick out a couple pairs of faded jeans along with two pairs of shorts. On my way back to show him, I spot something out of the corner of my eye and smile as I pick it up and carry it behind my back.

"So, Mitch . . . are you a boxers or briefs kind of guy?"

He stops looking through the selection of shirts and turns to me with raised eyebrows and an amused look on his face, so I pull the item out from behind my back and toss it over at him. He catches it before it hits him in the face, dropping the shirts he was holding in his hands, making me laugh at him. "Hey!" he shouts, playfully. Then he looks at what's in his hands. It's a pair of boxer briefs with a smiley face right in the front, over where the, um . . . goods are.

He laughs. "Can you find me a t-shirt to match?" he jokes. Then he looks around and quietly adds, "I'll bet Don would give me anything I wanted if I showed up wearing only these." He winks at me. "At least you pegged me with the boxer briefs."

I try to get the image out of my head of him wearing the silly pair of underwear.

We continue to joke around as we put together his new wardrobe. Ten minutes later we call Don out and have him bag up Mitch's things.

Don looks at me and then at Mitch, almost like he has a private joke that he's unwilling to share. "Do you have any credits left, Kay?" He smiles devilishly at me awaiting my answer, and I think he must be up to something.

"Uh . . . I have one left," I answer cautiously. "Why?" I narrow my eyes at him.

"Well, I guess I could take one credit. I mean it's actually three books, but since it's a boxed set, I guess I could bend the rules for my favorite doctor and let you have them for the one." He bends down behind the counter to retrieve something while saying, "A lot of ladies have requested these. But I like you, Kay. You're good to me and you always fix me up nice, so I kept them for you." He pulls out a set of books that I recognize as a popular erotic trilogy and my face heats up faster than a match in lighter fluid.

I see Mitch's jaw drop open out of the corner of my eye. I contemplate rejecting the books, but I know I've struck gold with them so I embrace my shame and nod my head at Don to deduct my credit and quickly shove the books into my backpack.

"Thumbed through the books myself just to see what all the hype is about," Don says, and I sense he's about to add to my humiliation. I shake my head and silently pray for this to be over. "Whew," he says, fanning himself. "That Christian Grey fella really knows his stuff." Don looks from Mitch to me and then back to Mitch, smiling the entire time.

Mitch steps back and holds up his hands in surrender when he says, "What?"

Mortified, I turn and walk away, but not before I look back and yell a word of thanks to Don. He winks at me while he finishes up with Mitch.

Mitch catches up to me out on the front walk and elbows me with a smirk on his face.

"Not a word," I utter.

"I—" he starts.

"Ever!" I interrupt.

He laughs at me and the deep, rumbly sound coming from his chest sends a twinge through my insides.

"Ever!" I repeat, staring him down.

"Okay, okay," he acquiesces.

We walk in silence across the open courtyard and I sit down on a nearby bench to try and gather my composure.

Chapter Six

Mitch gives me a minute, probably more for himself so that he won't laugh at me. When he finally joins me on the bench he asks, "So, what now?"

"Well, normally new residents would come to the clinic for a physical, but we've pretty much done that. I guess I just need to know if you have any medical conditions that we didn't cover already."

"Such as . . . ?" he asks.

"Um, let's see. Family history of heart disease or cancer?" I ask him.

"No and no," he answers.

"History of asthma?"

"Nope."

"You don't smoke do you? I didn't smell it on you when you were brought in."

"You *smelled* me, Mikayla?" I know he's kidding by the way he says it, with a raised eyebrow and stupid grin on his face. But, dammit, when he put my name at the end of that sentence, it just oozed sensuality.

"Uh . . . yes. You know, to check for alcohol on your breath." I roll my eyes at myself. I really was checking for the smell of alcohol, but I do remember his rugged spicy smell and I momentarily wonder if that is his natural scent or if it was something he had recently washed with.

"Is that all?" he asks.

"What about other diseases. Anything I should know about?"

"What do you mean by other diseases?" he asks.

"You know, um . . ." *For Christ sake, you're a doctor, Mikayla. Spit it out.* "Uh . . . STDs." I feel another blush work its way up my face and I wonder if I will ever be able to not turn red in front of this man.

"Doctor, do you know your freckles all but disappear when you blush?" He laughs. "No. No STDs," he says.

I simply want to find that hole I thought about digging earlier for my head. Instead, I punch him in the arm.

He immediately stops laughing. I thought I may have hit him too hard. But he looks down at the front of his jeans and back up at me and says, "Oh, shit . . . at least I don't think so." And all of a sudden, he remembers his reality.

"Don't worry, Mitch," I say, trying to comfort him. "I really do think your amnesia is temporary. It's only been a few days. Your memory will come back. Maybe not all at once, but it'll come back." I hope the words I've spoken are true. Well, I'm pretty sure I hope they are true. Who knows what, or who, he will remember. I need to keep in mind the possibility that he may leave once his memory returns, so I can't rely too much on him at the clinic until that happens.

He nods his head and changes the subject. "Tell me about credits. How do they work?"

"Well, adults get two credits per week and children get one. Everyone gets the same, no matter what their job or contribution around camp. Even Colonel Andrews only gets two credits per week. It's not much, which is why you want to be friends with Don." I elbow him. "But, it looks like you already have that in the bag."

He blows a hot breath on his fingertips and shines them on his collar as if he had just won an Academy Award.

"Anyway," I continue, "you can spend your credits each week as you earn them or you can save them up for something more expensive."

"Can you give me an idea of what things cost? Apparently, books cost one credit." He winks at me and then wisely shifts himself away from my swinging fist before it makes contact with his arm.

I roll my eyes at him and explain, "It's all about supply and demand around here. It doesn't matter how big or expensive an item is; it's all about how many people want it. Take liquor and cigarettes for instance, a pack of cigarettes costs four credits, that's half a month's allotment. Liquor is right up there as well." I turn away slightly knowing I will blush and say, "So are condoms."

"Huh," he muses. "So, society hasn't changed much, I see. It's all about sex and drugs. Add in some rock and roll and it'll be like nothing ever happened."

"Oh, there's rock and roll all right—just not the kind that blares through the headphones of your iPod. You'll have the chance to see what I'm talking about after the softball game on Friday."

"I look forward to it," he says, smiling. "So, what about the other stuff at the PX? There was a ton of clothes there, and I saw a section for shampoo and shit like that."

"Clothes are plentiful and super cheap if you get them secondhand. New things are harder to come by and will cost you. Shampoo, body wash and shaving cream will usually run you around two credits or so. Occasionally there will be some food items. Most of the food goes to the base kitchen, but sometimes there are odds and ends of things that they will find, mostly snack food, that will be for sale." I laugh as I tell him that last month a box of Twinkies went for eight credits.

"So, does anyone provide services in exchange for credits? Say if I wanted a haircut or something?"

I nod. "Well, maybe not a haircut—which, by the way, I could do if you wanted—but other things, yes. Betty Livingston or Marge Crockett will do your laundry and mend your clothes every week for one credit a month."

"Good to know," he says. "On the clothes *and* the haircut. So, what else? You said there were other things, plural."

My face heats up before I can put a stop to it.

"Oh, this must be good, your freckles just disappeared again," he jokes.

"Well, there are a few um . . . ladies, who offer their . . . services," I choke out.

"Reeeeeeally," he draws out. "And what's the going rate for that?"

"Why, you interested?" I scold him with my eyes.

"Do I look like someone who has to *pay* for that, Mikayla?"

"I don't know, with a head *that* big, you are kind of disfigured, so you might have to."

He laughs at me and then stands up, pulling his large pack up off the ground. It occurs to me that we are both carrying quite a load after visiting the PX. "Let's go over to Austin's apartment and see if you can bunk with him."

We cross the street to the apartment building and enter the first floor breezeway. A short hallway later, I stop at Apartment F. Mitch has his hands full so I open the door and walk in. He gives me a look and I know what he's thinking. "We don't really need to lock up around here," I tell him.

"Oh, okaaaaay," he says, like he can't imagine a world where some don't desire what others possess.

The front door slams behind us and he opens his mouth to say something else, but instead, I hear, "Too fucking early!" Then a grouchy Austin emerges from his bedroom, rubbing his head and scratching at the front of his boxers. His large stature fills the entire doorway to his room.

"Afternoon, sunshine," I say to Austin before turning to Mitch. "He works nights patrolling the perimeter." I look back at Austin and say, "You can go back to bed, we just wanted to see if Mitch could have Craig's old bedroom."

Austin looks sleepily from me to Mitch. "Sure, whatever. She told you not to take a shit in the toilet, right?" Then he turns around and shuts his bedroom door. Seconds later we hear a big thump followed by a creak from his bed, causing Mitch and I to crack up as we walk further into his new apartment.

"Don't worry about him, he'll be in a better mood later." I point to a door opposite Austin's. "Your room is over there. I need to go check on a few patients and do some paperwork at the clinic. Why don't you relax and get settled in today. Then tomorrow if you are up for it, we'll tour the rest of the camp on horses."

He walks me to the front door of the apartment, his hands now free to open the door. "Sounds good, but when can I start working?"

"Let's play it by ear, maybe in a day or two." I walk through the door.

"Alright then. I'll see you in the morning. Thanks for all your help today, Mikayla."

"No problem. See you later," I say. I expect him to close the door, but he stays put and leans against the door frame.

"Yup, tomorrow," he replies, still not moving a muscle.

"Okay," I say, hoping he will retreat, but he simply crosses his arms and stares back at me.

I turn around and roll my eyes while taking the three steps across the hall to Apartment G. I open the door, walk through and steal a glance back at Mitch to see him smile as he finally retreats into his apartment.

Entering my apartment after a productive afternoon at the clinic, Holly jumps off the couch and grabs my arm. She pulls me over to sit at the kitchen table where there is a bottle of . . . something, sitting next to two shot glasses filled to the brim with clear liquid.

"Don't think, just do," she says, handing me one of the tiny tumblers.

I hesitantly take it from her. "You've been over at Harley's again, haven't you?" I ask, referring to our resident that has taken to making moonshine—not the good kind, but the worst kind of rotgut anyone has ever tasted.

"I pulled a tick out of his ass earlier today," she says, mimicking a gag. "Now bottoms up!" She clinks her glass to mine and we drink the liquid fire.

After our faces go through some involuntarily hideous twitches, I recover my power of speech and say, "What was that for?"

"For getting you to loosen up, Kay. Now spill."

"Spill what exactly?" I ask her.

"Oh, come on. The whole camp is talking about how Mitch pissed all over John, apparently marking his territory."

My mouth falls open. "What?!" I shriek. "That is not how it was at all. John was touching me inappropriately. Mitch saw it and saw that I didn't like it, so he stood up to him. That's all." I shake my head and murmur, "Marking his territory . . . where do they come up with this crap?"

"Well, what do you expect, Kay? There's nothing better to talk about around here now that Kelly Nelson's pregnancy is old news."

"Are you seriously equating Mitch's silly little standoff with John to Kelly getting knocked up by an army captain whose wife used to be her high school science teacher?" I close my eyes at the thought of me being new gossip fodder for the troops.

Holly eyes me suspiciously. "It really wasn't a big deal?" she questions me.

"No, Hol." I wipe out my glass with the bottom of my t-shirt figuring it doesn't need washing because the moonshine probably disinfected it properly. I place the shot glass back in the cabinet.

"So, he's not 'claiming his territory'?" she asks.

"There's nothing to claim, Holly," I say, becoming irritated with her, even in my now mildly inebriated state.

She finally blows out a conceding breath. "Fine. Want to play Monopoly? We can pick up where we left off last time."

Holly and I went to bed after a riveting few hours of hotel building and property trading.

I couldn't sleep, so I pulled my secret gem, my newfound lady leverage, my latest guilty pleasure, out from its hiding place under my nightstand. And, dammit, I was just getting to the good part of book one when I hear a muted scream. Not a high pitched blood-curdling scream from a bad horror movie, more like a deep rumble of turmoil-turned-panic scream from a man.

I jump out of bed and curse silently when I stub my big toe on the corner of my dresser on the way out to the living room. Everyone else is sleeping, so I swiftly follow the noise out of my apartment to find the source. I open the door to Austin's apartment knowing that since he works nights, Mitch must be the sufferer of this nightmare.

I go into Mitch's bedroom and see, by the moonlight coming through his window, that he is crouched in a corner, cowering as if a predator is set to attack him.

Knowing I could very well end up hurt if I approach him, I call out, "Mitch! Mitch, you're having a bad dream, wake up!" His eyes remain closed and he doesn't respond. I look down at the floor around me and pick a shoe up off the ground and throw it at him.

"Crap," I mutter to myself when he slides further down the wall, moving his face right in front of the shoe just as it makes contact. *That's gonna leave a mark.* I should have grabbed the sneaker, not the boot. Mitch opens his eyes but is disoriented.

"Huh . . . what . . ." he says, looking around the room.

Deeming it safe, I walk over and help him stand up, being careful not to look down just in case he sleeps in the nude. He lets me guide him to bed. I pull the sheet over him and get up to leave when he grabs my hand. "Thanks, Doc. You saved me—I'll never forget you."

"Uh . . . it's okay, Mitch. You're okay now," I say, but he's already fast asleep, his chest moving up and down in a slow and regular pattern.

As I slip back into my bed and get out my paper and pen, I wonder just what it was that I saved him from.

Dear Jeff,

Is that what it's like for you over there? Are you having bad dreams every night? Is there someone there to help you if you are?

It feels like forever since I've been able to look into your big brown eyes and run my fingers through your wavy blonde hair. I didn't even mind that you had to cut it so short for the army. I've almost forgotten what it looks like short, but as I've said before, I won't give in to the temptation to look at your pictures. It wouldn't be fair to the others.

Oh, speaking of things nobody else knows about, Jamie found my journal with all the letters to you. She made fun of me for writing so many of them. I know it's silly that I still do it after all this time, but it makes me feel closer to you somehow. Although I feel bad that her fiancé died, at least she has closure, she knows for sure, and because of that I can't help be a little envious as strange as that sounds. Holly, in her usual crazy-yet-lovable fashion, almost laid Jamie out for invading my privacy.

It's so bizarre to have a life here that I don't share with you. I tell you about my friends, yet you've never met them. You've never even heard of them. My one wish, other than you making your way back to me, is that you are surrounded by people that love you as well. I know from your e-mails that you established some incredible friendships over there and I have to trust that those will help pull you through this.

Until next time. All my love,

Kay

Chapter Seven

This morning, Mitch and I are off to the stables so I can give him a full tour of the grounds.

He doesn't mention the nightmare he had or even that he remembers anything about me coming into his room last night. I casually ask him, "How'd you get the pretty shiner?"

He reaches up to lightly touch the blue and red bruise high on his cheek bone and replies, "Hell if I know, I woke up with it. Maybe John paid me a visit in my sleep." He elbows me and I realize that we kind of have a thing now. Every time we tease each other, the elbows come out. It's our thing. We have a thing. I suck on my bottom lip contemplating if I'm comfortable with this or not.

His eyes light up when he sees all the horses in the stables behind the barracks.

"We built it by hand," I say. "There are no nail guns and electric saws anymore. Everything is done the old-fashioned way. It's amazing how it brought everyone in the community together."

I walk him over to the horses to introduce him to a few of them. "This is Sassy, she's my favorite. We understand each other."

"Sassy?" he questions, looking amused.

I nod at him and move to the next stall. "This here is Buck. Ordinarily, I'd have you ride him, but considering your medical condition, I'd say it's not a very good idea today. Buck tends to throw off riders occasionally. I've stitched up quite a few lacerations caused by that one. No, today you should ride Rose. She's gentle and won't scramble your brains any more than they already have been." *Elbow down, elbow down*, I repeat to myself.

Mitch gives me a look so I say, "What . . . you can dish it out but you can't take it?"

He smiles at me. "Oh, I can take it alright. Give me your best shot, doctor." He stares at me long and hard. His unmanageable black hair falls into his eyes and I have the urge to reach out and brush it away. Our eyes are locked together. I shouldn't be looking at another man like this. I try to pull my gaze away from his for the fear of drowning in those bewitching sapphires.

"Dr. Kay," someone says behind me, and the trance is broken. I turn to see Brad, the stable hand. "You takin' her out today?"

"Yes." I nod. "Brad, this is Mitch Matheson. He's new here and I'm taking him on a tour of the grounds. Is it okay if he rides Rose?"

"You bet," Brad says, as he shakes Mitch's hand. "She hasn't been ridden in a few days, so it'll do her good." He saddles up Rose and Sassy for us.

Brad puts the stool next to Sassy and I slip my left foot into the stirrup then I swing my right leg over the top of her. When Brad and I look over at Rose, we see that Mitch has already mounted her and is walking her around to get her used to his weight. "Ahhh, he's a natural, I see," Brad says. I smile looking over at Mitch who appears to be very much at home on the mare.

Mitch takes Rose through some turns and maneuvers as I watch in awe of how he has easily won her over. It's like he has a power over her and I wonder if that extends to all females or just the four-legged kind. I'm not sure how long I've been staring when Brad pats my leg and says, "You two kids stay out of trouble now." He lets out a chuckle as I glance over at Mitch who winks at me.

I gently squeeze Sassy with my legs, prompting her to walk out the gate and into the grassy field that lines the back of the stables. Mitch brings Rose up alongside me as we set out to explore the northeast side of the camp that is lined with acres of grazing ground for the cattle that we raise. It will take a while to reach the far east side of the perimeter that borders the springs, and I find myself lagging behind and staring at the man riding in front of me.

His broad shoulders fill out the tight t-shirt he is wearing and when he moves, I can see ripples of muscle across his back. His wavy hair almost touches the collar of his shirt where it curls up and bounces slightly with each step of his horse. The dark stubble on his face and the tattoo on his bicep that peeks out from under his shirt almost complete his rugged bad-boy look. I can practically envision him wearing a cowboy hat, and the thought of that has me taking in a deep breath and then slowly blowing it out.

I realize where my mind is going and I try to snap out of it. I haven't done anything wrong. I'm only staring at him. So why do I feel so guilty about it?

It occurs to me that we've not spoken a word since we left the stables, yet it's a comfortable silence. Still, I'm trying to think of something to say when Mitch beats me to it.

"So, is he your boyfriend?"

"Is who my boyfriend?" I ask, trying to figure out who he could be referring to.

"Austin," he says in a sharp tone, as if he's angry.

I delight in the fact that Austin didn't divulge personal details about me despite the fact that they live together now. Knowing

Austin, however, he probably withheld information just to bug the crap out of Mitch.

I shake my head at him. "No. Austin and I aren't together, but he is one of my dearest friends."

Mitch nods at me in silence.

"My boyfriend, Jeff, is over in Afghanistan."

His eyes close and he shakes his head slightly. "Oh God, Mikayla, that's horrible. I'm so sorry. Hasn't there been any word about our troops overseas?"

"No. We barely know anything about the current state of affairs in our own country, let alone others. But Jeff isn't one of the troops. He's a doctor; a surgeon. He was only supposed to be over there for four months and was just a few weeks away from coming home when it all happened."

"It must be awful for you and everyone else here to not know about your loved ones over there."

I study him for a second then I tell him, "It's no worse than you not knowing about your family, Mitch. It must be gut-wrenching to lose two whole years of your life and not know if you have someone waiting for you somewhere."

"Yeah, I guess so," he says. "But what I don't understand is how I ended up in Florida of all places. I've never once been here and I don't know anyone who lives here. Well, I don't think I do, anyway." He laughs. "And how the hell did I get here from Afghanistan, or at the very least, from California?"

I realize that our horses have stopped walking and are waiting on us to tell them what to do. Mitch continues, "But still, I have this nagging feeling that there is someone I was looking for."

Of course he was looking for someone, he was alone. But why does the thought of him looking for a woman make my heart sink into my stomach? Maybe he wasn't looking for a woman. Maybe he was looking for a friend, or a family member; his brother's family perhaps.

I give Sassy a squeeze with my legs and we continue on toward the east pasture. "So, if you don't know who you might have been looking for, does that mean you weren't . . . um, that you didn't . . . uh . . ." I stumble over the words that won't come out.

A smirk flashes across Mitch's face. "Mikayla, are you trying to ask me if I'm married or have a girlfriend? Because if you are, just come out and say it."

A blush creeps up my face once again, as I roll my eyes at him and snap, "Whatever, Matheson. You are the one who started it."

"You're right," he says. He turns Rose around and expertly walks her backwards alongside me so we are almost face to face. "I guess it's only fair that I tell you then."

As he tells me about his ex-girlfriend, Gina, who he was with for two years, I notice that his hand goes up to absentmindedly grab at his chest again. It makes me wonder if she has something to do with this unconscious habit.

Rose complains about walking backwards so he turns her around before continuing his story. "So I started hearing from her less frequently and when I finished my first tour and returned home to Sacramento, I found out that she had run off with my best friend."

He purses his lips and shakes his head, and I can see that he's still hurt even though it happened so long ago. Three years ago to be exact, but to him it only seems like less than a year has passed since she dumped him. I wonder if maybe he ended up getting back with her and that she is the person he's been looking for. Then again, I can't imagine anyone taking back an ex who had exhibited such betrayal.

"I'm so sorry, Mitch." There's nothing else I can say. I have no words of wisdom or encouragement for him in a world where so many uncertainties exist.

In our renewed quiet, I look around at the beautiful pasture and take in a deep breath to inhale the sweet scent of the purple petunias that are growing faster than the cows can eat them. My eyes are drawn to the hummingbirds that circle around the aromatic plants, looking for a place to land. I view the countryside and think back to how different my life was before everything happened. I try to remember a time when I was doing something that wasn't related to work or school. I rack my brain and I can't even come up with one instance.

Mitch asked me earlier if I had any hobbies. If asked that same question a year ago, the answer would have been very different. I had none. No interests outside of medicine. Even the rare times when Jeff and I were alone together, we were always talking about patients, new surgical techniques, or my residency exams. These days, I can rattle off a list of hobbies that make life worth living. Horses, reading, softball, stargazing, music. There are so many things that fill my days now that I never took the time to appreciate before. So many things that contribute to my existence that is no longer singular, but multi-faceted and colorful. In fact, if it weren't for Jeff missing from my life, I might even go so far as to say I'm happy with the way things are.

My eyes wander back to Mitch and I see him lovingly talking to Rose while maintaining our leisurely stroll. I wonder if Jeff were here, would he be as enamored as Mitch and I are with these wonderful creatures? Would Jeff like to sneak out at night, as I often do, to the soft grassy courtyard across from the apartments to lie down in complete darkness just to stare in wonderment up at the amazing night sky? Would he get excited every Friday, knowing that after work, all our friends gather for a weekly softball game followed by a bonfire and sing-a-long at The Oasis? These are all such simple things. Yet, Jeff was never a simple person. Driven, that's what I would call him. But driven is good. It's why he grew to be an incredible surgeon. It's why he was such a good mentor for me when I first started med school. It's why I think I was initially attracted to him.

So, why then, as I watch Mitch interact with the beautiful animal he sits on top of, am I thinking that a man who loves a horse is just about the sexiest thing I've ever seen?

" . . . Mikayla? . . . Dr. Kay . . . hello?" Mitch pulls me back from my deep and inappropriate thoughts.

"Sorry, just daydreaming I guess," I say, hoping I wasn't blatantly staring at him the entire time he was trying to get my attention.

"I was asking you how much farther it is to the springs."

Mentally shaking my previous thoughts out of my head, I answer him. "I'd say about a mile." I gesture toward the open grassy areas. "And it's a whole lot more of this the entire way."

He narrows his eyes at me and lifts a hand to rub the stubble on his chin. Then he leans over and calmly says to his horse, "I think we can take 'em, Rose." His eyes flutter back to me momentarily, full of challenge and I realize what he means a microsecond before he yells, "Yah!" And before I can react, they are almost in a full-out gallop.

He may be good with horses, but he doesn't know that Sassy is about the fastest mare of the bunch. It doesn't take me long to catch up to them, and in no time we've got wind flying through our hair and smiles plastered on our faces. By the time we close in on the far reaches of the camp, we're riding neck and neck, laughing like a couple of teenagers on a joy ride.

Mitch calls it a draw and we slow the girls down to a steady walking pace. I find myself reveling in the foreign feeling coursing through my body. What is it . . . exhilaration . . . joy? Whatever it is, I like it. I want more of it. But I fear the man next to me may be the sole reason for it and that reality is not okay with my conscience. And again, guilt washes over me as I close my eyes and try to picture Jeff. My boyfriend. My love. The brilliant man that is the missing piece of my life.

Mitch stops laughing when he notices my change in demeanor. "Everything okay, Mikayla?" He circles Rose around me and the horses nuzzle each other while he awaits my reply.

"Yeah, just tired from the race," I reply. "And I'm thinking that was probably a bad idea, what with your possible *brain injury* and all." I raise my eyebrows, scolding him.

He simply shrugs his shoulders at me as we dismount the horses and lead them over to the water. I explain the aquifer to Mitch and show him how we have directed a supply of fresh water into the heart of camp. We pass by a few of the soldiers stationed along the back perimeter and I stop to introduce Mitch to them.

After giving Sassy and Rose time to recover from our race, we go over our plan to explore the southeast stretch of camp that houses the crops. Mitch helps me re-mount Sassy and then effortlessly mounts Rose as I watch his strong arms pull him up and over the top of her.

We settle into a steady pace as we zig-zag our way through the different farming areas that encompass the largest part of the camp's acreage.

Suddenly, Sassy gets spooked, rising up on her hind legs, dislodging me from the stirrups and throwing me backwards onto the ground. I wince as I fall onto my right ankle and I'm instantly sure that I've caused some damage to it.

"Shit!" Mitch calls out, watching me in horror as he quickly jumps off Rose. He runs over to where I came to rest in the mound of dirt that tried, unsuccessfully, to break my fall. On his way to me, he spots the culprit that sent Sassy running for the hills. "Looks like a Southern Diamondback—extremely poisonous. I hope the horse didn't get bit." He looks around and finds a large stick and expertly drives it through the head of the rattlesnake. Then he walks towards me, eyes on my now swollen ankle that I have removed from my boot.

He crouches down next to me and leans over to try and take my foot into his hands. I raise a brow at him and say, "I'm the doctor here, you know. I'm perfectly capable of tending to my own injury."

"Right." He rolls his eyes. "You do know what they say about doctors, don't you?" he asks.

"What, that they are the worst patients?"

He laughs. "Okay, that, too. But I was talking about the fact that they say you should never self-diagnose."

"It's no big deal, just a strain," I run my hand over the now tender flesh on my ankle. "Alright, maybe a sprain. But definitely not broken."

"Stubborn woman," he murmurs under his breath. He stares me down, then he holds out his hands and says, "Whenever you are ready for me to have a look."

I raise my leg in acquiescence and he carefully takes it into his lap. He runs his hands up and down my calf, and he gently palpates the bones in my foot and ankle. His touch is surprisingly light and slow as he thoughtfully regards my injury. His eyes snap up to mine and I wonder if he can feel the electricity that seems to be running from his fingers all the way up my legs and into my stomach, causing me to shiver involuntarily.

He lightly places my foot back down while smiling to himself. He turns his head, surveying our surroundings and then he stands up and proceeds to remove his shirt.

Huh? What the hell? If he thinks I'm going to be a quick romp in the field, he had better think again. Just because I felt a spark when he touched me, doesn't mean I want him. I'd probably feel a spark being touched by *any* man after all this time. But, then John's face quickly flashes through my mind and I know that is not the case. No, not just any man makes my insides melt. Still, just because my body has some kind of unintentional reaction to him, I don't have to act on it. I won't act on it. I straighten my back and gather my courage to tell him, "Mitch, I don't know what you think you're—"

The sound of the tearing fabric of his shirt cuts me off and I stop mid-sentence as I watch him rip his t-shirt into even strips. When I realize that he has removed his shirt to make a wrap for my ankle and not to seduce me in this field, I feel more than a little bit stupid. *Really, Mikayla?* I can't believe that for a minute I thought he was coming on to me. He said that he thought someone might be out there for him, so why would he all of a sudden set his sights on me? I need to get out of my own head and back into reality.

I try not to watch the way his biceps and ab muscles flex every time he tears another strip from his shirt. Then I try not to feel anything when he lifts my leg into his lap and gently, yet securely, wraps the pieces of fabric around my ankle. As a doctor, I can't help being a little awestruck over his quick resourceful thinking. I imagine that comes from being a combat medic and always having to make do with what you have.

"How does that feel? It's not too tight, is it?" he asks me when he's finished.

I shake my head at him. Little does he know that while he was wrapping my ankle and I was trying to ignore the erotic sensations shooting up my leg, I looked around to see where Sassy may have ended up. I became acutely aware that in her absence, considering my current state, that Mitch and I just might be riding back together on Rose. And the thought completely renders me speechless.

Minutes later, after Mitch retrieves Rose from her unexpected feast on some of the nearby crops, he is helping me up into the front part of the saddle. "You're small enough that we can both use the same saddle," he says. "It'll be more comfortable than one of us trying to ride bareback."

All I can think is, *God, I hate it when I'm right.*

When he bends down to grab my boot off the ground, I gasp when I see his naked back. There are about a dozen long, thin, crisscrossed scars spanning his broad shoulder blades and extending to the bottom of his rib cage.

He must hear my reaction because he stands up and twists his head around so I can see the huge smile on his face. "See something you like, Mikayla?"

"Uh . . . no, it's not that. I mean, I wasn't ogling your ass if that's what you think. I was um . . ." I don't want to make him feel self-conscious about the scars, but I also don't want him misunderstanding my reaction. "What happened to your back, Mitch?"

He wrinkles his brow at me, clearly confused by my question. "What do you mean?"

My face pales when I realize that he has no idea about the scars on him. That must mean they happened within the past few years. But they are well healed—so much so that Holly and I missed them when we did our quick visual exam in the dim light when he was brought into the clinic. However, here in the bright sunlight, they are easy to see.

It dawns on me that maybe this is why his memory hasn't returned yet. He could be suppressing the memory of a horrible event that happened to him. If I tell him about the scars, will it trigger his memory? And if so, what will happen?

"Mikayla?" He gets my attention again. "What's on my back? Tell me," he demands. "You look just like you did the other day when you realized I had amnesia." He stretches his arms around himself as far as they will go and runs his hands down one of the raised scars. "What is that?" His wide eyes appeal to me for answers.

"Mitch, you have several long scars across your back." He turns around to give me a better look. "They are all well healed and appear to be at least a year or two old."

He narrows his eyes, still feeling around, twisting his arms to get more of a reach. "What do you think happened to me?"

I search my mind for possible answers. "I don't really know. Maybe you were in a fight. I suppose it could have been an animal attack. Or . . ." I bite the inside of my cheek to suppress a smile.

"Or what, Mikayla?" he asks, looking slightly worried.

I try hard to keep a straight face when I say, "Or you were into some pretty kinky shit, Matheson. You know, whips, cattails, canes . . . everything one can find in a 'red room of pain'."

"In a *what* room of *what*?" He playfully swats my thigh. "I think you read too much for your own good, doctor."

At least we're both laughing again. Between my ankle and his scars, I wasn't sure that would happen.

I tell him that Sassy will most likely find her way back to the stable on her own so he ties my boot onto the girth ring and expertly hoists himself up onto Rose's back. "Let's head back and get you fitted for some crutches then," he says.

As he settles into position behind me, I can feel the heat radiating off his thighs as they press around the outside of my legs. I reach for the reigns at the same time as Mitch does and his hands fall onto the top of mine. We both pull back and he says, "Sorry, you go."

"No, that's okay, you can do it," I tell him. I figure it's safer this way . . . physically . . . emotionally. If he's holding onto the reigns, he won't have to hold. onto me. But when he reaches around me again to take hold of them, I realize he has no other option but to rest his forearms on my thighs.

Mitch turns Rose around and brings her to a slow walk. Much slower than before, presumably to keep my ankle from getting too jostled around.

As we leisurely make our way back, I become increasingly aware of his bare chest pressing against my back, his legs capturing mine, and his hot breath caressing my ear when he speaks. He tells me about his dad who is a dentist and his mom who's a school teacher. His older brother, Mark, followed in his dad's footsteps and he and his dental hygienist wife went on to have three adorable girls including a set of seven-year-old twins. The tone of his voice tells me that he is sad speaking of them, but I urge him to continue and I listen intently, hanging on every word, trying to distract myself from the sensations flowing through my body.

Rose stumbles on a bed of rocks and Mitch's hand instinctively presses against my stomach. His large hand lands on the strip of exposed flesh between my jeans and top, holding me tightly against him, sending what feels like a shot of adrenaline straight into my heart. I wonder briefly if he felt it, too. He lets out a long, hot breath that trickles down my neck as his hand lingers longer than necessary before he removes it.

When we finally reach the stables I find myself feeling sad. I tell myself that it's because of my leg, because I'm destined to hobble around on crutches all week. I close my eyes and shake off the little voice in my head that tells me it's because when I get off this horse, I will re-enter reality. That because the man sitting behind me—the man who is absentmindedly rubbing his pinky along the inseam of my jeans—has made me feel more alive today than I've ever felt in my twenty-seven years.

Chapter Eight

I lie in bed this morning, having only gotten a few fleeting hours of sleep. My mind was too busy thinking about the man across the hall and what possibilities lie therein. I didn't even realize how lonely I was until Mitch showed up. Yesterday . . . this whole week in fact, my loneliness was alleviated simply by being around him. He seems to fill a void that I didn't know was there— or maybe I just refused to acknowledge its existence.

I don't think I misread his cues. The way he touched my leg as he examined it . . . the way his eyes followed my lips when I spoke . . . the brief caress of my skin when his hand was on my belly.

Does he want more than just a friendship? *Do I?* I'm so confused. The lines are all blurred now. What is allowed? When do we give up hope? Hope of Mitch's memory returning. Hope of Jeff coming back to me.

I'm not ready to give up yet. But, I'm not rolling over to die, either. I know no one would fault me for moving on. But the real question is—would I be able to live with myself?

"Kaykay, up." Little hands tug on my sheets as Rachel tries to climb up on my bed.

I reach over and pull her up so she can lie next to me. She snuggles into me as I lie on my side and I realize how comforting it is to have this tiny human pressed against me. Fine auburn hairs are tickling my face as I breathe in the sweet smell of her.

Moments later, her mom comes into my room with an apology. "Sorry, Kay. I hope she didn't wake you."

"Are you kidding?" I say to Amanda while smiling at her precious little girl. "This is the best way to wake up. I wasn't actually sleeping anyway. I didn't do much but lie here all night."

"Your ankle is really hurting you, huh?"

"Mmm . . . something like that," I mumble.

Holly sticks her head into my room and says with a big grin, "Kay, someone is at the door for you."

I don't even have to ask who it is. I know he must be eager to start work today. "Tell him I'll be out in a minute."

I emerge from my room a few minutes later, hobbling on crutches while trying to put on my backpack. Mitch walks over and takes the pack from me, swinging it up onto his shoulder.

"Thanks," I say, turning away from him so he doesn't get a shot of my morning breath. "Uh . . . I need to shower and brush my teeth on the way."

He holds up his own backpack. "Me too, I'll walk you over. How's the ankle? Did it keep you up last night?"

"Not so much," I say. My eyes wander over to Amanda, who is looking at me suspiciously while sitting at the table with Rachel and Holly as all of them silently watch our exchange. "Uh, Holly, you coming?"

"I'll catch up with you at the clinic. You kids go on ahead," she says, flashing us an award-winning smile. I give her my 'I know what you're up to' stare before Mitch and I walk out the door.

~ ~ ~

Thirty minutes later, Mitch and I open up the clinic and check the whiteboard on the door for messages. I explain that people can make an appointment by using it, or they can leave any of the medical staff a message.

"Hmm . . ." I read a message from Kelly Nelson. "She's getting close," I say. I explain to him that Kelly is about thirty-seven weeks pregnant and has been having stronger Braxton Hicks contractions lately. "She's a frequent flyer at the clinic. It's her first child so she comes in every other day with questions about one thing or another. Even after Don gave her a book on pregnancy, she still needs constant reassurance." He laughs when I tell him that she thought she was dying when she felt the baby hiccupping for the first time.

"Have you delivered a lot of babies?" he asks.

I shake my head. "No, not many. One during residency and one about four months ago, but it was an easy delivery. By the time Carla sent her friend to get me, she was crowning."

"Wow, only two deliveries?" he cocks his head at me in disbelief. "Even *I've* delivered more babies than that, Mikayla. How is it that a full-fledged doctor hasn't had more experience than that?"

"Well, I wouldn't say I'm a *full-fledged* doctor." I shrug my shoulders and continue. "I was just finishing up my second year of residency when everything happened."

"That explains it then," he says.

"Explains what?"

"I was thinking you must have been some kind of child prodigy, becoming a doctor so young. What are you, twenty-six?"

"Twenty-seven," I correct him.

"Huh . . . me, too," he says. "So, what specialty were you going for?"

"Pediatric emergency medicine."

He nods his head at me. "Two specialties in one. Pretty hard core," he says.

"Yeah, well, I was kind of single-minded and solely focused back then."

"And now?" he asks.

I think about our ride yesterday and all the things I've done over the past year that separate me from my former self. "Now I have other interests as well." And although there was no hidden meaning to my words, I realize I was looking straight into his eyes when I said them, and I feel a heated blush sweep up my face at the unintentional insinuation.

He holds my gaze while a smile forms on his lips. Then he says, "So, doctor, can I have the grand tour of the clinic? I want to carry my weight around here, or I'll have Major Burnell putting my ass in a sling."

An hour later, we're in the back room going through the filing system that I set up when a low voice calls out from the front, "Dr. Parker, you here?"

Mitch and I walk out into the reception area to see Colonel Andrews helping Claire Taylor through the clinic entrance. He is holding a blood-soaked towel securely around her arm.

Despite her injury, I notice Claire's eyes light up when she sees Mitch behind me. She looks between Mitch and me and then whispers something to the colonel to which he nods his head.

"Claire, what happened?" I ask, quickly making my way to her and helping her into an exam room.

"I was slicing potatoes when someone dropped a pot on the floor behind me. The noise scared me half to death and the knife slipped and caught my arm."

Colonel Andrews adds, "It's a pretty deep gash. She needs stitches."

"Let's take a look," I say. I squirt sanitizer on my hands and slowly peel back the towel covering her wound. It has stopped bleeding, but as the colonel suspected, it will need seven or eight stitches.

"Aren't you going to introduce us?" Claire asks. I look up at her to see that she is eyeing Mitch standing behind me.

"Oh, sorry," I say. "Mitch Matheson, this is Claire Taylor, my . . . uh—"

"Friend," Claire interrupts me, reaching out with her uninjured hand to shake his outstretched one.

I'm not sure why she didn't let me say that she is Jeff's mom. I mean, yes, she is my friend, but still.

"We'll be right back, Claire." I turn to Mitch and say, "I'll show you where we keep the sterilized trays we use for minor procedures."

As I'm collecting the supplies we need, I watch Claire and the colonel through the glass in the exam room door. I wonder why he was the one to bring her to the clinic. I suspect he was simply eating in the mess hall when it happened and graciously offered to help her. I see Claire lean over to whisper something in his ear before he turns his head to look in our direction.

Mitch and I return to the exam room to set up for the procedure when Colonel Andrews asks to speak with me in the hallway. I tell Mitch, "Use the iodine to clean the wound and I'll be right back."

In the hall, the colonel asks me to keep a close eye on Mitch for a few weeks, having him only work my shifts so that I can assess his medical skills and figure out how he can best contribute around the clinic. "Of course," I tell Colonel Andrews. I take a second to figure out if I'm delighted or dismayed at the thought of having Mitch constantly by my side.

"Ah, Colonel?" Mitch sticks his head in the hallway to get the colonel's attention before he leaves. "When can I expect to get outside the gates? I'm eager to see the outside world, sir."

Colonel Andrews nods, sympathetic to Mitch's memory loss. "Soon, Sergeant. You can tag along on next week's supply run if it suits you."

"That will suit me fine, sir. Thank you."

The colonel waves goodbye to Claire through the exam room window. It doesn't escape me that Claire gives him a wink as he leaves the clinic.

"Mikayla," Mitch addresses me as I re-enter the room. My eyes snap to Claire to see that, yes, her raised brow tells me that she did catch the way he used my full name. "Would you mind if I do the stitches?" he asks.

"On your first day, Mitch? I don't know if that's such a good idea," I say.

"You know, I'm pretty good at them," he says. "In fact, they are kind of my specialty."

I look at Claire to see her smiling face following our conversation. She says, "Kay, dear, let him do it. He has to prove himself sometime."

He quickly sanitizes his hands and puts on a pair of latex gloves. Then he holds a hand out for the syringe of lidocaine I'm holding.

"Fine," I say, putting the syringe in his hand. I turn to Claire and say, "But if you have an ugly scar, don't whine to me about it."

"She'll hardly have a scar at all. I'm that good," Mitch assures both of us.

I remove an elastic band from my wrist and secure my hair back in a ponytail so I can lean down and watch carefully. I notice Mitch staring at the nape of my neck as I gather up and tie my hair back. Then I glance over at Claire to see a large smile spread across her face.

I watch him expertly stitch up Claire's arm. But, I'm not about to tell him that I think he did a better job than I would have done. His head is big enough as it is without me adding to it.

"I barely felt anything at all, Mitch. You are very talented," Claire says. "And you have such a soft touch for a man. Don't you think he has a soft touch, Kay?"

"Uh . . . I guess," I say, remembering his hands on me yesterday. I turn away so I don't give Claire the satisfaction of my blush. I hear her quietly laugh under her breath.

Besides Claire, Kelly Nelson was the only other person who showed up at the clinic today. Kelly thought her water broke, but it turns out she just peed her pants when she sneezed. Mitch and I got a lot accomplished thanks to the peace and quiet.

I loathe sitting in the bleachers watching everyone else play softball. I hope by next week my ankle will be strong enough for me to play again. The team I play for, the 'Civvies,' is on the field. Of my friends, Amanda, Pam and Craig are also on the team.

Austin, Tom and Holly play for the army team, as well as John and Lt. Camden, who folks teasingly call 'Lt. Latrine.' Mitch has joined the army team and I can't keep my eyes from following his every move as he wears another one of his tight t-shirts and a pair of snug baseball pants, compliments of Don, who is also watching in the stands with me. I realize that watching him distracts me from missing Jeff—as wrong as that may seem.

"Kay, I didn't think you'd be here tonight with your injury and all," I hear Jamie say as she makes her way to the top bleacher, not even trying to be modest in the short skirt she is wearing. I don't recall ever seeing Jamie show up at a game. She has never indicated the slightest bit of interest in sports.

"I still want to cheer for my team, Jamie."

"Oh. Well, I'll be cheering for Army tonight," she informs me. She turns to Don and says, "Bravo, Don. I'm assuming you outfitted that hunk of man out there?"

I roll my eyes at the two of them so obviously ogling Mitch. But then again, am I any different? Isn't that what I'm sitting here doing even though I'm not so vocal about it?

Two hours later, after Army beats us by a large gap, I smile at myself wondering if my absence was the reason for the big loss. I never had time for sports before, but over the last year, I've taken to just about any outdoor activity I can find. I try to maneuver myself down from the second level of bleachers when one of my crutches falls out of my reach. Mitch runs over, climbs up the two steps and helps me down before retrieving the crutch for me.

"Such a gentleman," Jamie says coming up behind us. "And a great softball player, too." She tries to work herself in between me and Mitch. She grabs Mitch and laces her arm around his elbow. "How about walking me over to the bonfire, Mitch?"

He looks between the two of us. "Well, I was going to make sure Mikayla made it over there, Jamie. But you can walk with us if you'd like."

"It's only a little sprain, Mitch. I'm sure Kay can make her own way over there. Austin is here to help her if she needs it. Isn't that right, Kay?"

Well, what am I supposed to say to that? *I saw him first* comes to mind. I can't think of a plausible reason to get Mitch to walk me, so I say, "Yeah, I'm okay. I'll just wait for Austin. You guys can go ahead."

I think I see a hint of confusion flash across Mitch's face before he says, "If you're sure, Mikayla."

"Yup," I say. Then Jamie pulls him away and starts gushing about how adept he was at running the bases and pitching the softball. I shake my head and silently curse myself for the twinge of jealousy I feel as I watch them walk away arm in arm.

The bonfire is in full swing when we arrive. The Oasis is packed; its outside seating area filled with adults and children. I think there must be a hundred people out on this beautiful, mild spring evening.

Don graciously offers me his chair since the rest are occupied. Normally, I would never accept it, but my ankle is throbbing from hobbling around all day at the clinic.

I'm not a big dancer, but sometimes the girls and I have been known to let off steam that way. But not tonight. Tonight I'm destined to be a bystander, an onlooker of the festivities, just as I was at the softball game.

As I listen to the music, courtesy of a drummer and a few guys playing guitars, I look around to see who is here, telling myself that I'm not trying to find anyone in particular. I wave as I make eye contact with Evan, one of the men who found Mitch that first day; and Georgia, the sweet old lady who knit me a sweater last winter after I helped her husband battle a bad stomach bug. When I spy Mitch sitting next to Jamie, across the open expanse that houses the bonfire, I wonder how they are getting along. He is perusing the crowd, taking it all in. This is the first time he's seen so many of our residents in one place. Jamie, on the other hand, is only looking at Mitch.

"They aren't on a date, are they?" Holly spits out behind me. I turn around to see her, Pam and Amanda along with Tom and Craig as they all stand gathered around the back of my chair.

"No," I say. "She kind of made him walk her over here after the softball game."

"Does Jamie know they aren't on a date? 'Cause it doesn't seem like she does," Holly says.

I look back over at them and see Jamie fawning over Mitch as he looks slightly uncomfortable. When his eyes find mine, he shifts away from her and adjusts his chair so her thigh is not pressed against his. I wonder if it's all women he doesn't want touching him or just her.

There is a break in the music and some people get up to visit the latrine. Others generously pass around bottles of liquor to their friends. A few soldiers sneak away to share cigarettes off to the side of the building.

It's fairly quiet during the break and I can hear Peter Richards, a guy from the band, ask Mitch if he plays guitar. Mitch laughs and shakes his head. "I wish," he says. "I always wanted to learn how to play." Then he gets a pensive look on his face while he stares at Peter's guitar. "Uh, would you mind if I gave it a shot?"

"No, go ahead man, I'm taking a breather." Peter leaves his guitar with Mitch and walks away.

Mitch picks up the guitar and places it on his thighs. He closes his eyes and feels the strings along the neck with the fingers of his left hand. Then he starts strumming and out comes perfectly played chords followed by a very surprised look on Mitch's face. He immediately looks up to where I sit. He smiles and shrugs his shoulders at me. I give him an encouraging nod, hoping that this may be what jogs his memory.

"Mitch, play us a song!" Don yells, coming back from the bathroom.

"Okay, but cut me some slack. I'm winging it," Mitch says, drawing a laugh from the crowd.

He starts to play and falls into a song like he's played it every day of his life. He closes his eyes and smiles while dozens of people jump up to dance to the catchy tune he is playing. I can see Mitch's lips moving to the words, but I can't hear him over all the singing voices in the crowd. A frown erases my smile when I remember that Jeff used to play guitar. It's one of the only things he ever did outside of medicine. I'm not sure he even enjoyed it. I think he did it purely to keep the dexterity in his fingers. *A surgeon's fingers need to be strong*, he would say.

I try to remember if I ever longed for Jeff's hands to play me just as I'm longing for Mitch's hands to dance across my body like they are dancing across the strings of the guitar. It was different when Jeff played. He didn't play with passion; he didn't let the music in. But the way Mitch looks right now, it's like the music is flowing through him, controlling him, freeing him. He looks . . . at peace. All I can think of is that I've never seen anything sexier than a man getting lost in music.

The song ends and the crowd erupts with applause. Men walk by and pat him on the back. Women scream cat calls. Mitch doesn't even look uncomfortable with all the attention. He still looks dumfounded, however, so I don't think he has remembered anything.

"Hey, Whiskey!" shouts a man from the crowd, referring to the nickname sometimes given to army medics, "play something slow so I can dance with my girl."

Mitch looks deep in thought and I wonder if he even knows what other songs he can play. After a minute of silence and crowd anticipation, he locks eyes with me and begins to play. After a few strums of the guitar I realize what song it is. I remember it from a few years ago. It's a song about a man who has feelings for a woman, but he's afraid to ask her to be with him. He is afraid that she will turn him away and his heart would break because he's been burned once before. As Mitch quietly sings the lyrics, other voices pipe in and project the song for everyone to hear. I find myself unable to tear my eyes away from his. It's like there's a magnetic pull holding my stare to Mitch's. I can see his lips still moving, singing the chorus about the man asking the woman to take a chance on him.

All of a sudden it hits me and I realize that I can't deny it any longer. I want him. I want him so badly, my body is shivering. I may even need him. I'm drawn to him like I've never been to anyone or anything before.

My eyes become blurry as an image of Jeff races through my mind. The spell is broken when someone spills drops of liquid onto my hands and I break our stare. I look into my lap only to realize that tears had slipped from my eyes. I feel like I've betrayed

Jeff merely with my thoughts. I reach around to grab my crutches and hobble away before the song is even over.

Holly walks along after me. "Kay? Are you alright? What *was* that back there?"

I stop and quickly wipe my eyes. "What do you mean?" I ask, trying to sound like I wasn't just crying.

"Well, Jamie was looking at Mitch and John was looking at you, but you and Mitch couldn't pull your eyes away from each other. Hell, there were so many pheromones oozing from you two that I think *everyone* here will get laid tonight." She laughs. "I don't even think Mitch noticed that Jamie left in a huff halfway through the song. He sure as shit noticed when you got up, though. I think he only stayed put when he saw me come after you."

I remain quiet so she studies my face in the moonlight. "Oh, crap, Kay. Are you crying? What's the matter?"

"I don't know, Hol. I'm having all these feelings that I don't want to be having. I feel like a terrible person. I don't know what to do."

She nods her head at me in understanding. Then she pulls me into a hug. "You sleep on it, Kay. Then you do what feels right. You do what your heart tells you to do."

Chapter Nine

For the second night in a row, I can't sleep. I quietly get up and leave the apartment to do the one thing that I know will help my insomnia.

I slowly make my way across the parking lot, carefully placing my crutches so I don't fall down. When I get over to the courtyard and approach my usual spot, I see movement on the grass. Someone is there.

Damn. I turn around to head back inside when I hear. "Mikayla?" My heart skips a beat when the low familiar voice speaks to me.

"Sorry, I didn't mean to bother you," I say. "Uh, how did you know it was me?"

"You're not bothering me, Mikayla." Mitch stands up and walks over to me. "Your crutches squeak every time you put weight on them. You can't sneak up on anyone using those things." He laughs. "Do you need help getting to the latrines or something?"

"No. I was just, um . . . I was uh . . . coming out to look at the stars," I say, sure that he will find my pastime ridiculously silly.

"You're kidding," he says.

"I know. It's stupid, but it relaxes me. They are so bright without any street lights to obscure them. You should try it sometime."

"What do you think *I* was doing out here?" He smiles.

"Really?" I didn't mean to sound so surprised that a man—a man in the army no less—would take the time to appreciate such things.

"I started doing it on my first tour. It's so dark over there. No street lights. No illumination from a nearby city. Just darkness, dotted with incredible stars and constellations. It was the only way I found calm in the madness."

I find myself wondering just who this man is and why is he turning my world upside down.

"Come here," he says, gently tugging on one of my crutches. "Lie down with me. The sky is so clear tonight and I'd hate for you to miss out."

I sit down and put my crutches to the side. I lay my head back and look up at the beautiful night sky. We don't talk, but I'm painfully aware of his presence mere inches from me. I can hear him breathe. I can hear the grass rustle when he moves his leg. I can hear the hitch of his breath when I move my arm and it brushes against his.

Finally, our silence is broken when he asks, "So how did you come to be at Camp Brady? You weren't living here when you were in residency, were you?"

My mind goes back to March 31st of last year. It's a day I try not to think about. The death, the destruction, the sheer panic.

He must sense my hesitation. "It's okay, Mikayla, you don't have to talk about it if you don't want to."

I contemplate not telling him my story. Then I feel guilty because I have memories of that day while Mitch has none. He woke up in a transformed world unaware of what happened to him or those he loves. So, for the first time in almost a year, I tell my story.

"No, I didn't live here. When Jeff joined the Army Reserve several years ago, they put him through training. I think the training scared him a little because that's when he started talking about disasters and how we would deal with them. Hurricanes, acts of war, terrorism—joining the army made all of those seem like real possibilities to him. So one day, he sat me down and told me that if anything like that ever happened when we were apart, I was to go to Camp Brady and he would find me there. It was only about forty miles from Gainesville where we lived. He knew they would have emergency supplies and means to care for people. But I never really took it seriously. I was young. I never thought anything like that would happen to us. A bad hurricane maybe, we do live in Florida, but beyond that, I couldn't imagine."

"Jeff was smart to prepare you," Mitch says. I look over to see him on his side, propped up on his elbow. A piece of hair falls into my eyes and he reaches out to brush it behind my ear. That small movement, that tiny gesture, has my heart racing and blood pumping in my ears.

I look back at the night sky and continue my story. "It was early on Easter morning and I was getting ready to go to the hospital. I had volunteered to work the holiday. The thought of all the kids in pediatrics getting a visit from the Easter Bunny . . ." I stop talking because I can no longer get words past the lump in my throat. God, I haven't thought about this in so long. I'd completely blocked it from my mind.

I feel Mitch's finger wipe a tear that escaped my eye and was rolling down the side of my head. I take a deep breath and tell him, "When everything went dark—the lights, my laptop, my cell phone—and the world got eerily quiet, I went outside my apartment where others had started gathering. Of course we thought it was just an outage, but a neighbor said that an outage wouldn't render all our phones dead and useless. Then it happened." I close my eyes as I tell him the rest. "The explosion. We heard the loud popping noises as transformers sparked everywhere. People screamed as a plume of smoke and fire mushroomed in the sky only a short distance away. It was the hospital. I know now that the solar flares caused an electrical surge that sparked fires all over the place. But the hospital, with all the oxygen tanks, just exploded. Gone . . . in the blink of an eye.

"We were all speechless, stunned, in shock even. A short time later, people came running from that direction saying it was all gone. There was nothing left of it but fire and rubble. A few men told the group of us that we were probably under attack and that it was nuclear weapons that rendered all electronics useless. They said we should find our families and prepare for the worst. When I saw a plane fall from the sky and realized all but a few cars had stopped moving on the street, I remembered what Jeff said. Knowing it would be pointless for me to even try to help at the hospital, I went into my apartment and gathered up a few things.

"I put some clothes in a backpack, along with some energy bars and a few bottles of water. I packed a small first aid kit and my cell phone—I wasn't yet convinced that it wouldn't come in handy. Then I rode my bike over to Claire's house."

"Oh, so you knew each other before?" Mitch asks.

I nod. "Yes. She is Jeff's mom. I waited there for a few hours thinking that she and Jeff's dad had gone to church. Claire didn't work and Jeffrey was a surgeon. I was sure that with his seniority, he wouldn't have been at the hospital on Easter Sunday. I ended up leaving a note, telling them where I had gone and asking them to come as soon as possible.

"The bike ride was as bad as I thought it would be. I had read a few books back in high school about the aftermath of war and thought I might come across terrible things, but it still didn't prepare me for what I saw. I ran into some people on the back roads who had abandoned their useless cars. I told them about Camp Brady and a few said they would head that way. Everyone was in a state of panic and a couple of men tried to grab my bike away from me. After that, I didn't stop for anyone or anything.

"I saw a few houses on fire along the way. I heard pleading cries from countless people on the side of the road and it gutted me to not stop and offer help. I even saw one man with a tire iron robbing a helpless family. Then I rode past the horrific wreckage of another plane crash. By the time I got here a few hours later, I was numb. I was sure it was all a bad dream that I would soon wake up from. In a state of shock, I collapsed into Austin's arms at the front gate."

I turn to Mitch. "So, that's it. That's how I got here." I attempt to slow my breathing as anxiety tries to take control of me. Then I realize that Mitch is holding my hand. He must have taken it in his to comfort me.

"And Claire's husband?" he hesitantly asks.

"No. Turns out he *was* in the hospital after all." I lower my eyes.

"I'm so sorry, Mikayla. That must have been so awful for all of you."

I remain quiet for a minute, lost in the sensation of his thumb rubbing soothingly across the back of my hand.

"I'm sorry too, Mitch," I say to him, turning on my side so that we are face-to-face. "I'm sorry you can't remember what happened. I'm sorry you don't know how you got here and that you have no idea who or what you were looking for." I give his hand a squeeze and ask, "What's it like for you—losing two years?"

He thoughtfully regards my question. "I guess it's kind of how you described your ordeal. It's like being in a dream. I'm completely numb." He slides closer and whispers in my ear, "Except when I'm with you."

In the moonlight, our eyes lock together. Our faces are inches apart. My heart is ready to explode with emotion. Mitch leans over and presses his forehead to mine. Our hot breath mingles. He stares into my eyes and everything else in my world is forgotten.

He pulls away smiling and leans up to press a kiss on my forehead. As his lips part from my skin, sensations flood my body and I momentarily wonder if one can orgasm without so much as a touch, but with only this desperate feeling of intense wanting.

I shake away the thought and ask, "Have you had any more bad dreams?"

I realize my faux pas when he arches a brow and looks at me curiously. "How do you know I have nightmares, Mikayla?"

Crap. I can't think up a quick lie, so I come clean. "I kind of witnessed one the other night." I bite my lip and wrinkle my nose.

"And . . . ?" he asks.

"And, I kind of threw a shoe at you to wake you up."

"You threw a shoe at me?" he asks, reaching up to feel the bruise under his eye.

"Well, a boot, actually. I was aiming at your chest," I say, wrinkling my nose. "But you moved and it hit your face instead. So, if you think about it, it's kind of your fault."

Suddenly, I'm trapped beneath him as he rolls me onto my back and sits on top of me, his legs straddling mine. "*You* did this to me?" he asks, playfully.

"Not on purpose, Matheson," I squeak out, surprised that I can complete a coherent sentence considering our bodies are touching in such an intimate way.

He looks down into my eyes as he holds my hands captive on the sides of my head. He stares at my lips. Then he shakes his head and closes his eyes like he's having an internal struggle. "So, what now?" he asks.

"What do you mean?"

"You know what I mean, Mikayla. We are both unsure of what is out there waiting for us . . . *who* is out there waiting for us." He sets my hands free and I find myself placing them on his thighs. He looks at where they have come to rest on him. "It's obvious we have this connection," he says. "We can keep fighting these feelings, or . . ."

"Or what?" I ask, nervously chewing on my bottom lip.

He reaches down and pulls my lip out from between my teeth. Then he runs his thumb over my mouth. "Or we can see what happens next. No guilt, no pressure, no strings."

"I, uh . . ."

"You don't have to decide right this minute," he assures me. "I just wanted to put it out there." He moves himself off my lap, back to his original position of lying next to me.

We both concentrate on the stars again. Then he says, "Cereal." I turn to look at him in confusion and he laughs. "No more nightmares, but I did dream of cereal."

"Oh," I say. "For me, it's pizza. God, I'd kill for a slice of deep dish with extra cheese."

"Yeah, but the strange thing is—I don't even like cereal," he says. Then he gets up to leave, turning around one last time when he says, "Goodnight, Mikayla. Sweet dreams."

I watch him turn into a silhouette shrouded by moonlight as he walks away into the dark of night.

An hour later, I go home and write a letter before I collapse with exhaustion.

Dear Jeff,

I can hear you now. If you could see me on crutches, you'd say, "I told you so, Kay." You were always telling me to be careful when I insisted on biking to the hospital every day. I remember the day my pager went off and I took my eyes off the road for a fraction of a second, and that's when I hit the parked car. God, I was humiliated when they brought me into the ER strapped onto a backboard.

Well, everything turned out okay then, and everything will be okay now. My ankle will heal, just as the bump on my head, along with my pride, healed then. But, I'll not give up riding horses as I gave up biking. I think that if you don't take chances in life, you'll simply miss out on all life has to offer.

Are you taking chances? Are you trying to find a boat that will bring you back to me? Are you exploring new and different things to enrich your life while we are apart? Are you letting another woman into your life and your heart?

I wish I knew what to do. You—you're the smart one. You always have an answer for everything. What would your answer be to this?

Until next time. All my love,

Kay

Chapter Ten

I arrive at work late today, courtesy of my late-night stargazing and letter writing. Sometimes I wonder how anyone gets anywhere on time these days without alarm clocks and cell phones telling us when to get up. As I hobble through the clinic doors, feeling marginally rejuvenated after my six hours of sleep, I see a gathering of people in one of the patient rooms. I walk over to see Kelly Nelson in bed, clearly in labor. I rush into the room as fast as my crutches will allow and ask, "Why didn't anyone come and get me?" I send a nasty look to Jamie, who was the nurse on call last night.

"Relax, doctor," Jamie says, pulling me out of the room. "If you recall I did four years as a labor and delivery nurse. Kelly is doing fine. She came in around midnight and is still only about seven centimeters dilated."

She motions over to Mitch who is talking with Kelly and her mom. "*He* wouldn't let me wake you, said something about you not getting enough sleep, whatever that means," she huffs. She rolls her eyes and gives me a full report on Kelly. Then she goes to say goodbye and wish luck to our patient. It doesn't escape me that when she says goodbye to Mitch, she runs her fingers down his arm rather seductively. However, I'm pretty sure I was meant to see it since she was looking right at me as if to say *game on*.

Mitch comes over when I'm checking out Kelly's chart. He says, "Morning, Mikayla. Did you sleep well?"

His smile fades when I spit out, "Mitch, you shouldn't have kept Jamie from sending for me. What if something went wrong? And you certainly don't need to give her personal details about my sleeping habits."

"What? Uh . . . did I miss something?" he asks. "We were perfectly capable of monitoring Kelly until you showed up. I promise, if anything had concerned me, I would have sent for you. Is everything okay, Mikayla?"

I take a deep breath and slowly let it out. I realize I'm pissed at Jamie and merely taking it out on Mitch. "I'm fine," I tell him with a small smile. "Thank you for letting me sleep in, it did me some good. Sorry I scolded you."

"Scolded me?" He raises an eyebrow suggestively. Suddenly I'm thinking of last night when he threw me on my back and straddled my lap. I feel the blush creep up my face. He whispers, "I'd give anything to know what you are thinking about right now, doctor." Then he walks out of the room leaving me a melted mess.

I take longer than necessary going over Kelly's chart to calm myself down; then I enter her room and proceed to examine my patient.

$$\sim \quad \sim \quad \sim$$

Hours later, Kelly's water breaks and her contractions are only a few minutes apart. She's nine centimeters dilated and almost fully effaced so it won't be long now. I send Kelly's friend to find either Nancy or Holly so we can have a nurse present when the baby arrives.

Kelly has her mom here, and some friends have come and gone over the course of the afternoon, but conspicuously absent is Captain Fields, the baby's father. Rumor is his wife forbade him from being present at the birth. They have been trying to re-build their marriage since his momentary indiscretion almost nine months ago. And while I commend him for trying to fix his marriage, I'm not altogether on board with him not being here to support Kelly. After all, he was partly responsible for what happened. It's not the first time someone strayed from his partner around here. You would think a disaster would bring couples closer together. However, if you listen to the rumor mill, affairs were running rampant those first few months after the outage. Some people were turning to just about anyone for comfort and solace. I've often wondered if the same thing happened overseas. Maybe it was worse, all those people thinking they might never get back home.

I hear Kelly scream so I limp into the room. I feel terrible that I can't give her an epidural, but Dr. Jacobs and I agree that having an epidural could increase her chances for a C-section and we can't take the risk. We are simply not equipped for major surgery here. We have no anesthesiologist, no blood for a transfusion, not to mention I've never performed a C-section before. We can only pray for an uncomplicated delivery and a healthy baby.

Mitch is a big help. He has either delivered or assisted in the delivery of dozens of babies. Over in Afghanistan, the medics would help deliver the babies of local women who had gone their entire pregnancies without ever seeing a doctor. He gives me a nod and says, "I think she's ready to push."

My heart rate accelerates and I take a few calming breaths, knowing this will only be the third baby I've ever delivered. Mitch and Jamie had already set out all of the supplies that we could possibly need. Mitch and I gown and glove up and clear the room of everyone except Kelly's mom who has been Kelly's rock throughout her pregnancy.

Holly and Nancy both arrive to help. Nancy has had years of experience as a neonatal nurse which puts me slightly at ease. With a lack of proper delivery stirrups, the nurses each take one of Kelly's legs to hold while she pushes. Holly counts to ten each time Kelly pushes, and every time she pushes, I get a glimpse of dark hair before the head again recedes.

Mitch must notice my shaky hands and sweating brow. He pats my head with a towel and leans down to whisper, "Relax, Mikayla. This is the good stuff."

Yes, I think. He's right. This *is* the good stuff. In our world of destruction and devastation, bringing in a new life should offer us joy and hope for the future. I grasp onto that as I watch a precious new being enter the world. As Kelly pushes harder and harder, the tiny body emerges from her womb into my hands. I quickly suction the mouth and nose before putting her new little boy on her belly. Mitch cuts the cord among the tears of all of the women present in the room. I look up through my own blurred vision to see him beaming at me.

"Pretty great, huh?" he says.

All I can do is nod at him.

While I finish up with Kelly, Mitch and Nancy take the baby over to another patient bed we had brought into the room. The tiny cries from our newest resident bring laughter and more tears from all of us.

When Kelly has been tended to and all cleaned up, I turn to look at Mitch who is holding the new swaddled baby. His eyes glisten as he smiles down at the perfect little human that has just entered the world. I think to myself that a man holding a newborn baby is just about the sexiest thing I've ever seen.

Mitch hands the baby over to Kelly. Holly grabs my elbow and says, "Kay, why don't you take a minute. We'll monitor them for a while. They are both doing wonderfully."

Leaving my crutches, I gingerly walk into the other room, removing my bloody gown and gloves along the way, and I go to wash up. In the back, I'm overcome with emotion and I lean against the wall as tears run down my face. The door opens, letting light into the dimly-lit room as Mitch walks through it.

"You okay?" he asks, shutting the door behind him, making the room go dim once again.

I nod, unaware that he can't see my gesture in the relative darkness. He comes closer and puts a hand on my cheek. Feeling my tears, he wipes them away then runs his hands down my arms. He doesn't talk. He simply stands here and comforts me as I go through a range of emotions.

I finally say, "That was . . ." I can't finish because there are no words.

"Exhilarating? . . . Intoxicating? . . . Life-affirming?" he completes my every thought. He stares into my eyes, and even in the dim light of the room, I can see his blue irises becoming darker under his hooded gaze. My breathing accelerates along with my heartbeat, which I'm positive must be audible. He reaches around my head and removes the elastic band from my hair, causing it to flow freely over my shoulders. Then he pulls my hair away from my face and leans in to put his lips lightly on mine. "Mikayla," he whispers against my lips, right before he feathers kisses along my mouth. My eyes close and my head falls against the wall behind me as he trails kisses along my jaw up to my ear where he sucks on a spot on my neck that sends shivers down my spine.

His lips slowly work their way back to mine as my hands come up around him to run through his hair. I tug on his hair lightly, prompting him to deepen the kiss and run his tongue along my bottom lip. I open my mouth and our tongues weave together, exploring each other, tasting each other. One of his hands lowers from my head to caress my lower back and press our bodies even closer, and I can no longer hold back the pleasurable cries that my body demands I make.

He moans into my mouth as our kisses become more heated. More demanding. More desperate. It's as if we need this to continue breathing, to feel alive. Mitch grabs my thigh and pulls my leg up, causing even more delightful friction against our pleasure centers. His hips grind into mine with abandon and I willingly accept every stimulating thrust.

His hand runs up under my shirt, leaving a trail of flames against my bare skin. When he grabs my breast, my body shudders involuntarily against his and I feel his lips smile against mine. "Oh, God," I moan.

He pulls back and leans his forehead to mine, speaking softly and out of breath when he says, "I was wrong. *This* is life-affirming." Then his thumb pulls the cup of my bra down and his fingers find my nipple.

"Miiitch," I say, drawing out his name while arching my back into his hand as tingles of pleasure shoot through my body under his expert manipulation.

"God, Mikayla. I've never heard anyone say my name that way," he says, kissing another trail up to my ear. "You are so sexy.

So beautiful." He sucks on my earlobe before he says, "I want you so much."

In this moment, I feel exactly the same way. I've never wanted anything as much or as desperately as I want him. His hand works its way to the top of my jeans where he slips his fingers underneath the material to caress my stomach. I want him to go faster. I need him to go faster. I'm building up so quickly I feel I will explode. I'm about ready to tell him to rip off the buttons when a strip of light blinds me from a cracked doorway.

"Oh, sorry," an embarrassed Nancy covers her mouth in surprise and turns to hurry out and shut the door.

Suddenly, I remember where we are. Ashamed of losing such control at work, I push Mitch away and try to quickly fix my disheveled appearance. The reality of what we almost did weighs heavily on me as I smooth down my hair. Why has my body betrayed my mind like this? How could I have let this happen? What about Jeff?

"I, uh . . ." I'm at a loss for words after what I just experienced. Not able to find my hair tie that he removed, I pull another one from my wrist and hastily secure my hair into a new ponytail. "I have to go check on everyone."

I hobble the few steps to the door before I hear him call out, "Mikayla?"

I keep walking, refusing to acknowledge him and what happened. I return to Kelly's room only to get curious stares from Holly and Nancy. Everyone else, however, was seemingly taken with the new baby and didn't even notice our absence.

A few minutes pass before Mitch re-joins us. I see Holly looking from Mitch to me and back to Mitch again. I can feel him staring a hole into the back of my head. I try to focus on my job. I assess Kelly and her baby once more simply to keep my hands and my mind busy. I'm glad there are multiple people coming and going from her room because there can be no awkward silence this way.

Thirty minutes later, our shift comes to an end. Nancy agrees to work second shift with Holly coming back for the overnight. I tell all the guests that they need to leave to let our patients get some rest. And luckily, this gives me an excuse to walk out of the clinic accompanied by several people.

I know he is watching me as I walk ahead of him in a small group. Holly keeps looking at me with a raised eyebrow and a smirk on her smug little face. I know she is itching to find out exactly what happened. But I can't talk about it. I have to clear my head. I tell her and the others I have something to do and walk away. I look back at Mitch and see him shake his head and close his eyes in frustration while his hand comes up to work the front of his shirt over his chest like he's done many times before.

We lock eyes. Then he nods, giving me a look of acceptance and understanding before he turns and walks towards his apartment.

I walk towards the barracks, and the stables behind them.

"How did you manage Sassy with your wonky ankle?"

I turn around to see that Claire has snuck up on me, out here in the meadow beyond the east pasture. I can't believe I didn't even hear her ride up. I guess I've been lost in my own world out here. This is where I come to think. Just as lying under the stars at night relaxes me; being out here in this meadow—with the tall wispy grass, the sounds of nature, and the smell of flowers—brings clarity to my life.

"Brad helped me get up on her," I say. "How did you know I'd be here?"

"I went by your apartment to see how you were holding up after I heard about Kelly's baby. I know that must have been stressful for you."

"It wasn't. It was incredible."

"I know," she says.

"You know?" I raise an inquisitive eyebrow.

"I ran into Mitch outside your apartment."

She doesn't need to say anymore. I can see it in her eyes. She has an uncanny ability to read people. To get past the bullshit and really find out what makes them tick. I'm one-hundred-percent sure that she got Mitch to say something about us and how we feel about each other. And I'm one-thousand-percent sure that I feel guilty as hell about it. She must be so mad at me for contemplating being with another man.

"What if this is it, Claire? What if we're all that's left? I know there are other groups out there somewhere, but we still don't know how many. It's been almost a year. How long do we wait? Are we supposed to sit around and let life pass us by while we wait for people who may never come back?" I belatedly realize that I'm talking about her only son. "Oh, God, Claire. I'm sorry, I don't mean for it to sound like I've given up because I haven't. I love him."

She brings her horse up next to mine. "I know you do sweetie, and I love you for it. You are one of the few people that still have hope. However, you shouldn't let that hope guilt you into missing out on life."

"But how do I know when it's time to move on? And how do I move on when he could still be out there?"

She sighs. "Oh, Kay, it's different for everyone. I'm not sure you'll ever know exactly when the right time is, but I see the way you look at Mitch. I've watched you two together. You are happy when he is around. You shouldn't feel guilty about that. Jeff wouldn't want you to stop living."

I stare at the ground. "How can you even stand to look at me, Claire? I'm sitting here thinking about being with another man. Don't you hate me for that?"

"Absolutely not, and neither would Jeff. Kay, you need to get over the guilt if you want a chance at happiness. I know—it was the same for me."

My eyes go wide as they find hers. "For you . . . what do you mean?"

"Well, dear, we haven't outright told anyone yet, but we've decided to stop hiding it." She smiles and shrugs her shoulders.

Then it dawns on me. "The colonel," I say, nodding. It makes sense. He brought her to the clinic when she was injured. The whispers between them. The wink when he left. I narrow my eyes at her. "You—you're the reason the colonel told me to work closely with Mitch every day, aren't you?"

A smile brightens her face. "Guilty," she says, not even having the decency to look slightly ashamed. "Listen, Kay, it took me a while to get over the guilt of moving on after Jeffrey. For months, I wasn't sure if I could. Thank God James persisted."

I reach over to touch her hand, "I'm so happy for you, Claire." Then I pull back. "But, it's not quite the same. Jeff could still be out there somewhere."

"Yes, he could, and I hope to God that he is. But nobody will fault you for moving on under these circumstances, sweetie." She smooths the back of my hair, just like a mother would. "What does your heart tell you, Kay?"

I cock my head to the side. "That's exactly what Holly asked me last night."

"Well then, maybe it's time that you listen to what it's saying."

Chapter Eleven

More than a week has passed since the kiss. It seems like yesterday, however, because I've relived it so many times in my dreams. Mitch has been giving me space, but that doesn't mean we still haven't come close to kissing a few times. It seems like we find excuses to touch each other whenever possible. I want him. I know this. But I want him without the guilt that comes along with it.

Happy to be free from my crutches, I stop by the PX to pick something up for Mitch, making me a little late for work. Figuring Mitch has already opened the clinic, I take my time getting there, enjoying the beautiful late March morning. When I get to the clinic though, I find it deserted.

Panic strikes me when I remember what yesterday was. It was the day Mitch went outside the gates for the first time. He went on a supply run with Evan's guys. My heart sinks. What if his memory was triggered and he decided to leave? What if he came to the conclusion that our little camp was not as great as I've made it out to be? What if he decided that waiting for me wasn't worth it anymore and moved on?

All kinds of scenarios are playing out in my head as I try to busy myself washing dirty linens from yesterday's patient. Finally, the front door opens and I hear, "You here, Mikayla?" My eyes close in a silent prayer of thanks as I try to keep myself from running out front and jumping into his arms.

"In the back," I say, trying not to reveal my sheer exuberance at his arrival. I pick up the package that I brought for him and walk out to the reception area. I see Mitch has a package in his hands, too.

"Hey," he says, beaming at me. He looks gorgeous. *Has he always looked this gorgeous?* He has another one of his trademark t-shirts on, paired with his faded jeans and work boots. He still hasn't asked me to cut his hair so it flops every which way, looking messy yet perfect at the same time.

"Hi." My heart is still somewhere in the vicinity of my throat so I can't manage to get more than the one word to come out.

"What's in the bag?" He motions to my hand and I look down at the package that I had all but forgotten I was holding.

"Oh, I got something for you." I walk over and hand it to him.

"Really?" he asks, his face brightening. "I got something for you, too." We stare at each other and laugh at the almost uncomfortable tension between us. Then we exchange packages.

He opens his bag first. He pulls out the t-shirts that I picked up for him. I got him a black one to replace the one he ripped up for me and a blue one because I thought it would go great with his sapphire eyes. "You got me clothes?" He looks up at me. "Nobody has ever gotten me clothes before. It's so . . . domestic."

I frown. "Sorry it wasn't something more exciting. I wanted to replace the shirt you ruined for me and the other one, well, I just thought it might look good on you."

"Don't be sorry, Mikayla. These are great. I meant domestic in a good way." He reaches out to run his hand down my arm.

"Thank you," he says, and nods to the small package in my hands. "Now you."

I unwrap a plain paper bag to reveal a book. I turn it over to see the cover that is dotted with stars in a night sky. "You got me a book about constellations?"

"Yeah. I found it yesterday when I was out with the guys. I couldn't think of anyone who would appreciate it more than you."

He was thinking of *me* when he was out seeing his new world for this first time? Here I was scared that he wouldn't come back, or that he had snuck away in the night to re-claim a life that he had once forgotten. A little piece of the wall I had put up around my heart crumbles. "Thank you, Mitch. This is the best gift I've gotten in a long time—maybe ever."

"Well, I hope not *ever*, but you're welcome." He picks up the packaging and folds it neatly. Then he puts it up on a shelf, already used to our recycling and reusing habits.

I look at the book in my hands and back up to him. "This isn't a going away present, is it?"

"Why, are you going somewhere?" He furrows his brow.

"Not me. I thought maybe going outside had triggered your memory and that you might be leaving us. To find something . . ." I frown again and add, "or . . . someone."

"I'm not leaving, Mikayla. Not until I figure out why I was down here."

"But what if you never figure that out?"

"Then I'll have a choice to make, I guess." He stares at me, his eyes caressing mine. "But life is all about making difficult choices, isn't it?"

I wonder if he is talking about him making the choice to stay or me making the choice to let go of Jeff.

"Hey, did you know there are 350 squirts in a gallon of milk?" he asks.

What? Where did that come from?

He laughs at me. "I'm just trying to lighten the mood, doctor. And while I've been avoiding you this week,"—he winks at me— "I've been learning a great deal about farming."

"You milked a cow?" My jaw falls open at the thought of this manly man crawling beneath a cow to repeatedly pull on its teats.

"I milked several of them. I also hung out with Craig who is teaching me about raising crops."

I eye him suspiciously. "Thinking of changing professions, are we?"

"I've got to have something to fall back on if you kick me to the curb," he teases me, giving me that familiar elbow to the ribs.

"I'm not kicking anyone anywhere, Mitch. But thank you for giving me time, you know, to figure things out."

As we go about our daily chores at the clinic, Mitch tells me about what he saw on the outside. It's just as I feared; not many other people around and plenty of neighborhoods left to pilfer— although they are having to go farther and farther out to get to them, wasting more of our precious fuel supply. The only good news was that they did run into a man who had biked from North Carolina and he said he heard rumors of the beginnings of a working government. I guess that's something.

$\sim \quad \sim \quad \sim$

"Help!" we hear, from where we sit in the file room. Mitch and I run out front to see Jared Williams helping his mother into the clinic. She is visibly sweating and looks pale. She can barely keep her feet beneath her. "I think she's having a heart attack!" Jared cries.

"Mitch, start the generator and hook up the EKG and oxygen and charge the defibrillator." Thank goodness we at least have a working AED. Still, we've lost more heart attack victims than we've saved. And since women generally don't have the classic symptoms of a heart attack, they tend to not seek help until it's too late.

"I'm on it," Mitch says, already making his way to the back of the clinic.

Jared and I get his mother, Monica, into an exam room and get her comfortable on a bed. I tell Jared, "Get her some water while I have her chew an Aspirin." She is barely able to chew it, but it does go down.

Mitch returns and we get her hooked up to the EKG and oxygen. People are starting to gather out in the reception area and Holly comes rushing in to help. Before the results of her EKG can be read, Monica goes into full cardiac arrest.

Oh, God, please let the AED have a charge.

"Holly, get Jared out of the room so we can work!" I yell over my shoulder.

Mitch unpacks the AED. "Hurry!" I snap at him as he opens the box and starts handing me the chest pads.

"I think it has a little charge, but we may not get much," he says.

"Then we'll do CPR until it charges back up," I tell him. "Whatever it takes, do you hear me?"

Holly returns, having found someone to stay with Jared outside the doors. "What can I do?"

"Bag her. We may have to do CPR for a while, so get ready."

I shock Monica with the AED and get no response. "CPR for two then shock again," I tell them. "I'll go first." They both understand that giving CPR is very physically taxing and it's best to take turns so one caregiver doesn't get exhausted. I'm pumping on her chest while Holly is giving her breaths with the Ambu bag. "Mitch, I want to give her a beta blocker and t-PA, go get those ready for me." He leaves the room and I turn to Holly and say, "It's the only therapy we can try, we have no other options."

"I know, Kay," she reassures me. "We will do what we can, everyone out there knows that."

Mitch returns before the two minutes are up. He places syringes on the table next to me and goes to sanitize his hands and start setting up an IV.

We shock her again. Still nothing. Mitch performs CPR this time while I finish her IV and administer the meds. We continue the cycle of CPR and AED for over thirty minutes. Holly and I both have tears running down our faces while Mitch continues to perform CPR even though we know it's too late.

I know it's time to call it. I put my hands over Mitch's to let him know to stop, but he just keeps going. Sweat trickles down his brow as he keeps pumping away despite the fact that Holly has stopped bagging her.

"Mitch, she's gone. There is nothing more we can do," I say to him. But it's like he doesn't even hear me. He doesn't miss a beat. I raise my voice and say, "Mitch, you have to stop now!"

Sweat drips off his nose down onto Monica's chest as he continues to try and resuscitate her. I lower my head and look into his eyes so that I can speak directly to him, but I see that his eyes are glazed over. "Mitch!" I yell, as I try to pull his hands away from Monica's chest.

"No!" he screams at me, batting my hand away. "She's not dead! She's not dead! She'll be okay. She has to be okay. Mom, please . . ." He keeps going on and on about his mother when it dawns on me that he must be reliving a memory. He told me his parents were alive and that his mom was a school teacher.

Oh, my God. He is remembering his mother's death.

"Holly, go get some guys to pull him off and take him in the other room. Give him a mild sedative if you have to. I'll deal with Jared."

I watch in horror as Mitch battles two large men when they pull him, kicking and screaming, off Monica's lifeless body. I try to ignore the commotion coming from the room they take him to so that I can comfort the man who just lost his mother. Then, I'll go comfort the other man who also just lost his.

Minutes later, after I break the news to Jared and his friends come in to sit with him; I leave to go talk to Mitch. I look through the window of the second exam room to see Holly sitting with him. He is lying on the bed, staring blankly at the wall beside him. Holly motions for me to come in and then she whispers to me, "I gave him a shot of Ativan so he might be out of it for a while."

"Can you take care of things out there?" I ask.

"Of course, you stay with Mitch. I'll handle it, Kay."

I sit by Mitch's side and he grabs my hand without looking at me. He's not unconscious, but he's not completely awake either. It reminds me of weeks ago when he was first brought in. I hold his hand and watch him drift off to sleep. I run my hand over his hair in an effort to comfort him. I can't imagine what that must have been like for him. I know he may be out for hours, so I ask Holly to grab me a book and a bottle of water. Then I sit and read to him, just like I did those first few nights. I don't know if he can hear me. I don't know if he can hear the shakiness of my voice as I read. I'm terrified of what will happen when he wakes up; of what he could have remembered. I want his memory to return . . . *don't I?* Even if it means him leaving here . . . leaving me?

Hours later, he finally stirs. Groggy eyes try to focus on me for a few minutes before he speaks. "Mikayla." He simply says my name. But that one word has me rejoicing ever so slightly. I'm not sure why I expected him to forget me when his memory returned. I know it's silly to think that would happen, but the mind is complicated. Then I brace myself for what he might say next.

"She's dead," he says. A tear falls from his eye and rolls down the side of his head.

I reach out to catch it. "I'm so sorry, Mitch. Do you want to tell me about it?"

He closes his eyes and sighs. "I was in Afghanistan when it happened. My CO pulled me aside after breakfast one day and said I'd been granted two weeks leave. He said my mom had a stroke and that I needed to go back to Sacramento to be with her. I knew it must have been pretty bad if they were making me go home. But, I was lucky. I made it home in time to say goodbye. My whole family was with her—my dad, my brother and his wife and daughters—we were all there when she died. She was only fifty-four."

He looks deep in thought and says, "I guess that's why I was back in the states." More tears blur his blue eyes. "I can't believe she's gone." He grips my hand tighter, pulling me down into a hug. I wrap my arm around him and rub the back of his neck. Even though this happened long ago, to him it feels like she just died. He is feeling every single emotion that he felt back then. "I need you, Mikayla," he cries his soft, broken words into my neck.

"I'm right here, Mitch." I climb into bed with him and he cuddles against me, spooning me in a way that feels so intimate yet not sensual. His body shakes as he silently sobs into my hair. I rub my hand over the arm that envelops me. We stay this way for hours.

I don't want to press him for more information, but my mind is screaming with selfish questions. *What happened next? Are you in love with someone? Will you leave now? Is this goodbye?* Yet, here he lies, spooning with me, after everything he remembers. This is good news. I relax into him and enjoy the comfort of his body pressed against mine.

He suddenly sits us up in bed and reveals, "Shit, Mikayla . . . it doesn't make sense. She died five months before the blackout."

"What doesn't make sense?"

"Her funeral. It's the last thing I remember. Why can't I remember anything after that?"

And there it is. My brain is on a roller coaster ride. Just when I think he's gotten his memory back and will not leave me, I find out there is still a large gap.

"It's okay, Mitch," I reassure him. "This is how it works sometimes. Memories are triggered by something you see, hear or feel and they may not all come back at once. But they usually come back in chronological order. This is a good start. And I'm sure you'll remember the rest in time."

"You're probably right. It's just so damn frustrating to have such a big chunk of my life that doesn't belong to me anymore." He looks around at the empty clinic. "I want to go back to my apartment now." He gets out of bed and I immediately feel the loss of his body against mine. I don't want him to leave. I want to be with him, comfort him, but I can't bring myself to say the words. As if he has read my thoughts, he puts a hand to my cheek and rubs his thumb along my jaw. "Will you stay with me, Mikayla? Will you just lie next to me tonight if I promise not to pressure you?"

I let out an audible sigh. "Of course I will." Then we walk out of the now darkened clinic together.

Much later, sometime in the middle of the night, I wake up in his arms. It is such a foreign feeling. I lie here and try to remember doing this with Jeff, but I can't. One or both of us was usually working. Our sleep was fleeting and the odd times when we were in bed together, we needed to sleep, not cuddle. Even sex was quick and most often planned into our busy schedules.

Being here, in bed with Mitch feels . . . peaceful . . . serene . . . right.

I can feel that my body craves his. I know that my heart craves his. But my mind . . . sometimes I just want to tell it to shut the hell up.

Chapter Twelve

I sneak out of Mitch's apartment early in the morning hoping he will be able to get some extra sleep. I told him last night that he should take a few days off. I know better than anyone how difficult losing a parent can be. It was hard watching him go through all those emotions yesterday and not relive the aftermath of the car crash that claimed my own parents when I was in college. But, yesterday was about him so I didn't burden him with my own grief as well.

When I get to the clinic, John is waiting outside the door. He smiles when I walk up. I inwardly roll my eyes and force my own smile when I say, "Good morning John, what brings you to the clinic?"

"Do I need a reason to come see you, Dr. Kay? Or do you only go by *Mikayla* now?" he spits out.

The way he says my name, like it's a bad word or something, has me wondering just what his problem is. I've never given him any indication that I'm interested in him so he has no reason to be jealous if I show feelings for another man. "Kay would be fine, John," I say, walking through the doors.

"Well, actually, I do have a reason. I haven't been feeling so hot for a few days. I think I might be coming down with something so I thought you should check me over."

"Okay. Why don't you head on into exam room one and I'll be there in a minute."

He nods at me and makes his way across the reception area to the exam room while I put my backpack away and get his chart. When I open the door to the exam room I'm surprised to see John sitting on the exam table—shirtless. "Oh, you didn't have to remove your shirt, John. I can take your vitals with it on."

"That's okay, Doc. I don't mind. I thought it would make it easier for you this way." He tells me his symptoms, which are all very vague and non-specific. I'm beginning to wonder if he really is sick, or if he's simply using this as an opportunity to get my undivided attention.

I walk around the exam table and put my stethoscope to his back, listening to his lungs. I take notice of the impeccable shape he's in. I'm not dead, after all. His broad shoulders and bulging muscles lead down to a tight and narrow waistline. Did he remove his shirt merely so I could see him? I think I hear him chuckle, but with the stethoscope in my ears, I can't be sure.

I come around front and listen to his chest. Then I place my fingers on his wrist to take his pulse. While I'm counting in my head, he raises his other hand and proceeds to rub it along the outside of my arm in a way that makes me very uncomfortable.

Before I can pull away, I hear someone behind me say, "Want to get your hands off the good doctor, Major?"

John smirks and cranes his head around me. "Do you mind, Sergeant? We are in the middle of an examination and would like some privacy." Then he raises his eyebrows at Mitch and says,

"And if you are insubordinate again, I'll take it up with the colonel."

"I don't mind at all, sir," Mitch says, walking over to get John's chart from the table. "I'm sure the colonel would be interested to hear about your inappropriate handling of the doctor here."

"Pfft!" John blows out. "I was merely helping her keep her balance, what with her bad ankle and all."

"Sure you were," Mitch snaps at him. "Mikayla, I'll take over now and finish up with him. You can go."

Refusing to be dismissed by any man—even though I understand his reason—I say, "Mitch, it's fine. I will finish the work-up."

"Yes, Sergeant," John bites at him, "why don't you go clean bedpans or whatever else nurses do."

I see Mitch's fists ball up as he ignores John's comment and turns to me. "No, Mikayla, you won't. I'll be handling the major's health issues from here on out."

Feeling there is way too much testosterone flying around this exam room, I say, "John, maybe you should go now. If you don't feel better in a few days—"

"You can come back and see *me*," Mitch interrupts. Then he steps in between John and me. I begin to panic when John jumps off the table and puffs out his chest. Mitch doesn't even flinch, however, and then John reaches around to grab his shirt and walks out of the clinic without ever putting it back on.

I turn to Mitch. "That was really unnecessary."

"Oh, it was necessary," he says. "I don't trust that asshole. I've heard people around camp talk about his erratic behavior. Major or not, I'll take him down if he touches you again." Then he frowns. "Unless you *want* him to touch you."

"No, Mitch." I roll my eyes. "I don't want him to touch me. But I can handle it. You didn't need to go all caveman on me."

"Caveman, huh?" he says. I can't help but relax when his lips curve upwards up into a seductive smile.

"So, are you doing okay today?" I ask. "You didn't have to come in to work, you know."

"Yes, I did. I can't just sit around and think about shit I can't do anything about. I need to stay busy," he says.

I start to walk out of the exam room when he grabs my hand, pulling me back to him. Hard. "You were gone," he says. "When I woke up, you were gone." He stares into me, his blue eyes darkening. "I didn't like it, Mikayla."

Oh! Hello again, Caveman. My insides tingle as he holds our bodies together.

"Dr. Parker?" a woman's voice calls out.

I reluctantly peel myself away from Mitch and go into the reception area. I see Rylee Tyner and her young son, Jack. Rylee nods at me, our signal that Jack is having trouble with his asthma and needs to be put on the nebulizer.

"Mitch, can you start up the generator please, and get Jack's super-power machine ready?"

"I'm on it," he says, smiling at the name we've dubbed the nebulizer to make it more fun for the little boy to sit through his half-hour treatment.

We get Jack all situated with the nebulizer and his mom settles in to read him a book. It's always the same routine with them.

I, too, have a routine I follow when they are here and the generator is running. "I'll be right back," I tell Mitch and I slip away to the back room to take care of something.

I lose my footing after I reach down to plug the charger in, and I end up sprawled out on the floor. Of course, Mitch picks this very second to come in the back. "You okay?" He comes over to give me a hand. "We need more albuterol out—"

He stops talking when his eyes catch the lit up screen of my charging cell phone. He shakes his head like he can't understand what he's seeing, like he couldn't possibly be looking at an actual working cell phone. I know, because it still affects me the same way when I see it myself.

"What the hell, Mikayla?" He eyes me suspiciously. "How do you have a working cell phone?"

"It doesn't actually work," I explain. "Well, not for calls and stuff."

"How did you get it?" he asks.

"It's a long story," I tell him.

"Oh, I see," he huffs, watching me hide it under a hospital gown while it charges.

"No, you don't, but I really can't—"

"Who else knows about this?" he says, cutting me off.

I shrug my shoulders knowing he won't like my answer. "Nobody. Nobody else knows."

"Kind of selfish, don't you think?" he asks. "Now, where's the albuterol? I have a patient out there."

"But I don't even u—"

"Where is it, doctor?" he asks, looking at me with disappointment.

"You have no right to judge me," I sneer at him. I stomp over to the cabinet where I keep the medicine he is asking for and grab a small plastic bottle of Albuterol. Then I turn around and throw it at him. *Hmmpf* . . . he didn't even give me a chance to explain. He automatically assumed the worst.

Mitch is standoffish with me for the rest of the morning. Even when he stitches up Harley Robertson's head and gets a pint of moonshine for his effort, he still doesn't so much as smile at me. He simply sticks the bottle in a drawer mumbling something about "for later."

One o'clock rolls around and Jamie walks through the front door, breaking the awkward silence in the clinic. "Kay, I know you've worked a lot lately so I thought I'd give you the afternoon off."

What's she up to? Jamie is *never* nice to me. As in, if I were on fire, the only fingers she would lift would be the ones roasting marshmallows.

Mitch walks out of the back and her eyes light up, just like the light bulb over my head does. Of course. She wants to be alone with Mitch. She had to pick the one day he is mad at me.

"Hi, Mitch." She pastes on a smile and raises the tone of her voice by an entire octave. "I've given Kay the rest of the day off, so it looks like it's just you and me all afternoon."

"Hey, Jamie." Mitch looks over at me and I shrug my shoulders. He tells her, "I don't know, I'm not sure I'm up for it, you know, with my mom dying and all." He shoots me a private, devious grin. "I think I'm going to just head out, too."

My jaw drops. He goes over and pulls the pint of moonshine from the drawer and walks past me as he says, "It's later." Then he winks at me.

I follow him out and shout over my shoulder, "Thanks, Jamie." I don't have to turn around and look to see her reaction. The sound of a bedpan hitting the floor alerts me to her tantrum.

Catching up to him, I ask, "Did you really just use the memory of your dead mother to get out of being with Jamie?"

"Yeah. I guess that was kind of morbid—but effective." He holds up the bottle. "You in? We could head over to The Oasis for an early happy hour."

I nod and smile because, apparently, all thoughts of cell phone secrets have been forgotten.

A pint of liquor may not be much to some, but I guarantee you sixteen ounces of Harley's firewater could kill a horse. I get the feeling that Mitch is all too happy to have it in his possession after yesterday's events.

We each down a swallow, followed by several choice words that don't usually come from my mouth. Mitch gives a few other patrons a drink as well. It doesn't matter what time of day it is, residents gravitate to The Oasis which has become the heart of our little community. If you can't find someone at home or work, odds are they'll be here.

"How about a game of pool?" Mitch nods his head in the direction of the community center.

"I don't know, you any good?" I ask him.

"I'm decent, I guess," he replies.

"Only if you take a few more shots of that first." I nod at the bottle on the table. "You know, to even the stakes." What he doesn't know is that sometimes we have Girls' Night there and I've had considerable practice knocking those little balls around on the green felt.

He raises the bottle to take a drink, but stops mid-motion. "Who is that guy over there?" he asks, pointing to a blonde-haired man sitting across the deck. "He's been looking at me the entire time we've been sitting here."

"That's Carson Withers. The brunette is his wife, Cassandra. I think they just got back to camp a few days ago. They left for a while to try to find her sister." As I'm telling him this, Carson and Cassandra get up and make their way over to us.

They stop in front of Mitch. "Mathews, ain't it?" Carson asks, in a thick southern drawl.

"No. Matheson. Mitch Matheson," he says, extending his hand.

Carson shakes it. "That's right. Staff Sergeant Matheson, from Sacramento. How the hell are you?"

His wife looks at Mitch and then at me and claps like a schoolgirl. "Oh, my God, is this her? Were you looking to find Mikayla Parker all along?"

Mitch and I look at each other and frown. He shakes his head at them as his hand absentmindedly comes up to grab the material of his shirt on his chest.

Cassandra says, "Aww, that's too bad. It would have made a great story to tell."

Mitch says, "I'm sorry, I was in an accident and I don't remember you, but you obviously know me. Would you mind joining us and filling me in on things?"

After I explain to the Withers about his amnesia, Carson proceeds to tell Mitch everything he can remember about their meeting.

"We was headed to Alabama to find Cassie's sister. We left with a few bikes and a couple weeks' worth of food and water. We was in the panhandle, just west of Tallahassee, when Cassie got a flat that we couldn't fix for nothin.' That's when you stopped to help. Most other folks we saw didn't bother to offer a hand, turnin' away as if they didn't even see us strugglin' with her bike. But you offered us a ride, even back-trackin' to help us find a sportin' goods place to rummage up a bike tire."

Cassandra puts a gentle hand on Mitch's arm and says, "We'll be forever grateful for that. I'm not sure we would have made it if it weren't for you."

"You're welcome, ma'am," Mitch says, staring at the couple intently as if they might hold all the answers to his existence.

"Anyway," Carson continues, "on the ride, we chatted some, but you was pretty tight-lipped so I cain't tell you much. Said you was searchin' for someone and that you would never stop lookin' because you had a promise to keep."

"You never did say if it was a woman," Cassandra adds. "But by the look on your face back then, we were sure it was." Carson nods, agreeing with his wife.

"You called me a Staff Sergeant?" Mitch asks.

"Well, that's what you told us your rank was," Carson says.

"Huh," he muses, looking at me with raised eyebrows. I smile, knowing he's pleasantly surprised to hold a rank higher than he thought. He looks back at Carson. "Can you tell me anything else?" Mitch asks.

"Let's see." Carson thinks for a second. "Oh, yeah, you said you was a medical somethin' or other and that you stopped to deliver a baby along the way. That's how you got the truck you had. The lady's husband was a mechanic who had retro-fitted some trucks with old re-built engines of some sort."

Mitch looks at me warily and then back to Carson. "Did I ever indicate to you that I was, um . . . married or anything?"

"Nah, you didn't say one way or 'nother, but you sure was intent on findin' whoever it was you was lookin' for."

Mitch leans over and whispers to me, "Breathe, Mikayla."

I let out the breath I wasn't aware I was holding. I'm not sure how to feel about this. Who was he looking for, and for the love of God, why couldn't he have told these people more? He wasn't going to stop looking until he found her. Well, maybe not *her*—but probably. That means he must have been in love with her. That means he has someone out there, just like I do.

"Oh, but I remember we told you about Camp Brady. You said the person you was tryin' to find was in central Florida so we gave you directions here. Figured it might be your best bet. I guess you made it. Sorry you didn't find who you was lookin' for though. Maybe there's still hope, you know, if you remember stuff eventually."

"Yeah, maybe," Mitch says, looking sad to not have all the gaps filled in. "Hey, thanks." Mitch shakes Carson's hand and the Withers walk away. Mitch calls out after them, "Did you find her— your sister?" he asks Cassandra. She shakes her head with a weak smile and turns around to walk away.

Mitch takes a long drink from the bottle and hands it to me. I take it willingly, attempting to squelch my own anxiety over what we just heard. "So, no pool today then."

He shakes his head. "Can I get a rain check on that? I think I'm going to take off for little while. Is it okay if I catch you later?"

"Of course," I say, trying to sound a tiny bit cheerful when I think I'm dying a little inside.

I watch him walk away toward the barracks and I wonder if he is sad because he can't remember, or because he now knows someone is waiting for him out there, or simply because the reality of someone else not finding who they were looking for just slapped him in the face.

I take one more drink from the bottle that Mitch abandoned on the table.

~ ~ ~

Dear Jeff,

People have left in search of loved ones only to come back empty-handed. They bring information of death and destruction amid small slivers of hope in the rumors they hear about the government making plans to help.

None of the missing have returned. No soldiers. No loved ones. And as each day goes by, I have to wonder if the chances of that happening get better or worse. More and more people are moving on from those they lost. I have found myself crossing lines that I never thought I would. Are you crossing your own lines? Does that make us bad people?

I delivered a baby last week. I haven't felt that alive since arriving here. It gave me hope. Hope for what, I don't know yet. But, I also lost a patient—one that could have been saved if I'd had the proper equipment.

Working here at the clinic has me thinking a lot lately about my past life and the direction it was heading. I like it here. Call me crazy, but I love the leisurely pace of our little community. I wonder if maybe I'm not cut out for the fast-paced life of emergency pediatrics. Is it wrong of me to simply want to set up a small practice someplace where all my clients feel like family?

The blackout has changed me. Has it changed you? Would we ever be able to be the Jeff and Kay that we once were? I guess the bigger question is . . . would we want to?

Until next time. All my love,

Kay

Chapter Thirteen

Hours pass with no sign of Mitch. I can't help but wonder if Carson helped trigger his memory. Dr. Jacobs told me that sometimes all it takes is a single event, item or even just a word and every lost memory will come flooding back.

My body goes into autopilot, understanding what I need and I end up at the stables. As Sassy carries me to the meadow, I think about the fact that Mitch has become such an integral part of my life. He hasn't even been here for a month, yet I already know my world would be incomplete without him.

I blink a few times as I see Mitch come into focus and I delight in my unexpected ability to make him materialize before me merely with my thoughts. I think I see a faint smile as he approaches and when I notice that he is riding Rose, memories of that first ride together flood my head sending a shiver down my spine.

"Hi," he says, bringing Rose to a stop next to me.

"Hey. You okay?" I ask.

He smiles and nods his head at me.

"If you're looking for a place to think, I know a good spot if you want me to show you. It's kind of off the beaten path."

"Sounds like exactly what I need. Lead the way, doctor."

I can feel Mitch's eyes bore into me as he follows me over to the meadow. It takes a few minutes to get there. Minutes that we spend in complete silence. Minutes of pure torture because I wonder what is going through his head. Minutes of overwhelming guilt because I want him for myself.

"So, here it is," I say, as our horses emerge from the tall trees into the serene grass and flower-lined prairie that has become my sanctuary. I turn Sassy around to leave. "Okay, well . . . maybe I'll see you later."

"Stay, Mikayla."

My eyes close in relief at his command. Those two little words increase my heart rate as if I've just run a marathon. I turn my horse back around and walk her over to him.

He lets out a deep sigh. "I feel so guilty."

I nod my head in understanding. "I know, Mitch. Me, too. It's okay. I know how you feel."

"No, Mikayla, I don't think you do." He inches Rose closer to me. "I don't feel guilty for wanting you. That's not it at all. I feel guilty because I don't want to be searching for anyone else. I don't want anyone out there waiting for me. I just want you."

His sincere eyes tell me he speaks the truth and I almost launch myself at him. Luckily, I remember we are sitting on horses and I come to my senses before injuring another ankle.

I quickly remind myself that he may feel that way now, but when he gets his memory back, I'm sure things will change. Still, we both harbor this guilt, for whatever our reasons, binding us together as we have yet another thing in common.

He holds my stare as he dismounts Rose. He walks both mares over to a tree and ties them together. Then he holds his hands up to help me down off Sassy.

I fall into his waiting arms, expecting him to place me firmly on the grass beneath my boots. Instead, he wraps me in an embrace, my feet inches from solid ground, my face meeting his. He moves us away from the horses and then just holds me to him, staring into my eyes that I'm sure are ablaze with want and need. He doesn't lean closer; he doesn't put his lips on mine. He is waiting for me to decide if this is okay. He's told me he wants me, and only me. However, I can't tell him the same in all certainty.

I see his tongue come out and swipe his bottom lip. This tiny movement, this unconscious gesture has me ignoring the battle in my head, silencing the voices when I lean in and softly place my lips on his. "Mitch," I breathe into his waiting mouth as I feel him release a relieved breath before he molds his mouth to mine.

It is only the second time we've kissed, but our lips fit together as if we've been doing this forever; as if our lips were specifically designed to fit so perfectly only with each other's. We nip, lick and touch each other with such fervor, such intensity, that I think it's not even possible that anyone else has ever shared a kiss such as this. My hands reach up to grab the hair that falls across his collar, weaving my fingers through the dark wavy locks. He moans into my mouth and then breaks our kiss to taste every inch of my neck, licking and nibbling his way along my jaw from ear to agonizing ear.

"Ahhh…" escapes my lips as he lightly nips at my earlobe.

His hands falter and I feel myself slipping out of his grip so my legs hitch up and wrap around his waist, bringing our hips together and drawing a pleasurable groan from deep inside him. His hands move down to support my bottom as our bodies mash together with impatience. I can feel the evidence of his arousal pressing into the apex of my thighs and it drives me higher.

Without a thought, I reach down to grab the hem of my halter top and boldly pull it over my head.

Mitch's expression quickly turns from shock to admiration as his heated stare first caresses my eyes and then my exposed breasts. "Mikayla," he whispers breathlessly, "you are so damn beautiful. I have to touch you."

He removes his hands from my backside and my body protests as I slip away from him, my feet finally reaching solid ground. He swiftly removes his shirt, exposing his own awe-worthy chest, spreading the shirt on the ground. Then he turns around and in an instant, he sweeps me up into his arms as if I'm lighter than air, and he leans over to deposit me on the material laid over the grass.

Oh! The Caveman returns.

He kneels next to me, his eyes running up and down my body. I momentarily wonder why I'm not embarrassed, being half naked in the daylight, but then I realize that with the way he's looking at me—the way he devours every inch of my exposed skin—there is no need for shame. His eyes tell me that despite my imperfections, he is appreciating my body like a priceless piece of art. His heated stare sends tingles through my body and I shudder to think what his touch is going to do to me.

He leans down to me and I stare at his mouth, wanting it to do so many things to me. He says, "I don't think I've ever seen anything as sexy as you lying here right now."

I can't wait another second to feel his touch. I reach up and grab his head and almost violently pull it to my mouth, our lips crashing together in heated passion. I can feel his smile against my mouth before he pulls back slightly. Then as if reading my mind, he murmurs into my mouth, "Who's the Caveman now, Mikayla?"

He reaches down to put my breasts in his hands and a moan escapes his throat, mirroring my own pleasurable sounds. He rolls my nipples between his fingers and my body arches into him as my eyes roll up into my head. He leans down to run his jaw up the side of my face and the scratchiness of his stubble just adds to the sensations shooting through my body. "I love the way your body responds to me," he whispers in my ear, his hot breath flowing over my neck.

His words turn me on every bit as much as his hands on my body. He looks into my eyes as a hand makes its way down to the top of my jeans. He works a finger under my waistband, leaving a blazing trail of sparks everywhere he touches. His eyes ask a question that I answer simply by raising my hips and pushing them into his hand. He wastes no time unbuttoning my jeans and reaching his hand down, working his fingers underneath my panties to where my body is aching for his touch.

When he finds my pulsating center, I hear, "Oh, God." I'm not entirely sure if the words came from Mitch or from me. He works a finger in and out of my slick flesh and my moans become muffled when I bury my face into his neck.

I'm building up so fast. My body is on fire under his touch. I writhe beneath him as I dig my nails into his arm. He works moisture up to my tiny bundle of nerves and I know I don't have long before I explode under his ministrations. He rubs circles with his thumb while a few fingers push deep inside my tight walls. "Mitch . . . God, yes!" I can't keep the pleasurable words from escaping my lips.

"You are so sexy, Mikayla. Your body feels so good. Let go for me, sweetheart," he breathes into my hair as his fingers bring me to a place that is my undoing. His words, his hands, his scent, his body . . . they all come together to push me over the edge into a place where heaven and earth collide as flashes of light shoot behind my eyelids and agonizing pleasure works down through my curling toes. He has me calling out his name along with garbled words of ecstasy as pulse after incredible pulse flows through me in never-ending waves.

Holy shit!

As I recover from what I can only describe as an out-of-body experience, I think that even though he's made me come before—in my guilt-ridden fantasies about him—this was, without a doubt, the best sexual experience of my entire life.

I gather my scattered wits and look up at Mitch who is beaming, no doubt at how he was able to reduce me to a quivering mess. I contemplate thanking him for such a pleasurable ride but instead, I reach my hand over and cup the large bulge in his jeans.

I'm taken aback when he removes my hand. "I want to return the favor, Mitch," I say, with a suggestive smile.

"No, Mikayla. You don't have to do that. That's not why I'm here," he says.

Not why he's here? I thought that's exactly why he was here. With what he just did to me, he's going to suffer a major case of blue balls if he doesn't let me touch him. I look at him in confusion.

He shakes his head at me and says, "I mean, yes, I'm sure that would be great . . ." He reaches a hand over my chest and places it above my heart. "But what I really want is this, Mikayla. Everything else is merely a bonus." His eyes soften and he runs a finger across my lips. "When you touch me like that—when you make me feel as good as you just felt—I want to know that it's *me* you are thinking of."

My heart sinks. "Mitch . . ." I don't know what to say. Everything he's said is true. Would I be thinking of him and only him if we went further . . . if we made love? It wouldn't be fair to him. It wouldn't be fair to Jeff.

"It's okay." He smiles down at me. "I'm not going anywhere."

We relax into each other and lie here, shirtless and in comfortable silence while our fingers intertwine.

"I want to tell you about the phone, Mitch," I say, eager to have him understand why I keep it so private. I also want him to know that I'm trying. I'm trying to give him more.

"No." I can feel him shake his head behind me. "I don't need to know," he says.

"But—"

"Mikayla," he says, rubbing a hand down my arm. "It doesn't matter to me. We all have our reasons for doing things. I really don't need to know."

We lie here until the sun begins to set and we realize we need to head back.

Halfway back to the stables, he pulls the horses to a stop, comes over close and reaches up to my hair. He shows me some blades of grass that were apparently stuck to the back of my head and I flush. "Sweetheart, your hair could be covered in mud and you'd still be beautiful," he says, leaning in to plant a sensuous kiss on my lips. When we part, his demeanor suddenly changes and he nods in the direction behind me.

I turn to see John in the distance. He's riding a horse close to the perimeter. I didn't realize he had any watch duties and I wonder if it's a coincidence that he's out here. I quickly remove a hair tie from my wrist and secure my locks into a messy bun. I wave at John, trying to be polite, but he simply stares daggers at Mitch.

"Well, I can't blame the guy for wanting you," he says with a shrug. "You *are* kind of irresistible. Especially now." He winks at me. "But if he even looks at you the wrong way, he's going down."

I shake my head at my Caveman. Then it strikes me that I've just thought of him as mine. *Mine*—I test the word again in my head. Could he be? Do I want him to be? The voices in my head are once again at war despite my repeated attempts to ignore them.

Chapter Fourteen

I narrow my eyes suspiciously at my best friends. I'm *good*, but I'm not this good. Why aren't they all vying for the little square packages, that are 'ribbed for our pleasure,' like they normally do?

"Okay," I slam my cards down on the card table, causing my drink to splash out of my cup and splatter all over my cards. "What the hell is wrong with you guys?" I eye the condoms on the table and then pick one up and examine it for quality control. "Have these been used or something?"

Holly, Pam and Amanda quickly look at each other before Holly says, "I have a goddamn yeast infection, so sex is the last thing on my mind." She nods to Pam. "And I guess she and Craig are in a fight at the moment."

I look from Holly to Pam. Wiping my cards off with my shirt, I say, "But these things are like gold. You can always use them later, you know."

I'm not sure, but I think Holly kicks Pam under the table. Pam says, "Maybe we're just all waiting until you raise the stakes."

"Raise the stakes? What do you mean? I've already lost five tampons and some nail polish." I really didn't want to bet the hot-pink nail polish, but it was the best thing I had when I drew a full

145

house so I had to go for it. *Damn Holly*. Her full house beat mine, her three tens to my nines.

Amanda pipes in, "They want your porn, Kay."

"Porn!?" I exclaim. I'm confused, but when they all stare me down with raised eyebrows, it dawns on me.

Aw, crap. "How the hell did you find out?" I ask. My face heats up knowing they are now privy to my guilty pleasure.

"Don asked me the other day if you were keeping Christian Grey all to yourself." Holly elbows me. "Well . . . ?" she asks. "Come on Kay, are you gonna share the dirty bastard or not?"

Hmmm. How do I handle this? They are my best friends after all. I'm trying to figure out what to do when Amanda asks, "Can we just finish this hand before getting into it? I have to pee." She glares at Holly and Pam and nods to the pot in the middle of the table.

"Oh, right," Holly says. "Okay, I call. What do you have?" They all lay down their cards which have to be the most pathetic cards I've seen all night.

I lay down my two queens, making me the winner of the hand, and I pull everything in the pot over to my side of the table. I inventory my winnings. Two condoms, a tube of lipstick—that I open up to see is my favorite color—and a sample-sized perfume.

Amanda smiles coyly at the other girls when she gets up to use the latrine.

"Hurry back for the last hand, Amanda," Pam calls after her.

"Last hand?" I ask. "It's not even ten o'clock."

"Yeah, but I hear they have great music tonight so I think we should all take shots and head over to The Oasis," Pam says, winking at Holly. What the hell is up with them tonight? Too much moonshine, I conclude.

"So . . . you were about to tell us if you will bet your precious Mr. Grey," Holly says, wide eyed and smiling in anticipation.

I look down at my stash and eye the condoms I was going to ante. I suppose I can just save them for next time. "I guess I can do that. But it's for a borrow only, not full ownership. Got it?"

"Geez." Pam rolls her eyes at me. "Awfully possessive of your porn, Kay." Then she mumbles something about wondering if Mitch knows of my erotic fantasies, causing her and Holly to burst into a fit of giggles.

As we wait for Amanda to return from the latrine, we fall into a familiar game of 'Best and Worst' that Pam came up with a while back. It's the way we rant and rave about life after the blackout.

"Okay, what's your best?" Holly asks.

"Not dealing with rush hour is super sweet," Pam says quickly. "My commute was hellish. Now it takes me thirty seconds to walk to work."

"No taxes!" I cry out, earning a 'halleluiah' from the other two.

"No pap smears," Holly adds.

"Hmm . . . I don't know about that one," Pam says. "My gynecologist was hot!" Holly and I laugh at her as Amanda walks back in.

"Oh, my turn," Amanda says. "My new hot bod is definitely a best!" She runs her hand down her body, displaying it like a model from a game show. "The blackout diet is the best damn diet I've ever been on."

The rest of us giggle and nod our heads in agreement.

Holly turns to Pam. "What's your worst, Pam? What do you miss the most?"

"Diet Coke," Pam says. "I've had some since, but warm DC is just not the same."

Amanda says longingly, "God, I miss 'The Bachelor.' What I wouldn't give for a night of TV."

I try to think of one I haven't used before. "Well, in keeping with Pam's beverage theme, I'd have to say Starbucks. I love Claire and all, but that coffee she mass produces in the mess hall is just *not* worthy."

We all look to Holly, who has a smirk on her face. "Oh, this is too easy. My vibrator."

Sweet Jesus, she never fails to come up with one that has the rest of us blushing. The last time we played this game, she said something about her pulsating shower head.

After one last hand of poker, Holly is all smiles, having 'won' a week-long borrow of my so-called porn. I roll my eyes and try not to think of how she plans to make use of it.

We pack up our winnings and head over to The Oasis for some late night music. The bonfire is in full swing when we get there. My eyes close and a smile invades my face when I hear the familiar guitar sounds of Mitch, who has become quite a regular entertainer around here. He spots me and when our eyes meet, a blush heats up my face as this is the first time we've laid eyes on each other since we were together in the meadow yesterday. He winks at me, prompting a few heads to turn in my direction to find the recipient of Mitch's gesture, which does nothing to ease the redness of my face.

We join a few other girls at a table in the back and pass around the remainder of Pam's liquor.

"So," Amanda wonders out loud to the rest of us, "I wonder what they have planned for the anniversary." She nods over to a table where Claire and Evan and a few others are sitting. They have formed a committee of sorts to plan an event for the upcoming one-year anniversary of the blackout. They've not revealed any details about it, other than we're supposed to all come to the center of town at dusk on Monday.

We are trying to speculate what they are planning when John walks over and stands in front of my chair. He says, "Dr. Parker . . . er, Kay, how about a dance?"

Not that I would dance with him under any circumstances, but certainly not when a slow song is playing—at the hands of Mitch, no less. "Uh, John," I say, giving him a weak smile, "thanks, but I don't think I'm up for a dance tonight."

He inches closer and leans down and I can smell the alcohol on his breath. "Aw, come on, Kay. It's just a dance."

"I'm flattered, John, but my answer it still no." I lean back as far as I can into my seat, putting more distance between us.

His eyes quickly flash to Mitch and back before he continues. "Why not, honey, don't you want to have fun?"

Honey? Alarm bells go off in my head and I glance over at Mitch who continues to play, but raises his eyebrows at me in question. I give him a little shake of my head. The last thing I need is for Mitch to go all caveman on me and create a scene.

"She said no, Major," Holly interjects. "Could you please leave now?"

Anger flashes across his face and he loses his footing when he tries to stand upright. He's more than a little drunk. He tells Holly, "Well, in my experience, no doesn't always mean no, now does it?" He looks back at me. "Isn't that right, Mikayla? Sometimes it means yes."

Gasps can be heard around the estrogen-laden table, but before anyone can properly react to his words, he grabs my arm and forcefully pulls me up against his chest. I hear chairs tumble over behind me as my friends quickly stand up to lend their assistance.

Turns out, however, they don't need to help because apparently, my caveman is already on top of things. "Want to get your fucking hands off her . . . *sir!*" Mitch yells, having come up right behind John.

I could swear I see a smirk on John's face before he releases me to turn around and take a swing at Mitch. Mitch dodges John's drunken attempt to assault him and in about two seconds flat, John is laid out on the ground, courtesy of Mitch's fist.

A crowd quickly gathers behind us, watching the excitement that our calm little camp has been devoid of for some time. So much for not creating a scene.

John sits on the floor of the deck and looks up at Mitch with a bloodied face. "Don't get too comfortable," he says. "I hope you've enjoyed your brief stay because you are so out of here. You can't hit an officer, you stupid prick." He doesn't even bother to wipe the bloody drool coming from his mouth.

"I didn't hit an officer, you low-life shithead. I hit a goddamn loser," Mitch says. Then, seeing that some men have come over to collect John, he walks away, holding his hand, muttering, "Fuck!"

I don't miss the fact that Mitch locks eyes with the colonel, who had apparently witnessed the entire debacle from the back of the deck. The colonel lifts his chin at Mitch as he walks by him and says, "You might want to have that hand looked at, son."

"Yes, sir. I'll do that," Mitch says. He throws a glance back at me as he walks away.

I see the colonel shake his head and chuckle as Mitch disappears into the darkness.

Craig comes up to the table all wide eyed and says to Pam, "What the hell did I miss?" Then he plants a very big, very publicly inappropriate kiss on her lips.

I narrow my eyes at them and say to her, "Fighting, huh?"

She shrugs her guilty shoulders at me as I replay the earlier events of the evening in my head. I turn around and point a finger at my three best friends. "You lost the hand on purpose, didn't you?"

Holly's jaw drops as she half-heartedly pretends to be insulted. "What? We have no idea what you are talking about, Kay."

Pam nods her head towards the dark shadow of the apartments. "Are you going to fix up your guy's hand, or what?"

My guy? Is this why they all conspired to put condoms in my hand, so I could sleep with Mitch? I look at Amanda. Surely *she* wasn't in on this. But she wrinkles her nose and looks anywhere but at me. "This is not over," I tell them.

I go by Mitch's apartment only to find it empty. I then try the clinic, thinking that maybe he wanted to fix up his hand himself, but I find it deserted as well. Unable to locate him, I walk out to the grassy courtyard by the apartments and plop myself down. I look for the constellation I was reading about last night.

I feel a hand on my arm and it startles me, especially after what happened with John earlier. I look up and smile. "Mitch! I was looking for you. I wanted to check out your hand."

He sits down and holds his arm out for me. I put it in my lap and I gently feel around all the bones in his wrist and hand. There's some swelling, but nothing feels broken to me. I go to lie back down and pull my hand away, but he grasps my hand in his and then I hear him draw in a sharp breath, indicating the true level of his pain when he intertwines our fingers. Still, he won't let me pull away.

"You didn't even hear me walk up," he says. "You must have been really deep in thought. Want to tell me what you were thinking about?"

"Pleiades," I tell him.

"You were thinking about that yoga crap?"

I giggle and he squeezes my hand. I make sure not to squeeze back. "No, silly, not Pilates . . . Pleiades. You know, The Seven Sisters constellation."

"Ahhh . . . so you've been reading the book I gave you." I can hear his smile in the darkness.

"It's actually pretty interesting. I could get lost in all the stories that have been told about the sky."

"Okay, I'll bite. Tell me about The Seven Sisters."

I gently take his hand and point with our joined fingers to the place in the sky where the constellation is visible. "Pleiades, or The Seven Sisters, is among the star clusters nearest to Earth and is the most visible to the naked eye." I try to draw it out for him with our entwined hands.

I close my eyes and try to remember the entire story. "There are many different versions of the mythical legend, but I'll tell you the one I like the best."

Mitch removes his hand from mine and I instantly feel the loss. He inches closer and lifts his arm and I instinctively cuddle into his side as he wraps his swollen hand around me. It's the first time we've lain like this out here on the grass, but it's as if we had maneuvered this way a thousand times before. My head nuzzles perfectly between his strong bicep and his chest, and his arm comes around me to rest on my waist. I breathe in his musky, manly aroma that has me swooning. Being with him is comfortable. It's relaxing. It's . . . right.

"I'll give you the Cliffs Notes version of it," I say, wondering how long I will even be able to speak coherently with his arm hugging me and his hot breath flowing across my hair. "The sisters were the daughters of Atlas, you know, the one with the weight of the world on his shoulders. So, Orion, the hunter, who also happened to be the most handsome of all men, saw the sisters and instantly fell in love with them. He chased them and pursued them relentlessly causing them to get frightened so they pleaded with Zeus to save them. Zeus turned the sisters into doves that flew up into the sky. He placed them in the night sky where Orion could see them, but could not touch them. In fact, legend is you can see his constellation chasing that of The Seven Sisters. But I haven't figured out which one is his yet."

Mitch is very quiet when I stop talking. I crane my head around to see that he is studying the sky. "Isn't it a great story?" I ask.

"No, it's not," he whines, petulantly. "So, Orion, stud of all studs, who fell hopelessly in love with them could look, but not touch. That is *not* a great story. Can't you tell a better one, like about the guy who rides the flying horse to stop the sea monster from eating that goddess?"

"That goddess would be Andromeda," I tell him, "but I think we have to wait a few months to see her constellation."

"Do you believe that?" he asks.

"What, the mythical legends?"

"No. Do you believe all that stuff about love at first sight? Like how Orion fell instantly for The Seven Sisters?" He squeezes my hip and I wonder if we've moved on from speaking of mythology.

"I don't think so," I say. My mind desperately wants to wander back to med school when I first saw Jeff, to when he became my mentor and shared his wealth of knowledge and skills with me. But my heart . . . my heart has me thinking of when I first laid eyes on Mitch.

"I think real love takes time," I tell him. "I mean, I guess you can love the way someone looks at first sight. But how can you truly love all of them without more concrete information to go on?"

"Concrete information . . ." he mutters, mulling the words over. "Always so scientific, doctor." He leans down to push my hair behind my ear and whispers, "Just because you don't believe in it, doesn't mean it can't happen."

My heart skips a beat.

It skips a thousand beats.

It may have actually stopped.

Did he just declare his love for me? Blood is rushing through my ears and I'm sure if Mitch looked closely, he would actually *see* my heart beating through my chest wall.

"Breathe, Mikayla," he says, laying his head down and glancing back up at the stars as if he didn't completely turn my world inside-out.

"You never did tell me about your family," he says, running his thumb in little circles on my hip, sending all-too-familiar sensations through my body. "Can I ask about them?"

When I am once again capable of putting enough words together to complete a sentence, I say, "You can ask, but there isn't much to tell. I'm an only child, raised by the world's best parents who died in a hit-and-run car crash when I was twenty."

He blows out a long breath and places a kiss on the top of my head. "I'm so sorry, Mikayla."

I know he understands, having just remembered the death of his own mother. He knows there is nothing else to say when you've lost such a huge part of your world.

"I dream about them a lot now," I say. "It's funny, but I think they would actually love it here. My mom was always talking about how technology was poisoning the health of society, and my dad loved to take us camping—you know, real camping in the middle of nowhere. We'd simply pitch a tent and see what we could scrounge up for dinner." I stretch my neck back and look at him out of the corner of my eye. "Have you ever eaten squirrel?"

He laughs, shaking his head. "They sound like great parents."

I nod, lost in the memories I've evoked speaking of them.

He brings me back when he starts talking about his own dreams. "I wish I dreamed of my parents. But, I'm still having weird dreams about cereal. For the life of me, I can't figure out why. I never even liked those colorful ones with the marshmallows when I was little."

"Well, maybe you need to try some now," I say. "You know, every once in a while a stray box will show up at the PX. Sometimes they haven't even gone stale yet."

"I guess it couldn't hurt," he says, "especially if it will get rid of these ridiculous dreams."

We lie here for hours, talking of parents, his brother, and our childhoods. He even lets me talk about Jeff and how we met. Before I realize how long we've been here, radiant streaks of red, pink and orange slowly overcome the dark-blue twilight of the horizon as dawn breaks. And I bask in the warm knowledge that we've just spent our second night together.

As I head back to my apartment, I wonder why he didn't make a move on me. Not one move other than holding me all night long.

Then a little voice in my head tells me that he was giving me concrete information to go on.

Chapter Fifteen

I haven't stayed up all night since my residency days before the blackout. I had almost forgotten what a toll it takes on a body. Luckily, I'm not expected at the clinic today. Still, it's not like I've been sleeping the day away. More like I've spent hours analyzing every conversation from last night.

I learned so much about Mitch. I'm not sure I even knew that much about Jeff after knowing him for almost six years. Goosebumps dot my skin when I remember Mitch's whisper in my ear about love at first sight. Was he talking about us? We've only known each other four weeks. Is that really enough time to love someone? It took almost a year for Jeff and me to admit our feelings.

I try to recall if I felt the same sensations when Jeff held me in his arms, but it's just been so long. We were great together weren't we? We were compatible, agreeable, safe . . . content.

I shake my head and realize that I could be describing my relationships with any of my friends. Were we merely a relationship of convenience? Surely not. I think I'm making things up in my head to justify my feelings for Mitch. I love Jeff. I was going to marry him one day for Christ's sake. How do I simply turn that off?

"Kaykay!" Little wet kisses cover my face as Rachel tries to wake me. "Unka Autin heya," she says in her adorable squeaky voice. For a one year old, she speaks incredibly well. I guess with nothing else to do but read books to kids these days, they develop a far better grasp on language.

"Uncle Austin is here?" I ask, happy to see my friend that I haven't spent time with in days.

"Up up!" she squeals.

"Alright, I'm coming, sweet girl." I throw on a pair of yoga pants and a t-shirt. I emerge from my room with Rachel on my hip to find Austin and Amanda sitting at the kitchen table, staring at me.

"Everything okay?" I ask, looking between their serious faces.

"Yes," Amanda says, plopping Rachel on the floor with a Sesame Street puzzle to keep her occupied. "We wanted to talk to you about Mitch."

Mitch?

Oh, of course. They probably know I was gone all night and they assume I'm sleeping with him. God, they probably hate me for contemplating switching teams from the *have-nots* to the *haves*. I lower my head in shame and ask, "Is this an intervention? Are you guys pissed because I was with Mitch all night? I didn't sleep with him, I promise."

Austin laughs. "Intervention?" he tries out the word. "Okay, yes, I guess that's what this is, just not in the way you think, Kay."

I look at them with a furrowed brow, confused by his words.

"Listen, Kay," Amanda says, "we see the way you guys are together. And Austin rooms with Mitch, so he hears things."

"Hears things?" I snap my eyes to Austin. "What does that mean, you hear things?"

Austin smiles suggestively and says, "Just because we're dudes doesn't mean we don't talk about shit. And sometimes he says your name in his sleep. He really likes you, Kay. The guy has it bad."

Once again, I recall Mitch's words from last night, *Just because you don't believe in it doesn't mean it can't happen*. I close my eyes as guilt washes over me for the millionth time in four short weeks. "I'm sorry."

"What are you sorry for?" Amanda asks me. "And why the hell *didn't* you sleep with him?"

I look up at her smiling face, still confused as to the direction of this conversation. "What? You *want* me to sleep with him?" Then I remember the condoms from our poker game last night. "Oh . . . you *do* want me to sleep with him. But, why?" I ask, looking between them for answers.

"Why?" Austin repeats. "Let's see, because you like him. Because he likes you. Because you guys are smokin' hot together. Because you are like two peas in a fucking pod. Do I need to continue?"

"But we're waiting. The three of us," I say, pointing my fingers between us. "We are some of the last ones to still have hope."

"Kay, moving on doesn't mean you're giving up hope," Amanda says. "Nobody expects you to hold vigil forever."

"You guys are. Why should I be any different?"

"Because you have found someone to love, Kay," Austin says.

Love? Do they think I'm in love with Mitch?

"I'm not in lo—"

"Kay, shut up and let me finish. You can fool yourself all you want, but you're not fooling anyone else." He motions a finger between him and Amanda and says, "Who's to say that if the tables were turned and someone came into our life, turning it upside down like Mitch has yours, that we wouldn't be contemplating the same thing."

I try to understand what they are telling me. "You mean to say that you could see yourselves moving on if the right person came along?"

"We aren't saying that exactly," Amanda says. "I think the point Austin is trying to get across is—never say never."

"Right," Austin says. "Kay, we know you don't need our permission to move on, that is between you and your own conscience. But you shouldn't feel guilty. Nobody is putting you up on a pedestal and expecting you to remain faithful to Jeff's memory."

Rachel, bored with the puzzle she has done a thousand times before, climbs into my lap and pulls a hair tie from my wrist. I brush her hair with my fingers and put in into a ponytail as I think about what my two friends have just told me.

"I think I need to go for a ride," I say.

I spend the rest of the afternoon talking with Sassy. Who knew she was such a great therapist?

∼ ∼ ∼

Dear Jeff,

I know it's been a while since I've written. I also know why. And I understand that you will never read these letters. Even if by some miracle you come back, you will never read them. What I once thought was for you, I now know is for me.

I write these letters only for myself. Maybe I write them to prove that I haven't given up hope for your return. Maybe I write them as a reminder to myself that I made a commitment to you. Maybe I *continue* to write them to try and abate the all-consuming guilt over my feelings for another.

Could what Austin said today be true? And, if so, is it possible to love two men at the same time? Because I love you, I do. I think I'll always love you. But why then, when I think about my future . . . when I try to picture my happily-ever-after, is it Orion that I see?

I can't bring myself to finish the letter. I fold it up, smearing the ink with my tears that fell onto the paper as I tuck it away in the box under my bed.

I kick myself when I wake up after a long night of much-needed sleep. Why did I not put myself on the schedule today? Of all days, I chose *today* to have free. What am I supposed to do with myself all day, just sit around and think about what happened one year ago, on arguably the worst day of everyone's life?

I tidy up the apartment that doesn't need tidying. I wash my laundry, take a shower, read a book, and do anything else I can think of until I can't take being alone anymore. So after lunch, I head to the place I know will make me smile. The clinic. Mitch is working solo today; just as he has been the last few times he's been on shift. Well, that's not entirely true. I seem to always find an excuse to go in when he's working, just as he does when *I'm* working, so half the time we end up working together anyway.

What I find when I get there is more than a little surprising. I can see into the exam room through the small window in the door, and what I see makes my jaw all but hit the ground. It's Jamie, and she's naked from the waist down. She is fluffing up her hair and arranging herself seductively on the bed.

What the hell?

Mitch comes from the back room and almost drops what he has in his hands when he sees me. His face turns a shade of red that most definitely does not flatter him, but it makes me all too nervous. He looks from the exam room over to me and he can't seem to find his words.

I'm about ready to turn around and run out of the clinic when he lets out a deep sigh and says, "Mikayla, thank God you're here."

Not exactly the reaction I was expecting.

"I need you to see Jamie." He shoves her chart at me like it's on fire. "I do not want to look in between that girl's legs. Who knows what's been there." He laughs, still blushing.

"She's a patient?" I ask, still trying to figure out what is happening.

"Of course she's a patient," he says. He looks through the window in the door to see Jamie displaying herself without an ounce of modesty. He looks back at me and quickly adds, "Oh God, you didn't think . . ." He can't finish the sentence because he breaks out in hysterics. He puts a hand on my shoulder and bends down because he is laughing so hard he can't catch a breath.

He finally looks up at me to see that I don't particularly find it funny. He says, "You did! You thought we were . . ." Again, he can't stop laughing and he looks so cute that I can't help giving into it and I start giggling along with him.

"Well, what do you expect?" I hit him playfully on his chest. "I mean, she's in there all sprawled out and you were here, all alone."

He stops laughing and puts both hands on my shoulders, looking me directly in the eyes. "Mikayla, don't you know by now how I feel about you?" He runs a hand down my jaw and cups my chin. "I don't want Jamie. I don't want anyone else. I just want you."

I melt.

I'm surprised there is anything left of me but a gooey mess on the floor. The way he's devouring me with his eyes right now, like I'm the only woman left in the world, has me utilizing all of my self-control so that I don't jump into his arms. If there weren't a half-naked woman in the next room, I would drag him in there myself.

Oh, right . . . there's a half-naked woman in the next room. I snap out of it.

"Wait, why *is* she half-naked and waiting for you in there?"

He shoves a pair of latex gloves at me. "She's not waiting for *me*, she's waiting for a medical consult. And now that you're here, *you* can do it." He leans against the desk and crosses his arms. "I can't wait to see the expression on her face when you walk in the room. That girl is seriously horny for me."

I try to ignore the fact that he knows Jamie is *seriously horny* for him, and ask, "What's her complaint?"

"Poison Oak," he says, with a smirk.

"Poison Oak . . . down there?" My eyes go wide.

He laughs while nodding at me. "She said she was in the woods and had to take a pee, and well . . . this happened."

"You're kidding," I say, laughing. "But she is a nurse. She knows how to treat this. Why did she need to come to the clinic?"

He raises his eyebrows at me.

"Oh, right," I say. "Looks like she's taking a page from the Major Burnell chronicles."

I grab the hydrocortisone cream and the antihistamine tablet from where Mitch had set them on the counter. I push the door to the exam room open and Jamie tosses her hair back and plasters on a huge smile.

Until she sees me.

Then she closes her legs and quickly wipes the seductive grin off her face. She purses her lips and rolls her eyes at me before saying, "Kay, what are *you* doing here? Isn't it your day off?"

"Yes, it is. But it's lucky I stopped by so that you didn't have to have a man examine you. I know how uncomfortable that makes most women." I have to bite the inside of my mouth to keep from smiling.

"I'm a nurse, Kay. It doesn't bother me. If you want him to do it, I'm really okay with that," she says, hopefully.

"Well, now that I'm here. I might as well take a look."

Jamie jumps off the bed and grabs her panties, pulling them on in a huff. "It's actually feeling much better. I think I freaked out a little. You don't have to look at it."

"But, what if it's not Poison Oak? What if it's something else and you need a shot of antibiotics? Why don't you lie back down and I'll take a look to be sure."

"No, really. I'm okay. I'm pretty sure it's Poison Oak. I am a nurse, after all," she spits out at me.

"I don't mind." I pat the bed that she just vacated. "Come on. You took the time to come in and all." Oh, God, I may be going to hell, but it's so much fun playing her like this.

She rolls her eyes at me and shouts, "Kay, just gimmie the damn meds!" She holds out her hands after pulling her jeans on. I try not to look shocked when I see that one of her hands has a rash on it, and that it looks exactly like Poison Oak. She must have deliberately rubbed it on herself just so she could have Mitch see her, uh, goods. It takes every bit of willpower to suppress the laughter that is screaming to burst out of me.

Who gives herself Poison Oak to get a man's attention?

Biting my tongue, I place the pill and the lotion in her hand. Then she turns and stomps out of the clinic as I hear Mitch say, "Bye, Jamie. I hope you feel better."

We don't have much time to laugh about it however, because Tanya Brolin and her son, Timmy, are walking up to the clinic. Or should I say Timmy is dragging his shaking, sweating, belligerent mother in for treatment. I had told Mitch about her when I reviewed patient files with him. She is a raging alcoholic, but every few months, she runs out of liquor and goes through the DTs. Timmy brings her here and stays by her side until the worst is over. He is only eleven years old—too young to have this burden placed upon him, but his father was deployed so it's just the two of them.

"Hi, Timmy," I say, trying to sound cheerful for this distraught child. Mitch picks up an emaciated Tanya and takes her to exam room two. Timmy has grown up far too quickly. Tears roll down his cheeks as he runs down the list of symptoms his mom has. He always waits until she can't hold anything down before bringing her in because there is only so much we can do here and he knows it.

We only start the generator for a few minutes to get a baseline EKG. Then we get her hooked up to an IV and push a round of benzodiazepines. She'll probably stay here overnight, but Timmy will leave in a few hours when she is over the hump. The only time this poor child ever gets a break from his mom is when she's sobering up here at the clinic. Then the cycle starts all over again as soon as she figures out how to get more liquor, which usually involves sex of some sort. It's sad. The world may have changed, but people still have the same problems.

Mitch and I finish setting up Tanya and come out to comfort her son. He looks up at me with big grey eyes that are now red-rimmed, and he silently begs for the one thing that calms him while he's dealing with this insanity.

I nod and his lips curve up slightly before he turns to head into his mother's room. I can hear her yelling obscenities at her son when I go into the back room. Mitch follows me as we continue to discuss her case. His eyes go wide when I pull my cell phone from its hiding place deep in the file cabinet.

He looks at me in confusion and I say, "Just come." I take the phone into exam room two and place it into Timmy's waiting hands. He smiles brightly at me before giving me a hug. Then he looks warily at Mitch so I say, "Don't worry, he won't tell."

Timmy lets out a relieved breath and gets started paging through the games until he finds his favorite.

Mitch grabs my elbow and practically drags me out into the reception area. He stares at me in disbelief before saying, *"That's* what you use it for?" He shakes his head at himself in disgust. "God, I thought—"

"I told you not to judge me, Mitch. I did try to explain it to you once, you just wouldn't let me."

"So you don't use it for yourself?"

I shake my head. "No, I don't," I say with conviction. "Not once. Not ever. I don't think it's fair that I would get to use it when so many others can't."

"Your pictures?" he asks.

"Huh uh, not even those. Scouts honor."

He raises his eyebrows. "You were a girl scout?"

"Actually, no. I don't do well with large, organized group activities. I tend to prefer the one-on-one kind." *Oh, my God, I'm flirting with him.* Badly, I might add.

His eyes darken and he trails a finger down my arm, raising goose bumps all over my body. "Shit, Mikayla. You can't say things like that when we're at work," he says.

He shakes his head as if to rid it of all inappropriate thoughts. Then he asks, "How did you come to have a working cell phone? Did you get it from the Faraday cage?"

"It's kind of a long story."

"Well, how about we have a drink after work and you can tell me all about it. We'll have an hour to kill before the . . . what are we calling it, anyway? It's not a celebration."

"I'm not sure, a remembrance, maybe? The committee still hasn't said anything about it. I guess we'll all find out together. And, yes, a drink would be nice. I have a feeling we'll all need one." I lower my eyes to the ground, feeling sad again over the notorious significance this date will always hold.

Over the next few hours, Mitch and I keep ourselves busy taking turns with Tanya until Nancy comes to relieve us. I stow the cell phone away in its hiding place and we convince Timmy to let us take him to get something to eat before we walk him home.

When we finally get to Mitch's apartment, he opens a cabinet revealing his liquor stash, thanks to his new friend, Harley. I silently wonder if he has charmed *everyone* in camp. We sit at his kitchen table and I tell him about the phone.

"About six months ago, I was called off base in an emergency. It's the only time I've been outside the perimeter since the blackout. There was a bad accident and a man's truck had overturned, pinning his wife beneath it. She was losing blood fast and they couldn't move the truck so they had to bring me on the scene. They wanted to cut her leg off since she was dying and it was the only way to save her. But her husband was hysterical, saying they had to get their son from college and she needed her legs to get there. He begged me over and over to try to save her leg.

"By some miracle, I was able to stabilize her long enough for them to figure out how to lift the truck off her. Then, fortunately, I was able to save her leg. She had to stay at the clinic for three weeks and she will live with a pretty bad limp for the rest of her life, but she kept the leg and her husband was very grateful.

"So one day at the clinic, her husband asks me if I have a cell phone. I told him I did, but that it was buried in my closet somewhere. He asked if he could see it for a few days so I gave it to him. After all, what did I need it for? Then, just before he and his wife were going to leave to continue on their journey to find their son at college in Georgia, he pulls me aside and gives it to me, telling me to turn it on. I must have looked at him like he grew a third arm, but I did it anyway. I about fainted when the screen lit up and I saw a picture of my parents on it. I always kept their picture as my background.

"Turns out this couple had been prepared for this kind of disaster. Doomsday Preppers or something. They had tons of equipment that they had horded away and protected in a hardened bunker. They didn't have much with them on their journey to get their son, but he did have a microchip for my kind of phone. And he even snuck in back to charge it for me when the generator was running.

"He told me not to share it with anyone. He said it would cause chaos and everyone would want it for themselves and it would merely end up getting broken. For weeks, I wouldn't even pull the thing out. I felt guilty even knowing it existed. Then Timmy came in the clinic with his mom. He was hysterical. Tanya was sick and shouting mean things at him, but he refused to leave her side even though it was tearing him apart. So I got out the phone to distract him, and ever since, he gets to play games on it while she goes through withdrawal. It's our little secret, just Timmy and me . . . well, and now you."

My mouth is dry from talking so I take a shot of the horrible swill sitting on the table.

Mitch kneels on the floor in front of my chair and puts his hands on either side of my face, rubbing his thumbs on my cheeks. "You are without a doubt, the most amazing person I have ever met in my entire life, Mikayla Parker."

He leans in and kisses me. He kisses me hard. He breathes his staccato words into my mouth between kisses. "I. Can't. Get. Enough. Of. You." Our lips explore each other's necks. Our hands explore each other's backs. Our eyes devour each other's bodies.

We don't even notice the door opening.

"Get a fucking room, you two," Austin says, chuckling. "Actually, don't. It's almost time for the . . . what are we calling it?"

Mitch and I laugh at his words that mirror Mitch's from this afternoon. Then we all take a shot and head out to attend the event that has yet to be named.

Chapter Sixteen

Candlelight service.

At least now we know what to call it. As our residents crowd into and around the open courtyard in the center of camp, there is a lot of speculation over what is going on. This is by far the largest gathering we've had in the year that we've all been together.

To the right of the courtyard, a massive white party tent has been erected, under which are hundreds, maybe thousands of helium balloons in every color imaginable. Next to the tent are dozens of tables that house numerous boxes of candles. Upon closer inspection, I recognize the candles as being similar to the small ones used by my former church on special occasions such as Christmas Eve.

We find Evan in the crowd and he tells us that over the past month, the supply runs have included stopping at every church and party store they could find to prepare for tonight's event.

"But balloons?" someone nearby asks in disgust. "This isn't a celebration, Evan."

Evan puts a comforting hand on the man's shoulder. "Just wait, George. Claire will explain everything in just a few minutes."

We gather around a podium and try to shush the children so everyone can hear Claire's voice in the absence of a microphone. Thank goodness for the bullhorn she has up to her mouth.

"Welcome, everyone," she starts. "Thank you for coming to our candlelight service. I don't need to explain why we are all here, so I'll get right to the gist of it since I can see you're all wondering about the balloons."

The crowd is eerily quiet as we wait for her explanation. "Of course, you can do as you wish, but the committee thought that the candles would be good to remember those loved ones that are missing. You may light a candle to show your continued hope of the return of a loved one. The flame represents life, life that we haven't yet given up on; life that we hope still burns brightly somewhere out there; life that we pray will someday make it back to us."

Already, there are audible sobs along with many more silent tears from most people in the crowd.

"The balloons signify those that we've lost. Now, I'm not going to preach to you or tell you what to believe. I can only speak for myself when I say that I will release a balloon for my husband, Jeffrey, in hopes that it reaches him in heaven where he is surely looking down upon me this very second." Her voice cracks and a tear slips out of her eye. "Most of us here never had the opportunity to say goodbye to a loved one. There were no burials to attend. No services at which to grieve. Let this be your closure. Let this also be the day we celebrate the lives of those that are still with us. Let us cherish what we have and not take anything or anyone for granted."

No one moves. I don't know if anyone is even breathing.

"Go on now," Claire waves us off. "Find your peace." She walks off the podium right into the colonel's arms and they both go over to release a balloon for their fallen spouses.

Mitch and I look at each other. I momentarily wonder if we are going to do this together. Would it seem strange to light a candle for Jeff with him by my side? Is he going to light a candle for the person that is waiting out there for him?

He mirrors my questioning expression; then he smiles and holds out his hand for me. It doesn't even take me a half-a-second to realize that, yes, I want to do this with him. I place my hand in his and he walks us over to the tent.

People are displaying every emotion imaginable. They are crying, yelling out in anger and frustration, even laughing. It's like this tent represents one massive funeral. I notice that people have been given Sharpie markers and are writing either the names of their fallen loved ones on the balloons, or messages to them.

We go over to select some balloons. Conspicuously missing from the various colors available is black. The balloons are bright, vibrant colors and the amazing sun-setting sky is becoming dotted with the brilliant colors. It's as if God himself chose today to display the most glorious sunset anyone has ever seen.

Mitch selects a purple balloon. "Mom's favorite color," he tells me. "Do you want to get a couple for your parents?"

"But they didn't die because of the blackout," I say.

"You heard Claire. It's up to us how we choose to do this. There are no rules here."

I nod my head and pick out a single balloon. Then I write both their names on it. "They are together forever, so I only need the one," I say, releasing it into the sky as a tear rolls down my cheek.

Mitch releases his as well and we stand, hand in hand, watching as our balloons weave and tangle their way through the myriad of others floating up through the comforting warmth and sweet embrace of the setting sun.

Part of me dreads walking over to the candle-filled tables. I'm not even sure what I'll feel when I light a candle for Jeff. Maybe I'll break down . . . maybe I'll smile thinking about the good times we had . . . maybe my heart will hurt with longing.

"There are so many people that I love who are missing," Mitch says. I think of his dad, his brother, his sister-in-law and three nieces, not to mention all his friends that may still be over in Afghanistan. He reaches for a candle. "I think I should only light *one* so I don't burn down the camp." He means it as a joke, but our eyes meet and the reality of the unknown fate of so many overwhelms us and we share an embrace before we continue on this emotional roller coaster.

He hands me a candle. "For Jeff," he says, with an understanding smile. "It's okay if you need to do this alone, Mikayla."

"No," I tell him. "Let's do it together."

I close my eyes and will myself not to fall apart as he takes a lighter from someone and ignites our candles. I stare at the flame. The flame that represents the life that Jeff still may live. I watch it flicker as the range of colors in the flame mirror that of the awe-inspiring sunset. Blue, red, orange, yellow . . . the flame mesmerizes me. I don't know how long I stand here and stare at it. My life with Jeff plays out before me. Every glorifying detail flashes through my head and I smile as I think of the stability, the generosity and the sincerity he brought to my life in the wake of losing my parents. But as my life with him dances through my memories, I realize that I'm missing him in the same way I miss my parents. I loved them dearly, just as I love him dearly, but in this moment, I know for certain, I'm no longer *in love* with him. In my highly emotional state, I'm fairly sure I hear myself let out an audible sob as relief flows through me.

I think I also hear Mitch say something like, "Okay, then." His voice is sad and sullen, and when my eyes flutter open for a brief second, I see him slip away, perhaps to put his candle in the receptacle.

Before I know it, sunset has turned to darkness and I'm still here, my cheeks wet and eyes swollen from the never-ending stream of tears running down my face courtesy of my epiphany. My candle has all but burned down to a nub and the hot wax dripping on my hand pulls me from my trance. I glance next to me to see that Mitch is no longer there. I look around, but I can't find him among the dwindling crowd. My eyes come across the large white tent, still with a good selection of balloons and I know what I have to do.

I walk over to the tent and grab one of the remaining balloons and walk out into the open courtyard. I get a Sharpie and write one last letter to Jeff on the side of the balloon. Well, it's not really a letter as much as a word.

Goodbye.

I stretch my arm up high over my head, holding the long string of the bright-blue balloon between my fingers, the balloon softly bobbing in the light spring breeze. As I release it, I'm releasing the guilt that I've burdened myself with. I'm freeing myself from my willful condemnation. I'm allowing myself the chance at happiness with another.

I watch the balloon get quickly swallowed up in the dark sky and as I walk away, I realize I'm ready to give myself over to the possibility of loving again. I suddenly stop walking as my heart splinters into my chest as if trying to tell me something. I decide to take the advice of my friends and listen to it. It's telling me what everyone else obviously knows. I'm *already* in love with him.

I can't get to him fast enough. This intense need I have to see him is driving my quickening steps as my feet fly across the fading stripes of the parking lot in front of the apartments.

I come around the corner and run straight into Holly, our foreheads smacking together. "Ouch!" she shouts. "Where's the fire, Kay?"

I rub my forehead, continuing to walk while I reply, "There's somewhere I need to be." I head towards Mitch's apartment.

"Ah . . . I see," she calls out over her shoulder, "the fire is in your pants." She laughs, walking away.

It doesn't even occur to me to knock on Mitch's door. I simply open it and plow through. I'm on a mission and two inches of steel is not going to stand in my way. The living room is deserted so I go back to his bedroom. "Mitch?" I walk into his room only to be disappointed by the emptiness of it.

"Kay?" I hear behind me and spin around to see Austin emerging from the kitchen. "He's not here. He didn't come back after the service. Did something happen?"

"Yes. No. I don't know," I say in frustration. "We were lighting candles and then he was gone. He didn't even tell me he was leaving."

"Well, you can hang out here if you want. I'm leaving for work," he says.

"No thanks. I'm going to see if I can find him."

I check the usual places—the clinic, The Oasis, the stables, our normal stargazing spot—but he's nowhere to be found. Maybe he doesn't *want* to be found. Maybe the service sparked his memory. Maybe I'm too late.

My heart sinks into the pit of my stomach while I make my way back to his apartment. I wait for him in his bed. It smells of him and I wrap my arms around his pillow as his scent envelops me.

"Mikayla?"

I startle awake in the darkness and wipe sleep from my eyes to see the moonlit shadow of Mitch standing next to the bed. "Mitch, I was waiting for you. I couldn't find you anywhere."

"Why are you here?" he asks with trepidation.

"Why am I here? Because I want you," I say, blushing in the darkness at my bold words. I reach out for him but he backs away.

"But I saw you. You were so distraught. You can't let him go. I know that now and I can't . . . I can't *do* this anymore." He turns to walk out.

"No!" I call out after him. "You don't understand, Mitch. I was crying *because* I let him go, not because I *couldn't*. I was so relieved that my emotions got the best of me. You left. You didn't see what happened. You didn't see me free myself from him. That's what I came here to tell you. That's why I had to find you."

I hear him turn around and step towards me. "You let him go? What does that mean?"

"Yes, I let him go, along with the balloon I released into the sky after you left." I reach for him again, but instead of pulling away, he lets me take his hand in mine. I pull him down on the bed. "It means that I want you and only you, Mitch."

Without warning, he flips me onto my back and climbs on top of me and I can't stifle the giggle that comes out at his Neanderthal tendencies. He pushes my hair away from my face and takes my head in his hands. He leans down to where our breath mingles. "Are you sure, Mikayla? Because I want to make love to you more than I want to take my next breath."

Oh my!

I arch my body into his, moaning my answer into his mouth as I lift my head and pull his lips to mine. Our kisses are demanding, impatient at first, but then they settle into a sensuous dance of unspoken promises.

I quickly reach for the hem of my shirt, wanting to rip it—and every other stitch of clothing that separates us—from my body. I feel him smile against my neck, where he is trailing kisses up to my ear. He whispers, "We have all the time in the world, Mikayla, and I plan on savoring every minute."

His words stroke my libido just as efficiently as his hands stroke my body. He pushes my shirt up and over my head then trails his fingers along the edge of my bra before pulling the cups down and freeing my breasts. I'm trussed up by my bra, heightening the sensation when his fingers tug at my stiff nipples.

"Oh, God," escapes me in a deep, throaty voice that I don't recognize. My hips involuntarily grind against his, seeking any friction that can relieve the ache that is building deep inside me.

"Mikayla, you are so sexy. Do you have any idea what you do to me?"

"Please, Mitch . . ." I reach for the button on his jeans. "I want to touch you." His jeans and shirt come off practically in one motion that would make me giggle if I weren't so strung out with want and passion.

I skim my hand along his perfectly toned abs as it makes its way under the tight cotton boxer briefs that hold in the very thing I seek. When I wrap my hand around his velvety steel length for the first time, he lets out a long, slow breath through his pursed lips. I move my hand up and down, listening to his breathing become shallow and quick as his hands continue to explore my breasts.

"You have too many clothes on, sweetheart," he says. "Let me take care of that." I reluctantly remove my hand from him while he strips me of my jeans and panties. Then he removes his own boxers and lies back down next to me. We fervently explore each other's bodies with our hands. I take the time to savor every ridge and ripple of his muscular frame before making my way back down to his throbbing manhood.

Strong fingers explore the apex of my thighs as pleasurable shock waves flow through me, pushing me up to the edge of the cliff I so desperately want to fall over. I feel a finger slip inside me. Then he gasps. "God, Mikayla, you are so ready for me. You feel so good. I don't think I can wait any longer."

I stiffen when I realize we are about to need a condom, which is tucked away in my closet with the rest of my poker stash. "What is it, sweetheart?"

"Uh . . . I think I need to go get something in my apartment."

He reaches over to the drawer in his bedside table and pulls out a little square package.

"You have a condom?" I ask, shocked at this revelation.

He laughs. "Don't be so surprised. I saved up and got one right after our night in the meadow. I knew right then that I had to have you someday." I see the moonlit silhouette of him rolling the condom down his length and I about detonate on the spot.

He arranges himself between my legs and hesitates.

"Please, Mitch . . ."

I hear his smile and then I hear pleasurable moans come from both of us as he pushes himself inside me. "Oh, my God. You feel so good," he murmurs into my neck. He looks into my eyes as he eases himself in and out, quickening his pace as our bodies demand gratification.

Looking up at him, I think that watching him make love to me is just about the sexiest thing I've ever seen. I arch my hips into his, seeking that last little something that will push me over the edge of the cliff. Reading my mind, he reaches a hand between us and rubs circles on the very place that will shatter me.

"Ahhh . . ." he leans down and moans into my shoulder. "You are incredible. I'm so close," he pants into my ear. Then he pulls back and locks eyes with me, not letting up the pleasurable thrusts or ministrations of his strong fingers. "Let go with me, baby."

My body explodes like it is a slave to his command. Every bit of my world is concentrated in the parts of our beings that are molded together and I perfectly convulse beneath him, screaming declarations of pure joy and satisfaction. He watches me come apart, our eyes and bodies connected, and he quickly joins me, falling over his own cliff into a freefall of pleasurable spasms.

He collapses on top of me and we lie this way, exchanging heated breaths, until we regain the ability to move at will.

"That was . . ." I can't even find the words.

"The best goddamn sex I've ever had in my life," he says, breathlessly completing my sentence. Then he stiffens a bit. "Oh, shit, Mikayla, please tell me it was the same for you."

I giggle, running my thumb over his bottom lip. "It was the same for me, Mitch. It was incredible."

Encased in his arms, I fall into sleep faster than I have in over a year. The last thing I remember is Mitch sleepily mumbling something about how glad he was to find me.

Morning light streaks through the window and dances on the wall in a prism of magnificent colors as it reflects through the glass of water on the sill.

I'm still drunk on the events of last night. I think it might actually qualify as the best night of my life. As I watch the quivering rainbow of light, I breathe in deeply to smell Mitch's scent that I've come to crave so desperately. I blush when I realize it is mixed with the distinct smell of our lovemaking.

Mitch is spooning me in what is now a comfortable and familiar embrace. My body moves of its own accord when I recall how his hands caressed me and how he felt when he moved deep inside me.

Mitch wakes and sleepily rubs his hand down my arm onto my bare thigh. I wiggle my bottom into his growing erection. He smiles into my hair and says, "Did you say you have another condom across the hall?"

I hold up two fingers and smile.

"Oh, sweetheart, you're going to be the death of me." He laughs, now fully awake and hopping up to pull on his pants and run a very quick errand.

Chapter Seventeen

We bask in our post-coital bliss for the second time this morning. Thank goodness Mitch ran into Holly in my apartment and asked her to cover for me at the clinic today.

"Maybe we should have saved one," Mitch says, looking over the edge of the bed. "You know . . . paced ourselves." I follow his gaze as he stares longingly at the three empty condom wrappers on the floor by the bed.

I laugh when I spot our pile of discarded clothes next to them. The pile is topped by the smiley-face boxer briefs that I threw at him that day at the PX. "You bought them?" I ask.

He reaches down to pick them up and throw them at me. "Of course I did. You obviously liked them. I just can't believe I was wearing them last night of all nights."

I retrieve them from where they landed on my chest and grin deviously at him as I seductively pull them up and over my hips. His eyes darken with passion as they follow my movements. "Shit, Mikayla, can you stop being so damn sexy? I'll never be able to wear those again without getting hard."

He gets up and puts on his jeans—commando—which is hot as hell. Then he pulls his t-shirt over my head and drags me along behind him to the kitchen. I stare at his broad muscular back along the way and when we sit, I ask, "Have you remembered anything about your scars?"

He shakes his head as he feeds me a bite of a stale granola bar. "No, but I've had some bad dreams about being hurt, so maybe I was in a fight or something."

I sigh and lower my head thinking of how awful that would have been. "I like my other theory much better." I think of the time I suggested that his scars were from some sort of intentional sexual gratification.

He raises a provocative brow. "Why doctor, are you proposing we experiment with that sort of thing? Do you have any of your own dreams that you'd like to share with me?"

Heat warms my face. "Uh . . ."

"I'm kidding, Mikayla," he says, laughing. Then he looks at me, deep in thought. "Well, maybe I'm not. I think I would do just about anything you asked me to, sweetheart."

I grab the last bit of breakfast out of his hand and pop it into my mouth. Do I really have that kind of power over him? It's a heady feeling.

He leans across the table and traces his finger across my nose and cheeks. "I could stare at this beautiful face forever," he says. "These freckles . . . they make you appear so young and innocent, when I now know you're anything but."

The way he plays with a lock of my light-brown hair, tickling my neck with it as his blue eyes seem to stare into my soul—I can't help but launch myself around the table and onto his lap. I straddle him and lean down, pressing my lips to his. Our tongues mingle without even a care that we've not yet brushed our teeth and probably have little bits of granola stuck in between them.

I grind myself into his lap, delighting in the feeling of his strong hands coming up to caress my behind through the thin material of his briefs. But as the tingles build up, so does the uncomfortable chafing feeling between my legs and I stiffen.

"What is it?" he asks, when I stop moving against him.

"Uh, I think you broke my vagina," I say, burying my head in his neck so he can't see my blush.

He laughs and kisses the top of my head. "Alright then, let's head out so I can get my woman some real food."

A smile touches my eyes at his declaration that I'm his woman. We go to his bedroom to gather our clothes so we can shower before going to the mess hall. I'm pushing his boxers off my hips when he says, "Why don't you keep them. I kind of like the idea of you wearing my underwear."

I try not to release the sigh that wants to come out of me. Must everything he says be so provocative and swoon-worthy? I dare not let him in on this little fact. "We could share them," I say, liking the notion that when we aren't together, we can have some small connection through these ridiculous smiley-face boxers.

"Fine, but don't wash them before you give them back," he says. He pulls me to him and whispers in my ear, "I want to be able to smell you on them."

Holy shit! Did he really just say that to me?

I'm sure I'm turning ten different shades of red.

Confirming my suspicions over my flushed appearance, he says, "There go those freckles again. You are so adorable when you blush, Mikayla."

After our showers and a much-needed laundering of Mitch's sheets, we go over to the mess hall for a late lunch. On the walk over he grabs my hand. It's a small gesture, one that happens millions of times to millions of people every day all over the world. But, somehow, him grabbing my hand and rubbing his thumb over the back of my knuckles has me grinning like a schoolgirl. And when I look at him out of the corner of my eye, he is doing the same thing. We both laugh because we know how this is affecting us. It's the first time we've been like this in public. Together. Intimately touching as if to announce our relationship status to the world.

When we walk into the mess hall hand-in-hand, we get stares from many tables. Damn rumor mill spreads like wildfire around here. Some people smile and nod as if to say, 'it's about time.' Claire spots me and comes over to give me a hug, whispering, "I'm so happy for you, Kay."

I even hear some clapping and a few cat-calls from the table where some of my softball team is dining. I roll my eyes at them, but my inner goddess really just wants to high-five every last one.

We get settled at a table with our lunch trays and go over our agenda for the day. "So, what shall we do on our unexpected day off?" Mitch asks.

"Well, I don't know about you, but I was thinking about calling in a few favors," I say.

"Favors? For what?" he asks, putting his apple on my tray in exchange for my beans that he knows I despise.

I shrug my shoulders and try to whisper in his ear without blushing. "Condoms," I say. "I think I can scrounge up one or two."

He closes his eyes briefly and when they open, they are hooded and darkening. "Sweetheart, you have got to stop saying

186

things like that in public." His eyes flash down to his lap where I can see a growing bulge in his pants and I revel in the knowledge that my mere words have affected him like this.

I giggle and ask him, "What about you, what do you want to do?"

"I was hoping to go for a ride. But, considering the state of things—" he motions to *my* lap "—maybe riding horses is not the best option."

I shake my head at him and excitedly say, "No! I want to ride. I'll deal with it. Plus, it's more on the inside anyway." I wrinkle my nose and wonder just how many times my face is going to heat up this morning.

He laughs and cups my chin with his hand. "So darn cute," he says. "Okay, we'll ride, but we'll take it real slow." The seductiveness in his voice makes me wonder if we're still talking about horses.

An hour later, Brad has saddled up Sassy and Rose. I don't think Mitch has ever ridden another horse since that first day I took him out. The thought lights up my face as I remember having to ride double with him.

We ride slowly, side-by-side and enjoy the lazy, peaceful, spring afternoon. We often catch each other staring and smile. He occasionally stops our horses to lean over and kiss me. We have conversations about anything and everything.

When I'm staring at him, longing to run my hands once again through his dark, wavy hair, I catch a glimpse of his tattoo as it peeks out from under his shirt sleeve. I ask him, "Did it hurt to get the tattoo?"

He stares down at it like the tattoo might have the answer to my question. "I don't know, exactly. I don't remember getting it. I'm actually opposed to tattoos." He shakes his head and laughs. "I know I'm in the army, so tattoos are practically a given, but I just never quite understood permanently marking one's skin." He looks suggestively at my body. "I know I don't have to ask you about yours because I now know firsthand that you don't have any." He winks at me and I will myself not to blush.

We are walking Sassy and Rose along the southeast side of camp, where massive amounts of crops are growing, when we spot Craig and he waves us over. While I look in wonder at the acres of strawberry, carrot and asparagus plants, Craig and Mitch talk in depth about tenderness, thickness, ripeness and other qualities of the fruits and vegetables growing in this quad. It amazes me that Mitch has learned so much about farming in such a short period of time. I've come to understand that when Mitch isn't working or socializing, he's out in the fields learning about raising crops. I remember thinking that first day we met that he would be one of those guys that just can't sit still, and he hasn't proven me wrong yet.

We are continuing on to the springs when Mitch pulls a few strawberries from his pocket that I didn't realize he had picked. He rinses them with his bottle of water then he beckons me over with a crook of his finger. He places a strawberry between his teeth motioning for me to take a bite.

Oh, I like playful Mitch.

I walk Sassy over and get as close as she will allow, then I lean towards him. My insides quiver as my lips touch his. Mitch and strawberries. Two of my favorite things. The fact that he remembers that strawberries are my fruit of choice melts my heart a little. We continue to kiss long after the sweetness of the strawberry is gone, until Rose and Sassy feel it's time to move on and pull us apart as our ravenous stares continue burn into each other.

"Tell me more about Gina," I say.

He rolls his eyes at me. "Way to kill the moment, sweetheart," he says, absentmindedly pinching his shirt over his chest. "Why would you want to know about her anyway?"

"Because I want to know everything about you. And because I need to get my mind off . . . other things," I say.

He laughs. "Okay, what do you want to know? My life is an open book." He frowns. "Well, most of it anyway." I can see he's still sad over the memories that have not returned.

"What was she like? What did she do? Was she prettier than me?" I giggle. "Wait, don't answer that last one, I don't want to know."

"She had short blond hair and brown eyes and was quite a bit taller than you are. She was pretty, yes, but not in the devastatingly beautiful way that you are, Mikayla. You are the most gorgeous woman I've ever seen." He smiles sincerely at me and I know he thinks it's true.

"Okay, let's see. She was cool for the most part, once you take away the whole running-off-with-my-best-friend scenario." He shakes his head in obvious irritation. "We knew each other in high school. We were all good friends, Gina, Dale and me."

"Dale?" I raise my brow in question.

"Yeah, Dale. He was my best friend." He blows out a breath like it physically hurt him to say that. "I never even considered Gina girlfriend material in school. She was a tomboy who liked to do everything that we did. I may have even looked at her as a sister then. But then we graduated and she went away to college so we lost touch. Dale and I both became EMTs together, even working for the same firehouse for several years. Then Gina came back to town and started working as an interior designer. She was not a tomboy anymore and I took notice of that. Dale was away on vacation when I asked her out and we quickly hit it off. When Dale got back he told me that he decided he was going to pursue Gina. When I told him I had beaten him to the punch, he took it like a true friend and just moved on to his next conquest.

"I didn't think anything of it when, after almost two years of dating, I joined the army and asked Dale to look after Gina while I was gone. Dale had dated numerous girls in that time and never again alluded to wanting her for himself. He promised me he wouldn't let anything bad happen to her. Before I left, she gave me a locket. It looked like dog tags, but it had a few pictures of her in it so I wouldn't forget her. Of course I couldn't wear it, I could only wear my real tags, but I thought it was a pretty cool going away present."

He grabs his chest again and now I'm positive that this unconscious gesture has something to do with Gina. It scares me, and I think once more that maybe she's the one he was searching for. I attempt to put it out of my mind and continue to hear him out. I did ask, after all.

Me and my big mouth.

"We wrote letters and e-mailed and Skyped and all that crap. I made it home a few times for a little R & R. It seemed like our time apart was not very difficult at all. So I told her that I was considering extending my tour for a few months. I should have known something was wrong when she was okay with that. I mean, what girlfriend doesn't want her guy back after he's been gone almost a year?

"I stayed in touch with Dale constantly. He would FaceTime me with all the guys in the firehouse. His e-mails would let me know that Gina was doing well and that I didn't have to worry about her. I really didn't have a fucking clue what they were doing.

Not until the day I returned from my first tour and they dropped the bomb on me."

I can see how much it still hurts him to talk about it and I suddenly feel guilty for bringing it up. "I'm so sorry, Mitch. I shouldn't have asked about her."

"It's okay," he says. "Yeah, it still hurts and part of me will always be pissed because I loved her, but I'm no longer sorry it happened." He reaches over to grab my hand. "I have you now." He smiles brightly. "And I actually think I'm more upset about losing Dale than Gina. I loved that guy like a brother and he totally screwed me over."

I smile back, but part of me is dying inside as '*I loved her*' plays over and over like a broken record in my head. If he remembers—*when* he remembers—will he still be in love with her if she's the one he was trying to find?

He must see my sad smile, because, as if reading my mind, he says, "Don't worry Mikayla. She is *not* who I was searching for. Believe me, I would never go back to someone who had hurt me like she did."

It provides me a sliver of relief hearing him say that. However, I'm certain I will be devastated no matter who turns out to be the mysterious recipient of Mitch's sworn promise that Carson Withers informed us about.

We ride in silence and I wonder if he's still thinking about her. I again chide myself for making him go there.

Mitch breaks our prolonged silence when he asks, "Can you get on the pill?"

Whoa! Not what I was expecting.

"Uh . . . I'm not sure," I say. "I suppose I could have the guys try to get some. I ran out of the supply we had on base long ago. Either way, I'm not sure I would trust pills that old."

"Let's get out the pharmacology book at the clinic and see how long they last. Then we wouldn't have to worry about condoms," he says, hopefully.

I point my finger at him and raise my eyebrows. "Oh, no! You're wearing condoms, buddy." I nod to his pants. "We don't know where that thing has been for the past two years."

He laughs. "Good point. Okay, condoms until my memory comes back. But get on the pill anyway. I want to feel *all* of you the second my memory returns." He brings Rose close and runs a hand along my inner thigh.

And suddenly, thoughts of everything else fade away as I think of what I want him to do to me. "Come on," I say. "Let's go cash in on those favors."

"Oh, hell yeah!" he says, turning us quickly in the direction of the stables.

Chapter Eighteen

I've been avoiding Mitch for the last twenty-four hours. I've done anything and everything I can think of to keep myself away from him. I'm not willing to risk it, because I know if he gets me alone, I'll throw caution to the wind. I'm not like this. I've never been like this. Calm, cool, calculated . . . *that* is the kind of person I am. Why does he make me want to do things, say things, *be* things that I've never considered before?

Damn it! Why did we have to go through all our condoms so quickly? I called in every favor this past week; traded everything I could part with—okay, not *the books*—but everything else. Mitch and I spent all our credits, even forgoing things such as shampoo, alcohol and shaving cream. What I wouldn't do for a freaking Visa card right now.

"You've been avoiding me." I almost jump out of my skin when his hot breath rolls over my neck from where he snuck up behind me.

I turn around and almost spontaneously combust when I see that dark, yummy hair and his sexy three-day stubble that I long to have scraping across my face.

He smirks at me. "Why doctor, I think you want me so badly that you don't trust yourself around me." He walks around me and stands in front of me, lightly running his hands up and down my arms while provocatively appraising me. "Am I right?"

"I—I've been busy, that's all." *I will admit to nothing.*

He chuckles in my ear. Then he licks my neck right below my earlobe where he knows it drives me wild. I'm melting into a hot mess of hormones right here in the clinic, but I refuse to succumb to his little game.

"I think you're lying to me, doctor," he breathes into my ear in between the kisses he is feathering across my neck.

"Huh uh . . ." I shake my head at him and sit down at the desk to concentrate on the patient files that need updating.

"You know," he says, spinning around the wheeled office chair, caging me in so I'm facing him, "just because we're out of condoms doesn't mean we can't have fun." He leans down and whispers in my ear, "There are many other ways to make you squirm beneath me, Mikayla."

Oh, God!

He leaves me wondering if I actually said that out loud when he laughs and kisses my head before he walks out to the front room.

What just happened? He's left me a damn mess back here thinking about exactly what he plans to do to make me squirm. He's wound me up like a toy and then he left before playing with me. Cruel . . . just plain cruel.

I hear the sweet cries of a tiny baby and snap out of my unfulfilled fantasy to join Mitch out front. When I come through the door, I find Mitch holding Kelly's three-week-old baby, Toby. He's smiling down at him making adorably silly faces at the newborn. I'm beaming at the picture before me. This big strong man is holding a tiny baby, calming him by rocking back and forth and humming a song that he has played on his guitar.

Something happens inside me and my world shifts on its axis when I realize how badly I want this—all of this. The man, the baby . . . the life I'm envisioning before me.

"Mikayla?" I look up to see his questioning eyes.

"Huh? Did you say something?"

Mitch and Kelly both laugh at me. I must have been out of it for a minute.

"I asked how many of these creatures you think you might want one day," he says.

My jaw drops slightly. I swear this man can read my mind. "Uh . . . I haven't really thought about it," I lie. "A couple I guess."

"A couple," he repeats back to me as if trying out the words. He looks down at Toby. "Yes, a couple would be nice."

Holy crap!

Did he just agree to father my future children? I look around the room. What alternate universe have I entered into and why is nobody else freaking out about this?

Despite the fact that my mind has been completely blown, I'm able to perform a well-baby exam on our newest resident. It doesn't escape me how Mitch looks at me when I hold Toby. It's the same way I was looking at him when the baby was in his arms—with longing, with awe, with pure unadulterated joy.

We have a few cases of the stomach flu come in, and then after lunch, Mitch expertly stitches up Brad's injury, courtesy of Buck. I'll never understand why these stubborn men continue to ride that horse knowing how many others have been injured doing so.

"Those are some damn fine stitches, Sergeant," Brad says, admiring Mitch's handiwork. "You sure you're not a doctor?"

"No, sir," Mitch replies. "But thanks for the compliment."

I, too, appreciate the proficiency of his efforts. Most doctors can't even stitch that well. When Brad leaves I ask Mitch, "How did a flight medic, who works under tremendous pressure and must do things on the fly, learn how to suture so well?"

"It's a gift," he says. He leans close to my ear and whispers, "Among my other talents." My face heats up and goose bumps prickle across my skin.

"Ugh!" I hear, and turn around to see Jamie walking in for her shift. "Would you mind keeping your PDAs to a minimum? This is a workplace, you know."

I roll my eyes at the person who, just a few short weeks ago, was spread-eagle on an exam table in this very same place of work.

I give Jamie the daily report before Mitch and I head out. I walk in the direction of the mess hall because it's approaching dinnertime, but he grabs my arm and jerks me the other way, toward the apartments.

"Aren't you hungry?" I ask.

"Very." He looks at me from under his hooded lids. "Just not for food."

Suddenly, he scoops me into his arms and carries me across the parking lot.

Oh!

"With the way you've been looking at me all day," he says, "undressing me with your eyes . . . do you really think food is what I crave?"

"Undressing you?" I pout. "What about *you*, with your whispers in my ear and all the leaning into me and brushing against me?" Just talking about what he did to me today makes me feel all warm and gooey in all the right places.

"Sweetheart, I don't care who started it as long as we both make it to the finish line."

We get to his apartment to find that, thankfully, Austin has already left for work. Mitch is still carrying me and doesn't put me down until he practically throws me on his bed.

Caveman.

He wastes no time at all tearing at my clothes. "Mitch, we're out of condoms," I remind him.

"Mikayla, if you think I'm going to let that stop me, you don't know me as well as you think you do."

"But we can't—"

"No, we can't," he cuts me off. "I promised you we'd stay safe. I keep my promises." He pulls my pants off and stares at my almost naked body. He runs his hands up my sides, all the way up to my head where he releases my hair from its captive tie. He works his fingers through my tresses and then pushes it behind my ears. He leans down to whisper, "I want to taste you, Mikayla . . . every inch of you."

I stiffen and my heart pounds so hard I think it might actually burst through my chest.

"Are you okay? Did I say something wrong?" he asks.

"No. It's just that . . . um . . ." I feel it coming, but I can do nothing to stop the deep crimson that I'm certain is working its way across my face. "I've never done that before." I throw my arm over my eyes in a childish manner, as if doing so will render him incapable of seeing me.

"What?" he asks, in utter disbelief.

Hiding under my protective arm, I say, "Uh . . . Jeff was kind of a germaphobe and he said that there was just too much bacteria to be safe. He said he saw some pretty disgusting things during his gynie rotation. So he never . . . I never . . . well, we just didn't."

"Okay, well, how do *you* feel about it?" he asks. He removes my arm from across my eyes and stares at me with want and passion. "Will you let me taste you, sweetheart? It's all I dream about. Well, that and cereal," he jokes.

Of course I want this. I've heard stuff. I've definitely *read* stuff. But I can't speak, I can only nod my head in agreement. His eyes light up then he kisses me long and hard, his lips and tongue sucking, swirling and licking—all a preview of what he plans to do to me and it has me squirming under him before he even makes it below my waist.

Ten minutes later, I'm staring up at the ceiling, unable to move after screaming exaltations to Mitch and to God and to whoever else might have been within earshot.

"Oh. My. God." There are simply no other words.

I feel Mitch smile against my stomach, where his head rested after bringing me to the best, quickest, and most earth-shattering two orgasms I've ever experienced.

"Well, thank you . . . thank you very much," he says, doing a terrible Elvis Presley impersonation, earning him a smack on the head.

"Ow," he says, feigning injury. He raises his head and looks up at me. "But, seriously, Mikayla, that was the hottest damn thing I've ever seen in my entire life."

My eyes go wide. "You *watched* me?" I ask, horrified by how I must have looked shaking and yelling under his ministrations.

"Hell yes I did." He removes the pillow I placed over my head in my embarrassment. "And you have nothing to be ashamed of, sweetheart. You were amazing. You *are* amazing. I will never get tired of watching you come apart beneath me."

I feel his erection press against my leg and know what I have to do. What I need to do. What, more than anything, I want to do. I reach out to grab him and maneuver myself so that he understands my intention.

"You don't have to do this, Mikayla. I don't expect you to do anything."

"I know you don't. That's one of the reasons I want to." I kiss him and taste my own juices on him which I find surprisingly erotic. "I want to see you come apart, too. I want to make you feel as good as I felt." I close my eyes and summon the courage to say one final thing. "I want to taste you, Mitch."

I could swear his eyes dilate on the spot at my words. His erection grows even harder and throbs in my hands as I lower myself and take him into my mouth for the first time.

"Sweet Jesus," he says, minutes later, coming down from his powerful release. "What did I ever do to deserve you?"

"So, it was okay then?" I ask.

"*Okay?* Shit, sweetheart, that was more than okay. It was incredible, phenomenal, life-changing. Are you sure that was your first time?"

I can't help the victorious grin that overtakes my face. "Yeah, but you'd be amazed at what you can pick up from books."

He laughs, coming up to kiss me, not even complaining about tasting himself. I lose myself in him once again.

We never do make it to dinner.

~ ~ ~

We walk hand-in-hand over to the softball field for our regular Friday night game. It's only been a couple of weeks, but it feels so comfortable, so incredibly right to be walking like this with him. Everyone has gotten over the initial shock of the town doctor now having a boyfriend. Everyone but John and Jamie, that is. Jamie is as spiteful as ever. Pam overhead her and a friend talking about Mitch being fair game until he puts a ring on my finger. Apparently Jamie said that even then, she still wouldn't count him out because that's when things really get interesting.

I know Mitch is not the least bit drawn to her. But she is gorgeous and thin and sexy and has big boobs—all the things men find hard to resist—so there is always going to be that insecure part of me that worries he will fall into her trap of seduction. I often wonder why she ever set her sights on Mitch when she could have just about any man in camp eating out of her hand. I think it stems back to the very beginning when she thought she would be in charge of the clinic with her years of advanced nursing experience. Then the green medical resident shows up and suddenly gets seniority over her. It's like high school all over again, and I hated it the *first* time.

Luckily, Jamie is working tonight so she is nowhere near the softball game. John, however never misses a game and he is not very discreet about loathing Mitch, either. If John and Jamie would get over themselves, they would see they are perfect for each other. They are both young, attractive, highly sexual and, of course— snakes in the grass. Kindred spirits I'd say. But they've set their sights on us and apparently, they don't like to lose.

In the seventh inning, Army is up by six and probably won't even lose the game if they try. We have a man on first and I'm up to bat. Mitch is pitching and smiles seductively at me right before he throws an easy lob right over the plate. I smack it out to left field and take off running. Mitch's eyes follow me the entire way. I make it to the base just in time to see Mitch double over and grab his leg.

He turns around and shouts at John, who threw the ball directly into his thigh, "What the fuck was that? The runner was going to second, even *I* know you don't have *that* bad of aim."

John smirks at him. "Well, if you were paying attention to the game instead of being so worried about your piece of ass over there, you would have seen it coming."

Mitch throws his glove down and walks quickly towards John. John throws *his* glove down and pushes his sleeves above his elbow. I don't miss the devious smile that forms on his lips.

Shit! This is not good.

Does John have a death wish or something? Mitch has taken him down once already and that was before we were even a couple. I have no doubt that Mitch would pulverize him to defend my honor. John may have bigger muscles, but Mitch is taller, broader and stronger than he is.

"What the fuck did you just call her?" Mitch yells at him, no longer bothering to address him properly after his display at The Oasis a few weeks ago.

Others take notice of what is about to happen and run over towards them.

"I just call it like I see it," John says. "That's what she is, right? A piece of ass until you get your memory back and move on to your *real* life."

Mitch's eyes flash over to mine before he all but runs the last few steps to John. Luckily, Austin and a few other guys get there first and push John and Mitch apart before they can throw any punches. I run over to them as well, but I keep my distance.

Austin pulls Mitch back and says, "Don't let him get to you, man. You know he's just trying to goad you, right?"

"Come on, John," one of the major's friends says. "It's not worth getting into a fight."

"Maybe not," John says, loud enough for everyone to hear. "But, have you seen her rack? I'd take a few punches over those any day."

Mitch breaks Austin's hold and balls his hands up into fists, pulling one back to take a swing at John. But, Austin is too quick for him and grabs Mitch from behind, forcefully restraining him from hitting John.

Mitch points a finger at John and yells, "Don't *talk* about her, don't *look* at her, don't even *think* about her, you piece of shit!"

The game obviously finished, some of the guys drag Mitch away and we all walk over to gather up our things.

"Don't worry, Mitch," John calls out over his shoulder. "I'll be here to pick up your sloppy seconds when you've moved on."

Mitch tries to turn around, but Tom and Austin have not released him from their hold. "Let it go, man," Tom says.

"Come on, let's go get a drink," Austin says to the group of us standing around Mitch and everyone murmurs their assent.

Holly whispers to me, "Jeez, testosterone much?"

I roll my eyes at her.

"Seriously, Kay . . . you need to watch out for John. He's picking a serious bone with Mitch and you seem to be the pawn. I'd stay as far away from him as you can get if I were you," Holly says.

Holly, Pam and I walk over to The Oasis together while the guys talk Mitch down. By the time we get there, Mitch has calmed down somewhat and we find a table while Craig and Holly go in search of much needed alcohol.

After a few shots, everyone settles down and we even manage to ignore the major and his friends who have chosen a table on the other side of the deck.

A slightly inebriated Mitch drags me out to dance when a slow song starts playing. I let him practically fondle me on the dance floor. I know it's for John's benefit. Mitch is marking his territory and for some reason, I'm more than happy to let him do that. I see John taking several shots while eyeing us dance. Luckily, he eventually gets drunk enough to pass out and some of his buddies take him home allowing the rest of us to enjoy the evening.

Mitch gets called up to play guitar. "Do you mind?" he asks.

I smile and shake my head. Do I mind?

Is he kidding?

Watching him play guitar is the most potent aphrodisiac in the world. While he plays, he locks eyes with me and it's as if each song he plays, he plays only for me, sings only to me. I think he's onto me, because he just feeds my fire with his selection of seductive songs.

Holly announces to the table loudly, "If you all hear noises coming from my bedroom, it's because I'm releasing the mountain of sexual tension oozing off these two." Everyone at the table laughs.

When Mitch comes back to join us, Pam puts a brown lunch-sized paper bag with a bow on top of it in front of me. I eye her suspiciously. "What's this?" I ask.

She motions to everyone sitting at our table except me and Mitch. "It's a little something from all of us. We pooled our resources to get you an early birthday present."

Oh! Okay . . . well, my birthday isn't for another week, but now I'm excited. I open the bag and reach in to pull out the contents. But, before I can completely reveal to everyone what I've been so generously given, a blush comes across my face and I stuff it back in the bag.

The others laugh and Mitch asks, "Well, what is it?"

"It's for you," I say, slapping the bag against his chest while I roll my eyes at my friends.

"For me . . . but I thought they said it was for your birthday." He opens the bag and looks inside. His face lights up like a Christmas tree when he sees the three-pack of condoms.

"Awww, guys, you shouldn't have," he says to them. Then he stands up quickly, causing his chair to fall over backwards. He throws me over his shoulder like a sack of potatoes. I scream at him to put me down, but he just grabs the paper bag off the table. "No, actually you should have. Gotta go now." He gets some high-fives from the guys on our way out.

I fully expect him to put me down when we get out of view, but my caveman won't have it and continues to carry me like this all the way to his apartment.

One condom, two hours and three orgasms later, we lie beside each other, panting, our bodies covered in a sheen of sweat. He says, "Best. Present. Ever."

I giggle and agree with him.

Chapter Nineteen

There was a lot of excitement around camp this week. A small convoy arrived, bringing information from the capital. The soldiers were making their way through Florida, finding groups of survivors and telling them the state of affairs. Apparently we have done pretty well for ourselves here at our little outpost. They chalked it up to good leadership and a remote location. Unfortunately, most groups didn't fare so well.

The U.S. took the hardest hit from the solar flares and EMP so it will take many years to rebuild the infrastructure that we had come to rely on. Some countries in the Far East came out nicely, but they are holding back help for political gain. Shipping companies are by far the business to be in nowadays as they are transporting new and rebuilt electronics overseas daily.

The soldiers told us of people hitching rides on ships. They heard that anyone who wanted passage would have to work on the docks for a month in exchange for the ride. Soldiers and others stationed abroad had started trickling in months ago. But there was much death and destruction overseas, especially in the places that were at war, and they weren't very optimistic about all the troops returning. Ironically, more people are leaving the country than are entering it, choosing to go in search of places overseas that don't have it quite so bad. With the massive reduction in world population, crossing borders into most countries doesn't seem to be an issue anymore, barring those far eastern countries that didn't take a big hit.

They said the primary objective of our government, other than the safety of our people, is to get the power up and running. At this point, they have limited power in the D.C. area with rolling outages. It is estimated that power will reach Florida in about a year.

They've told us to sit tight for now, but to also think about the future. They will need men to work the power grid when they get this far. The government has also started a program of deeding land to those who will participate in sharecropping. That too will work its way to us.

Medically, there is talk of people gravitating to the Jacksonville area where one of the largest hospitals is working to become a regional point of care.

Undoubtedly, we are devastated to hear that the projections were correct and that the population is a mere fraction of what it was just a year ago. That, in turn, led to another main objective of the government which is to prevent disease due to the millions of decomposing bodies around the country. This convoy is part of an initiative to recruit and set up remote bases for biological hazard containment. The colonel has graciously offered Camp Brady as a coordination site and many men here have volunteered their services.

Colonel Andrews is cautiously optimistic at this point and would like to maintain the status quo around here until we get further information.

The news has left many people stunned. I think some thought that one day the power would just come back on and it would go back to life as we knew it. Now, with the details these soldiers have provided and the stories they've told us about what has gone on for the past year, reality has finally hit some and hit them hard.

I'm not one of those. I like it here. I wouldn't really mind if things stayed like this forever. Growing up, I read all the 'Little House on the Prairie' books and I dreamed about being Laura Ingalls Wilder. Okay, yes, I do miss some of the conveniences from our former lives such as air conditioning, modern medicine, and most recently . . . readily available prophylactics. But, I've come to think that my mom was right. Technology *did* poison society. I see firsthand how relationships these days are stronger and more genuine without texting, e-mail and other electronic forms of communication that distance people from each other.

Mitch and I spent the night out in the meadow the day after we got the news. It's become our secret spot, our go-to place, our sanctuary. We took a blanket, a little food and some bottles of water along with birthday condom number two, and we simply enjoyed each other.

I've spent quite a lot of time this week figuring out if I want to be one of those who go to Jacksonville to participate in opening the new medical center. I want to help others, but my priorities have changed. I no longer want the high-paced, high-strung life of an E.R. doctor. I want to be able to ride horses, gaze at stars and participate in my own life more than I did before.

Tonight, Mitch is surprising me with something for my birthday. What, I can't possibly imagine, since we've spent every credit we had on condoms. He just told me to come to the mess hall at eight o'clock and to not eat first.

I've decided to dress up for the occasion with a borrowed above-the-knee skirt and cap sleeve blouse. Amanda lived on base so she has tons of clothes and, thank the Lord, we are the same size.

I walk into the deserted mess hall to find Claire waiting for me in the front. She gives me a big smile and escorts me back to a private area that dances with light from several flickering candles that I notice are from our candlelight service. I see a beautifully set table for two which she takes me over to. She holds out the chair for me before placing a napkin in my lap. The room is darkened, so if I didn't know it was an army camp mess hall, I would think I was in a five-star restaurant. The table has an elegant tablecloth and is set with beautiful china and crystal.

I look up at Claire with a million questions that she doesn't answer. She simply leans down to give me a hug and says, "Enjoy your night, Kay. You should know he planned the entire evening. And you deserve it more than anyone I know." She walks back into the kitchen as a single tear slips out of my eye.

I can't believe that this woman—the mother of the man I loved, the man who may still be out there somewhere—is helping Mitch with this wonderfully romantic evening for my birthday. *She* is the one who deserves this, not me.

A minute later, the door swings open again and Mitch comes into the dim light of the candles. He, too, is dressed up, wearing khakis and a polo shirt. He looks gorgeous. He smells gorgeous. My eyes follow his every step, his every move as he walks over and deposits a few more plates on the table. If I didn't know how much effort he put into this evening, I would jump into his arms and beg him to take me home this instant.

As if reading my mind, or maybe just the expression on my face, he says, "There'll be time for that later, doctor."

I blush of course, and along with my face, my insides heat up and tingle at the certainty of whose strong arms will be wrapped around me again tonight.

I take in his cleanly-shaven face for the first time. Although I also like his rugged look with the three-day stubble, spiffed-up Mitch is quite a delectable sight. "You look . . . this is . . ." I try to express my appreciation, but the words don't seem to come out.

He smiles and grabs my hands, pulling me up out of the chair as he lets his eyes wander over my body. "I see that we both borrowed clothes for the occasion," he says. "You look stunning, Mikayla, absolutely beautiful. I love seeing you in a skirt." He leans in and whispers, "I look forward to running my hands up under it later."

He kisses my forehead and pushes my speechless body back down into my chair. "But first, a birthday dinner," he says.

I finally allow my eyes to focus on the dish before me. It's a plate of chicken, potatoes and green beans. And it looks delicious. "Oh, Mitch, it looks wonderful. It's incredible what you've done here. These dishes . . . the fancy linens . . . you've made this into a real date. Our first date," I say.

He looks proud of himself when he says, "You'd be amazed what you can still find in the houses on base. Apparently, there's not a big demand for china and crystal these days. But, I figure you only turn twenty-eight once so I wanted to make it special. Claire even taught me how to cook."

My jaw drops. "You cooked this?" I ask, surprised at this man's growing list of talents.

"All of it. I even plucked the feathers off the chicken."

"And they let you do that? I mean, with the rations and all?"

"Let's just say there are certain perks to being tight with the mess hall manager, who also happens to be the colonel's girlfriend." He leans down to kiss me before taking his own seat, which is right next to me and not across the table. "There's more, but you'll have to wait."

More what? More food . . . more surprises . . . more of him seducing me? *Oh, yes!* All of them, I hope.

After we eat the delicious meal that he has expertly prepared under Claire's tutelage, he clears our plates and turns my chair away from the table. He walks over to get something out of the dark corner of the room.

A smile, that I'm sure he can hear as well as see, lights up my face when I see him come back with a guitar. I've never had anyone serenade me before. Even though Jeff played, he didn't ever play for *me*; he played to keep his fingers dexterous.

Over the next fifteen minutes, Mitch plays several songs, all my favorites, from those he has played at The Oasis, and none of which I ever told him affected me. He must have watched my reaction every time he played a song in order to compile this playlist. How he continues to get in my head amazes me. How he keeps burrowing deeper into my heart fascinates me.

How much I realize I love him scares me.

When he puts the guitar down, I crawl up on his lap, not even caring how unladylike I must look in my skirt. "Thank you. That was the best birthday present I have ever gotten." He reaches up, putting his hands in my hair, holding it back from my face. His eyes are burning into mine; they are filled with emotion, with desire . . . *with love?* Every thought in my head is about this man. Every fiber in my body is fine-tuned to this man. Every breath I take from here on out is because of this man. "God Mitch, I lo—"

His lips crash into mine before I get the chance to finish my declaration that was spontaneously falling from my mouth. *Oh,*

God. Was I really going to say it? I can't say it. I can't say it until I know that he loves me and not the person he was trying to find.

We spend the next few minutes tasting each other as if we haven't done it a hundred times before. Every kiss, every touch, every feeling is like the very first time with him.

Suddenly, he pulls back, laughing because my lips refuse to part from his so easily. "Sweetheart," he mumbles into my mouth, "I can't wait to get to this part of the evening, but there are a few more things we need to do first."

He stands up with me in his arms and places me back onto my chair. Then he sits back down in his own chair. And does nothing. So I say, "Uh, Mitch?"

"You don't think I'm going back in the kitchen like *this*, do you?" He motions to his lap. "I'm pretty sure Claire is still back there. So, just give me a sec. Jeez . . . so impatient," he teases. "Hey, before I forget, Don said we should go by the store tomorrow and you can pick out something for your birthday, courtesy of him. He did specify, however, that it *not* be a condom since he's running low."

When he finally, uh, calms down, he heads back to the kitchen only to emerge with a birthday cake, candles flaming and all, and he serenades me one last time.

I stare longingly at the chocolate confection, practically drooling over the memory of what things like this taste like.

"I told you . . . friends in high places," he says, feeding me a forkful of heaven as if it was our wedding cake. I can't speak. I can only relish the delightfully sweet taste as my eyes roll to the top of my head.

On our second piece of cake, Mitch brings up what has plagued my thoughts all week long. "Have you thought about what you are going to do when the colonel says it's safe to leave? Have you thought about Jacksonville?"

I nod my head, taking another bite. "Yes, I have, you?" I don't want to tell him my plans before he tells me his. I don't want to influence him in any way.

He chuckles and shakes his head at me. "Well, do you want to *share* what you've been thinking?"

"I don't know, do you?" I ask.

He rolls his eyes at me. "Okay, I'll go first." He puts his fork down and grabs my hand. Then he places our joined hands on the table. "I'm not really sure yet, to be honest. There's still so much I don't know. Until I know about my dad and my brother's family..."

Until he knows about the woman he was searching for.

I close my eyes and attempt to control my shaky breathing.

"Mikayla, look at me please." He squeezes my hand until I look into his eyes. "I don't know what I plan to do yet, but I do know that whatever it is, I want to do it with you."

I want so badly to believe this. But, it's not lost on me that he hasn't even alluded to being in love with me since that night under the stars. Maybe he wasn't talking about me back then after all. Maybe he still has doubts about whether or not he can love me after his memory returns. Is there any truth to the words John spoke at the softball game last week about me being someone he bides his time with until he gets his memory back?

He must see my frown. "What is it, sweetheart?" he asks.

"I just can't help worrying that you won't feel the same once you remember everything."

He runs his fingers down my arm and looks me square in the eye. "Mikayla, I can't think of anything in this world that would have me not wanting to be with you." He stands us up and nods to the door. "Now, Claire said she'd clean up, so what do you say we go celebrate your birthday and make good use of the one condom we have left?"

Chapter Twenty

Sleepy arms tighten around me as I wake up. I smile when I realize I've slept in Mitch's arms all night. "Morning, old lady," he says into the back of my head. "Can I call you that now that you are officially older than me?"

"By about ten minutes," I say, referring to our three month age difference. "And not if you want me to play with Little Mitch ever again."

He laughs. "Little Mitch? Is that what you call it?" He wiggles himself into my behind. "I'd prefer Big Mitch if you're taking suggestions."

After we shower and go for breakfast, Mitch and I go to the PX to cash in on my promised birthday gift from Don.

"Well, if it isn't my favorite couple," Don says when we walk in. "They got a name for you yet? You know like KayMit or something?"

"Ugh . . . no, Don," I say. "And I'd like to keep it that way if you don't mind."

"Sure thing, Doc. Go ahead and take a look around. I got some pretty jewelry and some new clothes in last week. Pick whatever you want. It's on the house. Well, almost whatever you want." He looks at Mitch. "You tell her the rules?"

My face heats up when I remember what I'm not allowed to get, and I walk away rolling my eyes at them as they laugh at me.

"Isn't she adorable when she blushes?" Mitch asks him.

"That she is, son. You got yourself a real keeper with that one," Don replies. "Too bad she doesn't have an older brother for me."

Their voices become more distant as I walk around the store perusing the aisles. Hmmm . . . what do I want? I pass by row after row of useless housewares. I look through his selection of books. I check out a few pretty tops that catch my eye. Then I see something across the store that makes me laugh.

As I quickly walk over to the food aisle, it dawns on me that I'm having a happy memory of Jeff without feeling the least bit of guilt.

Mitch must see me beeline to the food section. "Find something you like?" he asks, making his way across the store to join me.

"No, not really. I'm not going to get this, but it did make me laugh." I take the box off the shelf and turn it over and over in my hands, examining all sides of it. "It was just a silly nickname Jeff had for me. I've told you my middle name is Katherine, right?"

"Of course," he says. "It's a beautiful name."

"Well, Jeff said early on when we first got together that I must be pretty special for my parents to have put a K in all three of my names. So he started calling me Special Kay." I hold up the cereal box that reads '*Special K*' in big red letters. I continue to stare at it myself as I tell him the rest of the story. "It became a joke between us. He started buying boxes of it every time we went shopping until he had a cabinet full of it. After a while, it was almost like a habit for him. I was no longer just Kay to him, I was Special Kay. It was sweet."

I smile as I place the box back on the shelf among a few various other cereal boxes. When I turn to look at Mitch, I'm shocked at what I see. It looks like all the blood has drained from his face and he's leaning over, his hands bracing himself on his knees as if he might fall over. His breathing is shallow and quick, like he just ran a race.

"Mitch! Are you okay?" I walk towards him.

He looks up at me and says, "I think I'm gonna be sick." He runs out the front doors of the store. I go out after him just in time to see him lose his breakfast into the bushes that line the side of the building.

"Let me help you," I say, walking over to him. "Maybe you got some bad food at breakfast." I put my hand on my own stomach to see if I feel any gurgling.

"No!" he shouts, pointing at me to keep my distance. "I just need to get home." He doesn't even have the strength to look up at me as he slowly walks away.

The girlfriend in me wants to follow him home, rub his back and nurse him back to health. But, the doctor in me knows I have to go over to the dining hall and warn the others. "I'll run over to the mess hall to get you some water and see if anyone else is ill."

"No, you don't need to get me anything. I've got water at home," he says from across the lot.

"I'll see you soon," I say, heading in the opposite direction. I quickly make my way to the mess hall and find Claire to tell her what happened.

"Nobody else has complained that I know of," she says. "We served the same food all morning, for several hours and as far as I know, nobody else has gotten sick. But maybe you should check the clinic just in case."

"It's my next stop." I fill a few bottles of water before heading out. "And thanks for everything you did for us last night, it was very special."

"Well, you're a special girl," she says, giving me a hug before I reach the kitchen door to leave.

At the clinic, Holly tells me she's been there since seven this morning, but that nobody has come in with any kind of stomach trouble. I ask her to keep an eye out, explaining what happened to Mitch. We don't sit and chat, even though I know she wants to hear about last night. I just want to get to him and make sure that he is okay.

I know how some men can get about women watching them throw up. They think it emasculates them somehow, so I knock on his door instead of barging in. He doesn't answer right away so I knock again. I call out his name. "Mitch?" Still no response. I try the handle only to find it locked.

Locked?

We never lock doors around here. He must really be embarrassed that I saw him vomit. I knock louder, but then it dawns on me that he wouldn't be getting sick here in his apartment. He wouldn't risk stinking up the place. He would have gone over to the latrines, or out in the woods maybe. "Mitch!" I yell into the steel door.

Finally, I get a response. "Go away, Mikayla. I'm sick."

I quickly glance down both hallways to see if there is anyone else around to appreciate the irony in this situation. Then I say, "I'm a doctor, Mitch. I think I can handle it."

"I don't want to get you sick. I'll be fine here by myself."

"You won't get me sick, Mitch. I'm sure you just ate something bad. You do realize I'm around sick people all day, right?" I roll my eyes at the fact that I even have to remind him of this.

"Go home, Mikayla. Just let me sleep it off. I'm going to bed now."

"Mitch!"

He doesn't reply.

"Mitch!" I knock on the door again, but he must already be back in his bedroom. I shake my head. I don't quite understand why he doesn't want me here. Maybe he doesn't want me to view him as weak, seeing him sick. I remember how much he hated to stay at the clinic those first few days before we cleared him to leave.

I'm sure that's all it is. I decide to go back to the clinic to see if any other cases have come in. But before I go, I tape a note to Mitch's front door telling him where I'll be if he needs me.

$$\sim \quad \sim \quad \sim$$

"So, he still won't let you see him?" Holly asks.

"Nope. Not for two days now. He must be pretty sick. I guess I can appreciate the fact that he doesn't want his new girlfriend seeing him like that. I mean, if I were throwing up or worse . . . Ugh! I don't think I'd want him to see me. Kinda takes the romance out of it, you know?"

"Yeah, I guess. But two days? Jeez, I hope he's getting enough fluids. What does Austin say?"

"What *can* he say? I guess Mitch has been keeping to himself, sleeping all day and Austin works nights, so there's not much going on there. I'm sure he'll be better in a day or two. These bad stomach bugs usually don't last too long."

I busy myself going on rounds the rest of the day. I visit Kelly and that adorable little baby. I check on a few of our residents with high blood pressure issues. I drop by Timmy's apartment to see how he and his mom are holding up this week. I do everything I can to keep from thinking about lying in bed with Mitch. Sick or not, I want to be next to him.

Jamie comes to relieve me when my shift is over.

"Trouble in paradise so soon?" she asks.

"What are you talking about, Jamie?"

"It's just that you and Mitch usually have some body part stuck to each other's so I assumed with him being MIA . . ." I don't miss that she smiles while she's talking. "And he didn't show up for work yesterday."

"He's sick. I told you that, Jamie."

"Oh, right," she says with sarcasm. "I guess that's why I saw him eating a nice big breakfast after you left the dining hall today. He took it out the back door and sat by himself. He must really be pissed at you. That, or he's just had his fill. Either way, be sure to let him know I'll be happy to pick up where you left off." She spins around and walks into the back room without waiting for my reply.

He was eating breakfast out back? Maybe he thinks he's contagious or something. Why wouldn't he just come and talk to me about it? I have to get to the bottom of this.

I knock, but don't wait for a response. I open the door and let myself in his apartment. "Mitch!" I call out. "Are you feeling any better? I really don't think you need to avoid everyone anymore." I walk back to his room to see the door wide open but no trace of him. I look around his room and something seems off. His bed is made. His clothes are picked up and even freshly laundered. Did someone do this for him? I would have gladly done it myself.

I don't see any signs of sickness. No tissues strewn about or water bottles lying around. No rumpled clothing or even a simple container of pain relievers by the bed. What is going on here? I can't corner Austin because he's already left for work.

I will make myself crazy if I wait around here so I walk to the stables and saddle up Sassy. I trot her around a little since I've not been on her for a few days and Brad said she probably needs the exercise. We head out to the far crop quad. I close my eyes and enjoy the last bit of heat on my face before the sun falls behind the trees in the west. When I open them, I spot a few people walking between the tall rows of cornstalks in the distance.

I see Craig's trademark bright-orange Florida Gator's baseball cap that he rarely goes without. But I have to look twice when I think I see Mitch walking next to him. I squint my eyes and focus on the two of them walking in the other direction. I can't see his face, but that dark, wavy hair, the same unruly hair that I've weaved my fingers through a hundred times, is unmistakably his.

How did he get all the way out here if he is sick? I watch them talk and smile and joke around until I can't see them anymore. I sit, dumbfounded, on Sassy. If he was feeling better, why wouldn't he come find me? It's been two days since we've been together, doesn't he crave me like I crave him?

Then it hits me. It hits me hard. Maybe he got his memory back when he was sick in bed yesterday and now he knows who he was searching for. He knows there is someone waiting for him. Maybe he even knows that he loves that someone. He's avoiding me because he doesn't have the guts to break up with me. I start to get angry. After all we went through, how could he just up and walk away without so much as one word.

That jackass!

I run Sassy back to the stables as fast as I can through my tear-blurred vision and then I go find the one person who can comfort me like a mother.

~ ~ ~

"Shhh," Claire whispers into my ear as she hugs me. "Whatever it is, it will be okay, dear." She must wonder why I practically burst into her apartment with a tear-streaked face, almost diving into her arms.

She sits us down on her couch and comfortingly rubs a hand down my long hair as the colonel quietly slips out the door giving us a sad nod.

"H-he re-remembered," I stutter. "He must have remembered that he loves someone and now he can't even bring himself to face me." I tell her the whole story and she listens intently, holding my hand lovingly as if I were her own daughter. "M-maybe I deserved this—moving on too quickly. Maybe I don't deserve to be happy."

"Oh, Kay. Of course you deserve to be happy. We all deserve the chance to be happy in this unforgiving world we live in now." She blots my tears with a tissue. "I'm sure there is an explanation for this. Mitch loves you. I can see it. Everyone can see it. Even if he got his memory back, that doesn't mean he can simply turn those feelings off. Maybe he did remember something. And maybe he just needs time to sort out his feelings."

Everything she says makes sense. He could have remembered who he was trying to find and now he's deciding which one of us he wants. My heart drops into my stomach and I feel sick. I know that I have to give him time to work this out on his own. I have to stand back and watch the man I love determine if he wants to stay with me. I have to give him the space to figure out if he is going to shatter my heart into a million pieces.

How on earth am I going to get through this?

Claire lets me stay in their apartment all night, sleeping in the guest room. I'm floored by the care and compassion of a woman whose son I basically wrote off for dead. The way she continues to take me under her wing is astonishing. It saddens me that someday she won't be around to fill this role in my life. Surely she will go wherever the colonel ends up, which I'm certain won't be some little town in the middle of nowhere where I make house calls to check up on the local residents.

And right here, in the middle of the night in Claire's apartment, I decide my future. I don't want to go to Jacksonville and work in an emergency room. I don't want to re-join the rat-race even as slow as it may have become since the blackout. I want to continue to do everything I've come to love and appreciate this past year. I want to live my life, not let my life live me.

The only thing is . . . I want to do it all with Mitch.

Chapter Twenty-one

People are starting to stare and whisper. Women look at me with sad eyes. Men look at me with renewed hope. It's only been four days since I've spent time with him . . . smelled him . . . touched him. But, it seems like forever.

He's going out of his way to avoid me and I've been letting him. If he decides not to choose me, nothing I say or do can influence that. I love him, but I'm not going to put that burden of guilt on him if he can't reciprocate my feelings.

I saw him watching me from across the courtyard yesterday. He looked incredibly sad which left me trying to figure out if it was because he's decided not to be with me, or if it was because he misses me. It then occurred to me that the tables have turned. He is in the same exact position I was in a few weeks ago. It's because of this that I know he needs time, just as he gave me time. I only wish he wouldn't shut me out completely.

Evan walks into the clinic, breaking up the monotony of my day. "Hey, Dr. Parker," he says. "I think I found something that may belong to you on this morning's supply run."

How could he possibly have something that's mine? Did they sweep my apartment back in Gainesville? He pulls something from his pocket that, from where I'm standing across the room, looks to be a necklace. "What makes you think it's mine, Evan?"

"Well, the picture of you on the inside may have given it away," he says. "Don't know who the other gal is, or the fella', but I recognized you straight away. Funny thing, though, we finally got back to the place we ran into Mitch and found this on the floor of his smashed-up truck. Nothing else, no belongings, only this."

I'm stunned. A picture of me?

"I'll just leave it right here, Doc," he says, setting it on the table and walking out the front door.

I stare at the necklace as if I'm afraid of it. Does it hold the answers to my questions? I take a calming breath and walk over to the table where it lays. My breath hitches when I take it in. It looks like a set of dog tags, but it's actually a locket—just like the one Mitch described Gina giving to him. This is not mine, it belongs to Mitch.

I open it with shaky hands to see a very small picture of me on one side of the locket. On the other side is a picture of a beautiful woman—one I recognize as Gina based on the detailed description Mitch gave me. Her picture is old and faded like mine is. But, there is also a third picture that has come loose in the tiny frame as if it may have been placed over one of the other photos at some point. It flutters to the ground when I fully open the locket. I pick it up and take a look.

My heart jumps out of my chest. My face loses all color. My breathing stops.

It's a picture of Jeff.

I sit down and examine the locket that, ironically, is inscribed with 'always remember' on the back.

Why was Mitch carrying around a picture of Jeff and me along with one of Gina, in a locket that *she* gave him no less? A hundred questions are flying through my mind. How did he get the pictures . . . which picture in the locket was covered up . . . why was he coming to Florida?

All of a sudden, everything clicks together. The odd familiarity I sensed when Mitch was first brought into the clinic, the proficiency in which he learned to suture—as if he'd been trained by an expert—and the way he played guitar that reminded me of another. *Oh, God*—the way he suddenly got sick when I told him about 'Special Kay.'

He knew Jeff.

I can't stop myself from running to the back room and opening the file cabinet. I don't even hesitate. For the first time, I use the cell phone only for myself. I don't think twice about looking at the pictures Jeff sent me over a year ago. I know I'm right, yet I still need confirmation. I scroll through the pictures he sent me of his buddies where he was stationed in Afghanistan. Then I see him. I'd never miss that face anywhere. His hair is short and he looks a bit younger, but it's him. And now I know for sure who Mitch is.

He's Jeff's best friend.

Oh, my God. Oh, my God. Oh, my God. I can't think. How did this happen? How did I not know? Jeff talked about his best friend all the time in his phone calls and e-mails. But when you are stationed overseas, everyone has a nickname. Jeff's of course was 'Doc.' So how was I to know that Mitch, the same man who lost his memory and ended up on my doorstep; the same man that I fell in love with; the same man who may be about to crush my heart when he leaves to find Gina, is Jeff's best friend, 'Stitch.'

The second Holly walks into the clinic to relieve me, I throw my hand-written report at her as I run by. "Where are you off to so quickly?" she asks.

"I have to find him. I have to find him right now!" I say, practically yelling at her as I plow through the front door.

"It's about damn time!" she shouts back at me.

I run all over camp looking for him but come up empty-handed. I take one last shot and head to the stables. Seeing that Rose is not in her stall, I ask Brad, "Did Mitch take Rose out?"

He nods. "Nobody but. That boy refuses to ride any other horse. Strange attachment if you ask me. Kinda like you've got with Sassy."

I smile thinking that he still will only ride Rose, even if he *is* thinking of leaving me.

I don't know if he will be at the meadow, and if he's not, there are far too many acres of land to cover so I'll be out of luck. But, as I approach my favorite spot, I'm not disappointed. I find Rose tied up to a tree. I give her some company with Sassy and walk towards the clearing that we christened last week. I find Mitch sitting down, just staring at the ground where we made love.

"Hey," I say, startling him as I approach.

He looks up at me briefly with sad eyes but doesn't say anything. He just takes in a deep breath and blows it out slowly. It's a deep, agonizing kind of sigh that tells me something is definitely wrong.

"I need to talk to you," I say.

He gets up slowly and starts to walk away without uttering a single word.

I follow him and pull his elbow to make him turn around and face me. "I said I need to talk to you . . . . *Stitch*."

For the second time in a week, all the blood drains from his face as he pales at my words. "What . . . how?"

I hold out the locket for him to see. He closes his eyes and shakes his head when I tell him it's the only thing they found at the site of his accident.

"When were you planning on telling me you got your memory back?" I ask. "When were you planning on telling me you are leaving to find her?"

His eyes snap open and he finally looks directly at me. "Leaving to find who?"

"Gina," I say.

"I told you before, I don't *want* her. Why would you think I'm leaving to look for her?"

I throw the locket at him. "That's why!"

He opens it to see exactly what I saw, the pictures of two women with a loose picture of Jeff on top.

"It isn't what you think, Mikayla. My memory came back the other day when you told me the 'Special Kay' story. Every memory—every single detail—came flooding back as if I'd never forgotten. One second I didn't know, and then I just did. It was that fast." He looks back at the ground where he was just sitting. "I wasn't avoiding you because of Gina. I was avoiding you because of Jeff." He holds out the locket and says, "I had put his picture on top of hers to cover it up. It must have come loose."

I'm still confused. "But, if you weren't looking for Gina, what were you doing traveling all alone, and how did you end up here? And why do you have my picture?"

"I came here for you, Mikayla. Because of a promise I made to Jeff—a promise to make sure you were okay if anything ever happened to him. I don't know any more about his fate than you do right now. All I know for sure is that it was *you* I was trying to find all along." He shakes his head and sighs. "Can you believe that shit?"

My jaw drops at his revelation. "But if you were trying to find me, then why are you running away from me now?"

"Why?" he asks, as if I've just posed the stupidest question in the history of mankind. "Because I'm your boyfriend's best friend, that's why."

I shake my head vehemently. "No, Mitch, *you* are my boyfriend," I say. "Yes, the circumstances under which we met are strange . . . unbelievable even, but it doesn't change how I feel about you. I don't care that you were his best friend."

"But I do, Mikayla."

"So, that's it? Are we done now? Are you walking away from me?" I'm raising my voice to him as my anger increases over his stubbornness. He can't even stand to look at me. I reach out and pull his chin up so that we are eye to eye. "Why won't you look at me, Mitch?" I yell.

"Because I fucking love you, that's why!" he shouts. "Because he's my best friend. And because I'm not Dale."

My heart is now firmly lodged in my throat.

He loves me.

He's not looking for anyone else.

He was looking for me the whole time. *Me!*

A tear escapes my eye as I try to compose myself enough to get words past the enormous lump blocking my airway. "You are not like Dale at all. You didn't intentionally fall for your friend's girl. This is totally different. The world is different. He is never coming back. I know that now. Even if I didn't know that, it's still *you* I want." I step closer to him and put my hand over his heart. "I love you, too, Mitch."

He gasps. As he stares at me and absorbs the words I've spoken, I see a struggle going on behind his eyes. I can tell that he wants so desperately to give in to this powerful magnetism between us. But he also feels overwhelming loyalty towards a man that may no longer exist.

Finally, he wipes the tears rolling down my cheeks. "Are you sure, Mikayla?" He cups my face with his hands. "Because there is no going back. If you let me love you, I will love you forever. I'll never stop, that's a promise. And we both know I keep my promises, even when I don't remember them."

After that declaration, which is arguably the most romantic thing I've ever heard in my life, I struggle to get out the words I need him to hear. "*You* are the one I dream of, Mitch. I want *your* hands on my body. I want *your* heart feeding my soul. A part of me will always love him, but he was my past. You, Mitch . . . you are my future."

He picks me up and holds me to him. "Damn right I am, sweetheart," he says, right before his lips come crashing down on mine.

"I have so many questions," I say between our hungry kisses.

"And I have all the answers," he promises, "but right now, I have to have you." He picks me up and carries me over to our spot. "I want to bury myself in you. Will you let me make love to you?"

Oh, God. Just hearing him say that sends shockwaves through my body. But, is he really willing to take the risk? I never told him I went on the pill a few weeks ago. I don't want to break the spell by getting all clinical on him, but it would be irresponsible of me not to ask about his sexual past.

He must see the indecision on my face. He laughs and says, "Two women. I was with two women after Gina. Both were well over a year ago and I never once went without a condom. I'm clean. And I'm willing to accept whatever happens here." He leans down, still holding me in his arms and whispers close to me, "I said forever, Mikayla."

Oh my!

"Me, too, Mitch. I'm in this for good, too. But we don't have to worry about accepting anything right now, I'm on the pill."

His eyes go wide as a huge smile spreads across his face. I can practically see his brain trying to figure out how many times humans can have sex before collapsing from sheer exhaustion. I know this because I'm thinking the same damn thing. "Surprise!" I say, playfully.

He places me back on my feet, removes his shirt and spreads it out on the grass. "Sorry, no blanket this time," he apologizes. Little does he know, I would lay with him in a puddle of mud if it meant we could be together.

I quickly rid myself of my shirt. His eyes caress my half-naked body from head to toe, making me shiver simply from his provocative gaze. He closes the gap that separates us. He wraps his hands around me and unhooks my bra before watching it fall down my arms onto the ground.

He cups my breasts and they mold into his hands perfectly as if they were made just for him. I'm certain his thoughts mirror mine when he looks at them in wonder and then closes his eyes, punctuating the gesture with a deep sigh. With his eyes still closed and his hands still claiming my breasts, he leans into me and declares, "Mine."

His hot breath on my face, his strong hands on my body, his unique smell that I've craved for days, his possessive proclamation

. . . they all come together, stimulating each of my senses and taking my carnal need for him to a level I've never before experienced. "Please, Mitch . . ." I beg, working the button on his jeans.

"God, I've missed those words coming from your beautiful lips." He pulls off his jeans and boxer briefs all at once, leaving him gloriously naked in front of me. He then slowly peels my jeans down my body, stopping to kiss my stomach, my navel, my soft curls, my thighs, all in a slow seduction that is driving me to the brink of hedonistic insanity.

He kisses his way back up my body—my entire body— causing involuntary quivers of pleasure. As soon as he slips a finger inside me, I convulse around him and he must hold me up with his other hand as my knees attempt to buckle beneath my uncontrollable spasms.

"Mikayla, you are so sexy," he says, kissing me through my waning tremors. "I can't wait to be inside you. I need to feel all of you." He lays me down and hovers over me in contemplation as he picks a piece of grass from my hair and examines it. Then in one swift move, he maneuvers us so that he is lying on the ground with me straddling his hips.

Oh, how I've missed his barbaric ways.

"Is it okay like this, sweetheart?" he asks.

In answer, I smile and reach between us to rub my hand up and down him a few times before placing him at my entrance. His eyes glaze over as I lower myself onto him and begin to move. His mouth forms a perfect 'O' as he releases a slow breath. I now understand why he likes to watch me. The fact that my body can bring him to this heightened plane of existence is only fueling my own appetite for him.

"You are so beautiful. I could watch you like this forever," he says. I could have said the same words to him, but hearing him speak them in his deep, seductive voice merely drives me higher. He brings a hand down to where our bodies join and when his thumb finds me, I scream out his name as waves come crashing over me, pulling me under and tumbling me around before allowing me to come up for air.

"Mikayla!" I hear him shout as he joins me, grunting my name through his own release.

I collapse onto his chest and our panted breaths mingle while we come down from another extraordinary experience.

"Damn, sweetheart," his breathless voice proclaims, "every time with you is better than the last." He shakes his head as if trying to understand the inexplicable pull we have on one another.

I shake my own head, wondering if there has ever been another woman on earth who has ever loved a man as much as I love him.

Chapter Twenty-two

Later, when we are fully clothed, but still not ready to leave, we lie on our backs, enjoying the setting sun as he tells me about who he is—filling in all the blanks for me. Not that it matters in the least. I love him. Nothing he could reveal to me would change that.

He tells me that two weeks after his mom died, he went back to Afghanistan and joined up with another battalion where he met Jeff. They had medicine in common, but that's about as far as their relationship went, until something happened to solidify them as lifelong friends.

"Are you sure you want to know everything? This may be hard to hear, Mikayla."

"Yes. I want to hear it all. The good and the bad. I want to know everything about you." I sit up and pull his head into my lap. He looks up at me with hesitation. I can tell he's scared to divulge something. I smile and nod at him in encouragement as I join our hands over his chest.

"I had only known Jeff for a few weeks. It was December fifteenth. A Thursday—that's the day he became my brother."

I marvel over how he can remember the date, let alone the day of the week. Then as his eyes take on the expression of a frightened child, I know he only remembers it because it represents a day something terrible happened. Something unimaginable.

"A bomb had gone off in a civilian area, causing dozens of casualties and even more wounded. It was near a school and several of us, Jeff and me included, volunteered to go to the scene. It was pretty close to a hot zone, but when we heard kids were hurt, it didn't matter. Unfortunately, we never made it. Our convoy of three Humvees was ambushed. We lost six men immediately, all soldiers who were defending us. The remaining six of us were bound and taken to an abandoned warehouse."

As I listen to his every word, I have to remind myself to breathe. I can't imagine what they must have gone through. And Jeff had just arrived in Afghanistan only a few weeks before. Then it hits me—that was the week he didn't contact me. He said later it was due to some Com Link failure and I didn't even think to question him. What I realize next brings instant tears to my eyes.

"Oh, God—your scars," I cry. I run my fingers through his hair hoping that it provides a modicum of solace while he re-lives his terror for me.

He lifts a hand to catch my tears and asks me, "Sweetheart, are you sure you want to hear this?"

I nod. "Yes. I need to know."

"Okay." He brings my hand to his lips and kisses it tenderly before placing it back over his heart. "Yes, that's where my scars came from. We were all beaten. They made us watch each other as we were whipped with a long switch while our captors laughed and got drunk. Then a man came running in with a small child who was bleeding profusely. The man was delirious. He started shouting at us, saying it was our fault his son was dying, that if it weren't for the Americans trying to control the world, his family would be safe. He came over to where we were restrained by chains, unable to move, and he started shooting us one by one, execution style while our other captors just watched indifferently, like they were simply viewing a movie. The man still held his bleeding son while he killed four of us. We were all yelling at him to stop, begging for our lives. He put the barrel of the gun to my head and Jeff yelled 'Doctors! We're doctors, we can save your boy!' He kept yelling it over and over until the man heard him through his hysterics.

"Some of the men spoke English and Jeff told them if they could bring us the supplies from our convoy that we could save the man's son. Of course neither of us knew if that was true or not, but it bought us some time anyway. A few hours later, after Jeff had worked a miracle, the boy regained consciousness.

"But it didn't seem to escape one of our captors that I hadn't done much except assist Jeff. He took out a knife and said to Jeff, 'You claim your friend is a doctor. If you are lying, you'll bleed out and he will be shot.' Then he sliced Jeff's lower back practically from hip to hip where he wouldn't be able to fix himself up."

"Oh, my God, Mitch. No!" I cry, pulling a hand up to my mouth to cover my sob.

He squeezes my other hand. "Luckily, he didn't slice deep enough to cause any major damage, but it took over a hundred stitches to sew him up. I even had to put in some sub-dermal sutures, which, fortunately, flight medics are trained to do in emergency situations.

"After that, they started bringing some of their wounded to us and it became clear that we were being kept alive as long as they needed us to provide medical treatment. They continued beating us and constantly letting us know we didn't have too long to live. There were times when Jeff and I were alone, and that's when we bonded. We vowed to seek out each other's families if one of us made it out without the other. I vowed to find *you*, Mikayla.

"Jeff was incredible. I was scared to death that they would figure out I wasn't a doctor, but he kept making me do things that he thought I could handle so we could keep up the façade.

"A week after we were first captured, we were rescued. He saved my life, Mikayla. I can never repay him for that."

"It sounds like you ended up saving his, too," I say through the tears that haven't stopped falling since he spoke those first words.

"That's when we became brothers," he said. "You go through that with someone and it changes who you are. No matter what happens in life, we are connected in a way no others can be. When we returned to base, we were inseparable. He told me all about you and I told him about my family. We said that even though we made it out of that situation, we would still uphold the promise to find each other's loved ones if anything ever happened to one of us.

"So when the blackout happened just two weeks after my tour ended—knowing he was still over there—I knew that I had to find you. So after checking on my own family, who I'll tell you about later, I set out for Gainesville. I had no idea where to find you. I knew where you worked and where you lived, but after the outage, none of that mattered. Still, I had made him a promise and intended to honor it knowing that it would be difficult if not impossible for him to get to you."

"Thank you," I say, leaning down to place a chaste kiss on his lips.

"For what?" he asks.

"For everything. For helping Jeff. For being his friend. For keeping your promise . . . for finding me."

"Don't thank me, sweetheart, it was all him. I owe everything to Jeff Taylor." His eyes light up and he says, "We should name our first kid after him."

Holy shit!

My heart rate just went from zero to sixty at Mach Two. I laugh, pretending I'm not totally freaking out while simultaneously having visions of children running around this meadow with us. "I hardly want a daughter named Jeffrey," I joke.

"Okay then, Jeffrey for a boy, Taylor for a girl." He smiles up at me and runs a thumb across my face as he stares intently into my eyes. "She'll have your beautiful green eyes," he says.

"He'll have your dark, wavy hair," I say.

"She'll have your adorable freckles," he says.

"He'll have your strong hands," I say.

"She'll have your amazing heart," he says, and he pulls my head down to his, kissing me with so much passion that my heart hurts. It actually hurts—because it is bursting with my overwhelming love for this man.

After another round of life-affirming sex, I find myself absentmindedly tracing his tattoo with my finger while we lie side by side on the ground on top of our shirts.

"I got it shortly after we were rescued," he says. "I figured if being a medical professional saved my life, I might as well advertise it just in case I ever got taken again."

"That's brilliant," I say, leaning over to kiss it. "I love it."

When I look back up at him, he locks eyes with me. "I love you, Mikayla Katherine Parker," he declares.

"Promise?" I ask, smiling at him.

"Promise," he pledges, before leaning in to seal it with a kiss.

We find Claire upon our return to camp and he tells her the same story of their captivity and ensuing friendship. I can see in Claire's eyes that she has decided almost instantly to consider Mitch family, just as she does me.

Tears dot her shirt where they have landed after falling from her cheeks. She says, "I'm a big believer that everything in life happens for a reason. You two are meant to be with each other. God brought you and Jeff together for the sole purpose of you finding Mikayla." She takes Mitch's hand. "I can see it in your eyes. You love Kay, but you feel guilty for it. Well, don't, Mitch." She points between us and continues, choking slightly on her words. "This is a great love story. One you will tell your grandchildren. Things like this don't happen every day. In this life, you take every opportunity for happiness and I can see without a doubt that you've found that with each other. You certainly don't need my blessing, but for what it's worth, you have it."

We hug Claire and spend the remainder of the evening sharing funny stories about Jeff. I learn that he was the one who taught Mitch how to play guitar. Mitch tells us about pranks they would play on each other and I smile, thinking how un-Jeff-like that sounds. Mitch brought out the playful side of Jeff and Jeff taught Mitch how to perfect his stitches. I am so grateful that they had each other.

Later in bed, Mitch spends half the night telling me about what happened to him after the blackout.

"I was spending time with some buddies of mine in Lake Tahoe when it happened. We knew right away what was going on, so we gathered supplies and found some bikes to get us back to Sacramento where our families were. It was about a hundred miles and we were all in pretty good shape, but the terrain was rough—

up and down mountains almost the entire way—so it took a couple of days to get there.

"I headed straight to my dad's house, where I lived when I wasn't deployed. He wasn't anywhere to be found and it looked like he never made it home after the outage so I traced the route I knew he took from home to his dental office."

I can feel the tension in his body so I know what he will tell me isn't good.

"I found his car on the highway. It was mangled up with a semi-truck. I couldn't even get to his body to give him a proper burial."

"Mitch, I'm so sorry," I say, trying to comfort him while at the same time, reliving my own memories of the aftermath of my parent's accident.

He kisses the side of my head through my hair. "Just another thing we have in common now, huh?"

I lay my head on his chest as he continues the story.

"When I got back to my dad's house, my brother Mark was there, looking around for supplies. He and his wife and kids lived in the next town over and they were going to head to a fishing cabin back in Lake Tahoe that was owned by his wife's family. So we gathered up everything we could carry on our bikes. But before I headed out, I got a picture of you and Jeff that he had given me and I cut it up to fit in the locket from Gina. I figured I would need to know what you looked like if I was going to try to locate you. I wore the thing every day, and looked at it every night before bed. It became my inspiration to keep going when things got tough."

I think of all the times after he came to Camp Brady that I saw him grab at his chest. I was beginning to think it was some kind of tick. Now I know that it was his subconscious trying to remind him why he was here. He was simply reaching for the locket that held my picture.

I close my eyes. I still can't believe he was searching for me the whole time.

"I helped Mark, his wife, Grace, and the others get settled at the fishing cabin. I had to make sure my nieces were going to be okay. They were so young. Megan and Melanie were six-year-old twins and Katie was only three. It took a couple of months to go out and gather the supplies that would keep them fed and safe and then I told Mark I had a promise to keep and set out for Florida with just a bike and trailer.

"The first month wasn't bad because I had the bike. However, I quickly ran out of food and had to stop often to try to scrounge up something to eat. After a while, all the obvious places were stripped bare. I also started running into bad groups of people and ended up getting my bike and trailer stolen. Luckily, I got away with a backpack and my guns, but it was slow going after that because I stuck to back roads to avoid large groups.

"I would sometimes find generous people that would allow me to stay with them for a week or two to recover from the elements and to rest my legs. I would help them with whatever I could in exchange for a bed and some meager supplies to get me through another week or so out on the road.

"It wasn't until I had made it all the way to Alabama before I ran into Harold and Jenny Starke. They are the ones Carson told us about. I delivered her baby and he gave me the pickup truck I was driving when I crashed into the scouts from Camp Brady.

"So, that's it in a nutshell. That's how I found you, Mikayla."

I know he downplayed his journey for my benefit. It took him almost eight months to get here from Lake Tahoe. He went through eight months of hell to cross the entire country to find me.

All to keep a promise to a man he had known for what, sixteen weeks? Unbelievable.

I'm amazed by this man who, against all odds, set out to find me, not even knowing where to look and only having a general location to go on. I'm not sure I've ever met a person with more integrity, more sincerity, or more honesty than Mitch. Yes, this is the man I want to be with forever.

Like Claire said, we were meant to be. Nothing will ever change that.

Chapter Twenty-three

I spend most of the morning in the clinic, thinking about the events of the past few days and how unreal it all seems.

Everyone that comes in is talking about the future.

The future!

It's something we didn't think of much until recently. We simply worried about how to survive in the present. But now that the government is reaching out to people and setting up programs to get society functioning again, there is excitement in the air. Everyone is wondering where they will fit in. Some people fear they won't have any worth, especially those who worked in professions such as information technology. I suppose someday, we will need those folks again, but right now, the extent of today's technology needs consists of getting cars and generators to work.

I, too, wonder what use I can be, having only gotten part of the way through residency. It may be years if not longer before they will figure out a way to get medical schools and residency programs back on line.

Perhaps I should have learned another profession over the past year. Mitch has been out in the fields with Craig every chance he gets. He's smart like that. There is nothing my caveman can't do.

Maybe I could work as a psychic or something with my ability to merely think of Mitch and have him appear before me. I smile as he walks up the front sidewalk to the clinic.

"Hey, sweetheart," he says, coming over to plant a kiss on my lips. "What's so funny?" he asks when I giggle.

"Oh, nothing, just thinking of other professions I can try when we leave here," I say.

"Oh, really? Giving up on the whole doctor thing?" He winks.

"No, not really," I say. "Of course I still want to practice medicine, but I don't want to go to Jacksonville so I just wonder if I will even get to." I frown.

"Mikayla, doctors are needed everywhere, even lowly residents," he teases me. "I'm actually relieved you don't want to go to Jacksonville. It sounds like it's going to become very large, very quickly and I kind of like being out in the sticks."

"You do?" I ask enthusiastically, happy that he might feel the same way.

"Yes, I do. In fact, I want to participate in the sharecropping program. I think I'd make a damn good farmer, don't you?" he asks, pounding his chest like an ape.

"Yes, I do," I say, giggling. "But what about your family? Don't you want to find them?" I ask. "I know how important they are to you."

He nods. "Yes, of course I do."

"Okay then," I say.

"Okay then, what?" he asks.

"Okay, we'll go out west to find them," I say.

He looks shocked. "What? Uh . . ."

"They do have small towns that have farms out west, don't they?" I ask.

"Well, yes, but . . ." He shakes his head and furrows his brow. "You'd *do* that for me?"

"Of course I would. I don't have any family here," I say. "Well, there's Claire and my friends, but no blood relatives. It's important that you find them, so yes, we will go out west. Whenever you want to."

He stares at me in disbelief and then pulls me close. "What did I ever do to deserve you?" he asks. "I love you, Mikayla."

"Promise?" I ask.

"Promise," he vows.

$$\sim \quad \sim \quad \sim$$

Mitch stays with me to finish out my shift, then he heads to the showers after being in the fields all morning. We make plans to meet at the community center for a game of pool later. He's up by a few games in our ongoing tournament that we have every Wednesday night. We no longer play for material things. We play for, um . . . favors. So, even when we lose, we win. We chose Wednesdays because it's the one weeknight when everyone tends to gather at The Oasis for a mid-week bonfire with music and dancing. It's our time to be alone because the masses are otherwise engaged.

I quickly eat a light dinner and go over early to get in some practice. I'm *so* winning tonight's game.

It's getting dark inside the community center so I light my lamp. I hear the door open and smile because he's come early, too. "Couldn't stay away, huh?"

"I tried. But, no, doctor. I can't stay away from you," says a familiar voice that is most definitely not Mitch's. John comes out of the shadows and stands in front of me.

"John, what are you doing here? Isn't everyone at the bonfire?" I ask.

"Yup. Everyone," he says, inching closer.

Alarm bells go off in my head and I quickly say, "Mitch will be here soon for our regular game. Did you want to play?" I back away from him and walk over to the other side of the pool table.

He follows me and says, "Oh, I want to play. Just not billiards. And I just saw your little nurse friend heading to the mess hall, so he won't be here anytime soon. Looks like it's just you and me."

His breath washes over me as he comes closer. It smells putrid, like a mixture of alcohol and poor dental hygiene.

I put down the pool cue, which in hindsight was probably a mistake, and I walk toward the door. "I'm just going to go find him then," I say.

"I don't think so," he says, quickly stepping over to grab my arm.

"John, please let go of my arm," I say, still trying to make my way to the door.

"You think you can just tease me? String me along until someone better comes around that shows interest in you?"

I look closely at him and something is off. He reeks of alcohol, but even in the dim light, I can see that his pupils are practically pin holes, a sure sign of drug use and I wonder where he has gotten hold of something like heroin. Or maybe even morphine. We have a small amount of it under lock and key at the clinic, and he is an officer so he probably has the means to get it. If he's high, God only knows what he will do.

I have to get out of here!

"John, how about we head over to The Oasis and I'll dance with you," I say.

"How about you dance with me right here, doctor," he says, forcefully pulling me against his body.

I gasp and my entire body stiffens when he holds me against the erection in his pants. "J-John," I stutter, trying to calm my frantic words, "you're not thinking clearly." I look up and speak straight at him. "You do *not* want to do this, John."

He laughs in my face and his rancid breath, along with the thought of what he intends to do to me, makes me want to vomit.

"Oh, I want to do this all right," he says, half smiling down at me with a spaced-out look in his eyes. "I've wanted to do this since I first laid eyes on you. I was just waiting for the right time. I knew that you come here every week and that sometimes you come early and, lucky me, tonight was one of those times." As I struggle to get away, he pulls me over to the nearby couch and pushes me down onto it. Hard. "Now, do what I tell you or I'll beat the shit out of you. Then I'll beat the shit out of Mitch just for kicks. Don't think I can't do it, *Mikayla*. Just because he took me down once doesn't mean he'll do it again. I'm an officer. I know people who will do things for me. You just remember that and keep your pretty little mouth shut while we have some fun here."

He begins unbuttoning his pants and I take the opportunity to get up quickly and run for the door. He chases after me, catching me and picking me up by the waist as he drags me, kicking and screaming, back to the couch. He throws me down hard enough that my head snaps back and hits the solid railing behind the cushions. *Ouch!* My hand goes up to rub the back of my head as he climbs onto me.

Oh, my God, this is really going to happen.

He is so much bigger than me, at least twice my size, and his weight is holding me down. There is nothing I can do but scream and punch at him as he tears at my shirt.

Then I hear someone yell, "What the fuck is going on here?"

I cry out to my savior, "Mitch, Help!" I scream, as he runs across the room to me.

John stands up and takes a fighting stance as Mitch comes up on him. "She doesn't belong to you, Mitch!" John screams, now struggling to keep his footing.

"The hell she doesn't!" Mitch yells back, right before he tackles him to the ground, hitting him over and over until blood spatters all around us.

"Stop, Mitch!" I yell, before he kills John.

"Mitch, easy man," someone says to him. I look up to see Austin, pulling Mitch off John.

Then I see multiple people running over to lend their assistance. I could have sworn Mitch came in alone and through the other door. I didn't know we had an audience. But I'm grateful for anyone who can help out to make sure John is restrained.

What I see next has my head spinning as if I'd taken drugs myself.

There, walking side-by-side towards me, looking at the three of us and trying to figure out what they've come upon is Holly, Craig, Pam and some others along with Claire . . . and Claire's son.

Jeff.

Jeff is standing next to his mom. Jeff is here at Camp Brady and is standing with my friends as they come over to help me. His hair has grown out. He has a beard and he looks rough around the edges, but it's most definitely him.

A few men carry John over to the couch and detain him.

Jeff looks at me as if I'm not real, as if he can't believe that after all this time, I'm still here. I'm not sure, but I may look at him the same way. Then I look over at Mitch, who is watching me. Then Mitch looks at Jeff, then Jeff at me. Jeff looks back to Mitch and repeats his words back to him, "The hell she doesn't?" And then he walks right over to him and punches Mitch in the gut.

Mitch goes down without so much as a fight. Jeff climbs on top of Mitch and pulls his arm back, clearly getting ready to hit him again. I look down at Mitch. He lies lifeless on the ground. He's not lost consciousness, but he doesn't even lift a hand to defend himself, not even to protect his face when Jeff takes a swing at him. Mitch doesn't bother moving his head out of the way. He takes the punch and blood trails out of his mouth.

I run over, along with Austin, who picks up Jeff and removes him from on top of Mitch. Jeff paces around us, not bothering to look at me while he yells at Mitch. "What the fuck? Are you seriously screwing my girlfriend? When did you become such a traitor, you son of a bitch?" he asks.

Seeing Mitch lying bloody on the ground; seeing Jeff rant and use obscenities like I've never seen him; and seeing my would-be assailant lie restrained over on the couch all have me on the brink of hysterics.

Claire comes over and gets between all of us. "Now, let's all calm down. This is a lot to take in," she says, looking at me with incredibly sad eyes even though I know she is rejoicing at the return of her only child.

She waves Austin over and says, "Austin, you take Mitch to the clinic and get him cleaned up." Then she says over her shoulder to Holly, "Dear, would you please go with Kay back to your apartment for a while and make sure she is alright?"

She walks over to her son. "Jeff, let's take a few minutes. I know a lot has happened here, but you can't blame Mitch, son. Let's go walk around and get re-acquainted." She leads him out of the room; all the while he is shaking his head and muttering something about shitty best friends. "Let's all meet at my place in an hour to talk this through like real adults, shall we?" Claire says.

Meet at her place in an hour? All of us . . . as in Mitch, Jeff and I? I almost collapse at the thought of us being in the same room. What if Jeff tries to hurt Mitch again? What if they kill each other?

I hope Claire intends to have Austin come along as well.

I watch Jeff and his mom leave the community center. I can't help but stare after them until they are out of sight. Then I look over at Mitch and see the devastation on his face as he obviously saw me watching Jeff.

Holly grabs my elbow. "Come on, Kay. Let's go cool off for a bit. Nobody is going anywhere." She pulls me and I follow her reluctantly out of the building as I turn to see Mitch being tended to by Austin. His head is shaking repeatedly from side to side and his eyes are squeezed shut.

I wonder what he must be thinking. Is he thinking that I was almost raped and he saved me? Is he thinking that Jeff coming back means I'll leave him? Is he thinking that our happy world just came to an end? Is he thinking that he can no longer love me?

Before Holly pulls me out of Mitch's sight, I can almost hear his vow from earlier in my head . . .

Promise.

Chapter Twenty-four

On our way back to the apartment, it dawns on me that Jeff and I didn't so much as say a word to each other. I look around and see many unfamiliar faces. I realize he must have come in with a group.

I see Amanda sprinting across the courtyard. I follow her with my eyes and watch as she jumps into the arms of a waiting man, causing them to tumble to the grass. They kiss and laugh and cry, and I can't help my own tears from falling. She always said he would return. She was sure of it.

I turn to Holly. "How many came with him?" I ask.

"Forty or so," she says.

I hold my breath and ask about her husband. "Carter?"

She shakes her head.

"I'm sorry," I say, reaching down to take her hand. "Maybe he will come soon."

"Maybe," she says.

Amanda catches up to us and introduces us to her husband, Denny. They are both smiling from ear-to-ear and, understandably, can't keep their eyes and hands off each other. We only exchange pleasantries as they quickly head over to the daycare center so that

Denny can meet his daughter, Rachel, for the very first time. I'm so happy for them.

Why can't I be happy for *me*? I'm glad that Jeff is back, aren't I?

Of course I am. Claire must be over the moon. He is alive!

"Holy crap, Kay," Holly says as we enter our apartment. "What are you going to do?"

"What do you mean?" I ask.

"What do I mean? You've got two of the hottest guys left on the planet vying for you."

I shake my head at her. "Hol, I'm glad Jeff is back and that he seems to be okay. But, I love Mitch now. Jeff coming back doesn't change that."

"Poor Jeff," she says. "Did you see the way he went after Mitch? The guy still has it bad for you." She brings me a bottle of water. "So, hey . . . if you don't want him anymore, does that mean he's up for grabs?" she asks, wiggling her eyebrows at me.

I roll my eyes at her and laugh.

Then I realize I might be the tiniest bit jealous over what she just said. I didn't anticipate this. I love Mitch so why would I care if someone else wants Jeff? I try to shake it off, but I ignore Holly's question all the same.

"Oh, God, Kay!" She looks guiltily at me. "With all the excitement of Jeff showing up, I didn't even ask you. Are you okay?" she asks, patting my leg. "I mean, was that asshole John really going to do what I think he was going to do?"

Events from not quite an hour ago flood through my head making me cringe and feel sick all over again. "Yes, he was. It was terrible, Hol," I say, choking on my words. "He was drunk and probably high. He said he had been following me just waiting to get me alone."

Holly covers her mouth to stifle her cry. "Oh, my God!" She hits the pillow on the couch next to her. "That rat bastard better get put in jail. Oh, wait . . . do we even have a jail here?"

"I think there are some holding cells over in the officers' admin building. But, who knows, Hol. It comes down to his word against mine and he's an officer."

"An officer who everyone knows is a slime ball," she says. "You also have like ten witnesses who saw him holding you down on the couch before Mitch pummeled him. I'm sure the colonel will lock him up, I mean you're kind of like a daughter to him since he's with Claire and all."

"I hope so. Maybe Claire will be able to tell us something when we get to her apartment." Then I stiffen as I remember we will be going over there in a short while to meet with Jeff and Mitch. "God Holly, what am I going to do? I'm about to be in the same room with both of them. What if they kill each other? I'm scared to death."

She puts her arm around me. "I'll be there with you, Kay. Don't worry, it will all work out. You'll see."

I'm glad to see that *she* is so confident. I attempt to busy myself with meaningless tasks until it's time to go. I can't let myself think about what will happen in just a few minutes when my past and my future collide.

As soon as the door to her apartment swings open, Claire pulls me into a tight hug. "Sweetie, are you okay? It must have been awful for you, John forcing himself on you like that. James will be by in a little while to talk to you and Mitch about what happened. Then we are going to make sure he doesn't bother you again."

"Thanks, Claire. I'm okay," I whisper to her. "I'm more afraid of what is going to happen right here. Terrified is more like it."

She squeezes me and says, "Kay, it's going to be fine. Have a little faith."

"Are they both here?" I can barely ask her over the pounding of my heart.

"No, Mitch hasn't shown up yet. I'm sure he will be along shortly," she says. "Now, come on in." She has to pull on my hand to get me to follow her. Am I ready for this? Can I face the man who I let go so that I could love another?

I walk around the corner and see him. He looks good. Really good. It looks like he got a shower. His damp blonde hair curls up slightly at the nape of his neck and is longer than I've ever seen it. He trimmed his beard and now boasts a nice scruffy hint of one in its place. He was always in decent shape, but now he's downright fit, his new muscles complimenting his almost six-foot frame.

I can see him taking me in the same way. I try to remember what I looked like before he left. My hair was shorter and I was definitely more rounded. I'm down about twenty pounds now . . . along with most other people. He looks at me longingly and then stands up and walks over to me.

He hugs me and my heart skips a beat, not yet knowing if this is right or wrong.

I bring my arms up to return the hug and I feel this body, this unfamiliar body that belongs to a man I once knew every inch of so intimately.

"Kay," he says in my ear. It's the first word he's spoken directly to me in almost eighteen months. "God, I've missed you."

He holds onto me, prolonging the hug and I feel oddly uncomfortable considering we had been together for over five years.

The door shuts behind me, startling me. When I glance over, I see Mitch staring at us appraisingly. I'm hugging Jeff and he is holding me to him. I wonder if this upsets Mitch. I smile over at him, hoping he understands that the hug is just a friendly gesture on my part.

"I'm so glad you're okay, Jeff," I say, pulling myself back from him.

"Come in, Mitch. Austin," Claire says. "Everyone come sit in the living room please."

We all follow her into the room that has two couches and a chair. Jeff sits on one couch. Mitch sits on the other couch. I realize the predicament this puts me in and I walk over and sit down in the chair. I hear Holly giggle behind me as she and Austin join Mitch and Jeff on their respective couches. Claire pulls a kitchen chair next to me, plopping it down in the middle of the room, like she is the mediator. Maybe that's exactly what she is.

I stare at Mitch, but he won't look at me. He keeps his gaze fixed on the window even though it's dark outside and there is nothing to see. He has a cut on his jaw along with a bright red bruise that is starting to turn purple. He has a couple of steri-strips holding his skin together and I feel guilty that I wasn't the one tending to his injuries.

Claire introduces Jeff to Holly and Austin so I assume they hadn't met earlier which probably means Jeff had literally just arrived at camp when they found me. Then, after a minute of excruciatingly uncomfortable silence, Claire tells us, "I have explained to Jeff the circumstances behind Mitch's actions at the community center." She turns to Mitch and says, "He knows about your amnesia and that you weren't aware of who Kay was until a week ago." She puts a loving hand on my arm. "I told Jeff how hard this year has been for you and that you waited so long and were so patient and loyal to him, but that nobody could be expected to hold out hope forever."

Claire looks at Jeff, then at Mitch, then at me. "You all have some talking to do and I hope you can work this out as responsible adults. I love each one of you. I'm not taking sides. I'm here for all of you, whenever you need to talk. Does anyone have anything to say?"

I'm still trying to wrap my mind around the fact that forty people showed up today. I have so many questions, but the one I have to ask Jeff is, "Who came back with you? You had Amanda's husband with you. How did you find him? What about Austin's wife, or Holly and Pam's husbands. What do you know about them?"

I can't be sure, but I think Jeff is shocked at my question. Perhaps he thought I would throw myself at him and beg him to take me back after I'd betrayed him with Mitch. Maybe he thought I would want to know what he went through to get to me. He shakes his head, almost imperceptibly, and says, "People with similar interests found each other over there. We stayed with those who were trying to make their way back to certain geographical areas. We got to know each other over the past year, just as you all have." I don't miss that he sends a quick look of disgust to Mitch. "However, some groups of people left early on, thinking they would be better off leaving quickly, so we didn't get to know everyone you are looking for. I can tell you that Pam's husband died, along with several other spouses of people I've been told are living here." He turns to speak to Holly and Austin. "As you know by now, your spouses didn't arrive with us and I'm sorry to say that

I just don't have any information on them. They could be with another group. But, don't give up hope. There are still a lot of folks over there that are working to get across the pond."

"Pam's husband is dead," I repeat to myself. All I can think of is that I have to get to her. I stand up, but Holly intercepts me before I can leave.

"Pam is dealing with it, Kay," she says, pulling me back. "Craig is with her and she seems to be handling it. She's sad, but she had moved on. We will find her later. Right now you need to deal with *this*." She points back to the living room.

"There is nothing to deal with, Hol," I whisper to her. "I'm with Mitch and Jeff is going to have to accept that."

She leans in close to me. "Then why didn't you sit down next to Mitch?"

She has a good point. Why didn't I?

"I guess I didn't want to rub it in Jeff's face," I say. "But make no mistake, I still love Mitch."

"You might want to tell Mitch that, Kay," she says. "The way he looks right now, it's like he's sure you are going back to Jeff."

When she pulls me back into the room, I'm surprised to see Mitch talking to Jeff.

"I'm sorry," he frowns. "You have to know that if I had any idea who she was, I would not have laid a hand on her." His eyes flash momentarily to me. "I would never intentionally screw you over. You have to believe me, Jeff."

Jeff nods his head over and over, and chews on the inside of his cheek, thinking before he acknowledges Mitch. "I know. My mom explained everything. It's just so unbelievable how it all happened." He rubs his hands together. "Still, you have to give me a minute to take it in, man. It doesn't make it any less shocking thinking about you with her."

They are talking about me as if I'm not here so I butt in. "I'm standing right here, gentlemen. You don't have to talk about me like I'm not."

"Sorry, babe," Jeff says, like our relationship never missed a beat.

Holly, Austin and I all snap our heads over to Mitch and see his eyes close at the endearment Jeff used. Mitch lets out a deep sigh and stands. "Right," he says. "It'll take some adjustment on all our parts. It's been a long day and I think I'm going to head home."

Mitch walks out of the apartment without so much as a glance my way. I'm torn. I need to go after him, but I don't want to make Jeff feel badly. He called me 'babe.' Does he think I'm simply going to dump Mitch and get back with him?

I pull Claire aside. "Claire, what exactly did you tell Jeff about me and Mitch? Does he know we're in love?"

She shakes her head. "He knows that you are dating and that you have feelings for each other, but I didn't think it was my place to tell him just how deep those feelings go." She puts her arm around my shoulders. "You are in quite a position, Kay. You are between two amazing men who both obviously want you. But, you have to go with your heart. I have a feeling that means not being with my son and I'm okay with that. Jeff is a strong man. He'll bounce back. You can't be with him out of guilt or obligation, you know that, right?"

I nod at her. "I'm sorry, Claire," I say.

"No need to be sorry," she says, smiling back at me. "I have my son back. It's a glorious day. Everything will work out as it's meant to."

I wish I had her optimism.

"I have to go after him," I say, walking towards the door. "Please tell Jeff I'll find him tomorrow and then we can talk." I give her one last hug. "I'm so happy for you that he is back. I really am. Don't ever think I didn't want this to happen."

"I know, dear. Now go find your happily-ever-after," she says, waving me out the door.

Before I can go after him, however, Colonel Andrews catches me in the hallway and asks me to recount exactly what happened with John. He takes me for a walk around the courtyard while I tell him every detail of the horrible experience. Then he tells me that John is being detained based on the testimony of some of the people that walked in to see him holding me against my will. He said he may ask John to leave the base but would like to talk to Mitch and a few others first.

"Don't worry, Kay," he says. It's not lost on me that this is the first time he's ever called me by my first name. Perhaps he does think of me as a daughter now. "He won't lay a finger on you again. I promise."

There is that word again.

Promise.

And suddenly, I have to go after Mitch. Now. I can't wait another minute.

I don't even bother looking in his apartment. He won't be there. He's hurting. He's confused. He might even be angry. Like me, there are only two places he would be right now, and it's far too dark to take out the horses. I go out front, to where I know he will be. I find him lying on the grass, staring up at the sky and I quietly lie down next to him. I silently wonder if we are both looking at Orion and The Seven Sisters.

We lie here for minutes before either of us speaks.

"It's okay, Mikayla," he says. "You don't have to feel guilty. I get it. You and I have been together for five minutes. You were with him for five years. It makes sense. I won't try to fight him for you. You both mean too much to me to do that. He's still my friend even if he doesn't see it that way."

My jaw drops shockingly at his words. I sit up and look down at him. "Mitch, is that what you think I came out here for—to dump you?"

"Well . . . yes," he says. "Didn't you?"

"I love you, Mitch. That hasn't changed just because he came back. He never even said he wants me back. It's been a long time. His feelings may have changed as well."

He gives me a look that screams 'duh,' and says, "He called you 'babe,' Mikayla. Believe me, he wants you."

I shake my head. "That's merely a habit," I say. "We have both changed so much. I can see that even though we haven't really talked yet."

"You haven't talked?" he asks. "Then what have you been doing for the last hour?"

"Talking to the colonel. He came looking for both of us but you had left. I told him exactly what happened tonight with John."

He sits up quickly as if he suddenly remembered what happened earlier. He finally looks me in the eye. "I'm sorry," he says. "I'm sorry I didn't get to you sooner. If he had touched you. If he had hurt you. I would have killed him."

"You almost did, Mitch. If you recall, Austin had to pull you off him. It was a good thing he showed up." I can see his split jaw in the moonlight and I reach up to touch it gently, but he flinches and pulls away from me. "I'm so sorry I didn't get to tend to you myself."

"It's no big deal. I deserved it," he says.

I gasp. "What? Why would you say that?"

"Because I took his girl. I deserved every punch he was going to lay on me."

I grab his hand and tighten mine around it, not allowing him to pull away this time. "You deserved nothing. Is that why you didn't protect yourself? Because you thought you did something wrong?" I release his hand and reach out to turn his face towards mine. "Loving me is not wrong, Mitch."

I see his grimace. "Mikayla, I have to go. I need some time."

"Time for what? Time to figure out if I'm worth it?" I stand up angrily and start walking away. I turn around and say, "Because I am, Mitch Matheson. I'm worth it. And if you don't think so, you're a jackass."

I walk away but still hear him mumble, "That I am."

Chapter Twenty-five

Most people are rejoicing at the return of their loved ones. And I am, too. I am truly glad that Jeff has come back. But the tension it has created around here could be cut with a knife—or maybe a damn chain saw.

What's worse is that now Jeff is at the clinic every day. Every. Day. And Mitch is conspicuously *not*. He got permission from the colonel to help Craig and the other farmers out in the fields on the condition that if needed here, he would come right away.

So, for almost a week now, Jeff and I have been working side-by-side and Mitch has kept his distance. When I try to talk to Mitch, he gives me the same story about both of us needing time to figure things out. I was okay with that for a few days, but now I'm just pissed off. Figure out what exactly?

I love him. He loves me. End of story, right?

I get that he thinks he's like Dale. He thinks he's taking me away from Jeff if he allows our relationship to continue. I have to make him understand that's not the case. I also have to make Jeff understand that despite his repeated attempts to get close to me, my heart doesn't lie with him anymore. I'll always love Jeff. I just don't love him *that way*. And whether he does it consciously or not, he always ends up touching me, grabbing my hand, or making some comment that alludes to us being a couple. I try hard not to hurt his feelings, but it's starting to weigh on me.

"Did Mr. Stephens come in this morning, babe?" he asks, staring at a patient file.

"Jeff," I address him, closing my eyes briefly and sighing, "you have to stop calling me that. We're not together anymore."

"Right." He smiles over at me and winks. "But that won't stop me from trying."

"We've gone over this. I'm with Mitch now. You are wonderful and I'll always cherish what we had. But, please stop with the name calling and the flirting and the touching."

"Kay, we were together for years and I've just now been informed that we're not a couple any longer. Can you give me a little time to get used to it before you bite my head off?"

"Fine," I pout. "I know it's hard for you. Maybe if you and Mitch could try to be friends, it wouldn't be so bad. You guys shared something that bonds you for life. Can we please rise above this and try to all get along?"

He looks sad as he nods his head. "Yeah, okay. I'll try," he says. "For you, I'll try."

"What are your plans, Kay?" he asks, changing direction. "Do you think you'll head up to Jacksonville with us?"

"Us?" I ask, raising an eyebrow quizzically.

"Yeah. Holly, Jamie and I were talking yesterday about when would be a good time to go. I don't want to leave the camp without a doctor so we all agreed to stay on until the numbers dwindle down, but we really need to start thinking about the next step."

Since when does Holly confide in Jeff before me?

It all seems so real now. People are talking about leaving. Some already have, taking parcels of land that the government has been doling out for sharecropping. Some have left to go in search of loved ones now that it's becoming safer outside the gates. Some, like me, are unsure of their place in the world, and now with Mitch and I 'taking time to think,' I don't even know if we are still going west as we had planned. But one thing is for sure, whether Mitch is in my future or not, Jacksonville is not where I want to be.

"I don't think I want to go to Jacksonville, Jeff," I say. "I think I'd like to work in a small town."

He gives me a disapproving look. "How will you ever improve your skills doing that? And what about your residency?"

"It's not all about skills or being the best for me anymore. I've learned to enjoy my life outside of medicine and I want to keep it that way. And, my residency? I'm not sure there even *are* residency programs anymore. The bottom line is, I'm willing to take my chances. I like it here. I'll find somewhere to fit in."

"Well, don't be surprised if we all try to change your mind over the next few months," he says. "I see how tight you and Holly are and I know she wants you to go. Jamie, now that's something else altogether." We both laugh at her dislike of me that is so blatant that Jeff is already aware of it.

After work, I find Holly, Pam and Amanda and we head to The Oasis. I know it's a Wednesday and this isn't my usual routine, but I also know that Mitch won't be waiting for me at the pool hall. He won't be waiting for me anywhere.

Well, I'm tired of waiting for him to figure things out. So, I'm bringing my A game with me tonight. Craig has promised to get

Mitch to the bonfire and I plan to take full advantage of the situation.

It's awkward at first with me and the girls sitting at one table and Mitch and the guys at another. And thank goodness Jeff doesn't show up. I don't need the unbridled tension that surrounds the three of us whenever we are in the same place at the same time.

The more we drink, the less awkward it gets and the more I catch Mitch glancing over at me. The first part of Operation Seduction goes well, so I'm ready to set the wheels of the rest of my plan in motion.

I drag Holly out to the dance floor that is directly in front of the band, across the deck from where we were sitting, but close enough for Mitch to watch me. Then Holly and I start to dance. And by dance, I mean *dance*. I move my body in ways that I didn't even know I could. I run my hands up and down my sides provocatively. I wiggle my hips, put my arms in the air and close my eyes, getting lost in the music.

"Shit, Kay," Holly says, "keep it up and Mitch will take you right here on the dance floor. He hasn't stopped staring at you since we walked up here." She laughs and continues, "His eyes are practically popping out of his head like he's a carnivore and you're the only steak at a vegetarian buffet."

We giggle and then I not only keep it up, but ramp it up even more. I have needs. Needs that have gone unsatisfied for a week now. I have to feel his hands on me. I'm sure if I can get him alone he will break and finally realize he is being unreasonable.

My bladder screams at me after all the alcohol I've consumed. I tell Holly, "I'm heading to the latrine. Be back in a few." She nods and motions for someone else to come dance with her.

It's dark by the latrines, but I'm not scared anymore. Not since John left. He didn't put up much of a fight once word got around and he realized what a leper he had become in our little community.

Still, when I emerge from the toilet, I about jump out of my shoes when I run smack into someone. Then my body relaxes instantly when I smell him. Even before I see him clearly, I smell him. I'm glad it's dark because I can hardly contain my victorious smile, knowing he must have followed me here.

"Mitch!" I feign surprise, keeping my hand on his chest where it landed a moment ago.

"Mikayla . . ."

I can tell by his breathing that he's turned on. I am so in tune to his body it's like we are one person.

"What are you trying to do to me?" he asks.

I lean up to his ear and let my breath flow out over it a few times before I say in a low, sultry voice, "Is it working?" Then I place a kiss on his neck in the very spot that I know drives him wild. His body stiffens. I can tell he's having some kind of existential struggle. I try to make it easy for him when I put my lips on his and whisper "I want you . . . and only you."

"Fuck," he says, letting out an angry sigh into my mouth right before shoving his tongue between my lips, claiming my mouth with that familiar barbaric possessiveness that I've come to love about him.

He pushes me back against the wall of the latrine and holds his body tight against mine as our mouths hungrily explore each other. Our hands search for places to grab, seeking out any and every body part that we've both craved so much but have been denied.

My body is humming in a heightened state of arousal. I don't even care that we could be caught when I boldly reach for his jeans and slip my hand beneath his waistband.

I hear a noise behind us and then someone says, "Oh, sorry!" The intruder hurries away, scared off by our lewd public behavior.

Mitch pulls away and my body protests. "Shit!" he says, releasing my grip on him as he walks around to the other side of the latrines. "Shit, shit, shit!" he exclaims again, punching the latrine like he did John's face. "I can't do this to him."

"To *him*?" I cry. "What about to *me*, Mitch. What do you think you do to *me* when you pull away like this—when you deprive me of you?"

"I . . . I'm sorry," he says as he walks into the darkness. "I just can't do this, Kay."

Tears streak down my face and my body slumps to the ground like a rag doll. He's never called me Kay before. That's it then. He's made his decision.

My life without him flashes before my eyes.

No! I run after him, refusing to let him decide this for us.

I catch up to him outside the door to our apartments and pull him inside mine. "You have to talk to me. You can't just decide this for us. I'm in this, too," I say.

"There's nothing to discuss. I'm backing off. We all need some time to figure things out. It's the right thing to do, Mikayla," he says.

Well, at least he's using my rightful name again.

"Are you walking away?" I ask "Don't you remember our date? That night was perfect. It was one of the best nights of my life. You said to me that night that there wasn't anything in the world that would keep you from wanting to be with me."

"No. I said there wasn't anything I could *think* of," he corrects me. "I sure as hell didn't think of this." He shakes his head. He paces around again like he did by the latrines. Then he runs his hands through his hair in exasperation. "It's not that I don't *want* to be with you. It's that I *can't* be with you, Mikayla. Those are two different things."

"That's bullshit, Mitch," I cry to him. "You *can* be with me. I'm right here!" I point at myself like he can't see me. "I'm standing in front of you and I love you." I put my hand over his heart. "*You.* I love *you*," I say, trying to get through to him. "I love you *more* than him, can't you understand that?"

"But you loved him so much longer. That counts for something, too," he argues.

"Why are you coming up with reasons not to be with me?" I ask. "Don't you love me anymore?"

"Of course I love you!" he shouts, running his frustrated hands through his hair once again. "I told you I would never stop. I promised you. But I promised him first. I promised him I would take care of you if anything happened to him." He closes his eyes. "That promise didn't include screwing you."

I wince at his choice of words. "Mitch, it's *my* life. I get to choose who I want to live it with."

"No. It's not just your life. It's his, too," he says, blowing out a long breath. "It's Gina all over again. She chose him and he allowed it. It nearly killed me. I won't do that to Jeff. I'm not going to be like Dale."

My God, what do I have to do to get through to him?

"But, Jeff has accepted that I love you, Mitch."

His eyes snap up to mine and I think I see a trace of hope, like maybe I'm chipping away at his protective armor. He asks, "Has he, Mikayla? Have you told him in no uncertain terms that you love me more than you love him?"

I think back on all the conversations I've had with Jeff this week. I've told him numerous times that Mitch and I are together. I've told him to stop flirting with me, to stop trying to be around me all the time, to stop addressing me with his endearments. But, did I come right out and say I was in love with Mitch? I honestly can't remember. Full of guilt, my gaze shifts to the ground.

"I thought so," he says, his voice so defeated it sounds like it comes from a small child, not my big Neanderthal of a man.

"I'll tell him," I say. "I'll go tell him right now." I reach for the door.

"No." He pulls me back. "Let me talk to him," he says. "I'll talk to him tomorrow man to man. I've been avoiding him, but now I realize we need to have this conversation. Will you give me time to do that please?"

What can I say? Of course he needs to talk to Jeff. I've been pushing them to get together all week. I smile because he has just given me a sliver of optimism. Once they talk, Mitch will realize it's okay for us to be together. "Yes, I would like that," I say. "You two have been acting like jackasses not trying to reclaim your friendship. I think you two talking is just what we all need to get past this."

"Okay, then. I'll talk to him tomorrow," he says. He turns to leave, grabbing the door handle but then he hesitates, shaking his head slightly. Suddenly, he pivots back to me and plants a kiss on my forehead. "See you later, Mikayla."

I touch the place on my head where his lips met my skin, as if doing so will somehow keep him closer to me.

I get ready for bed, confident that this will be my last night spent without lying in Mitch's arms.

Chapter Twenty-six

Jeff is not scheduled to work today and Mitch is off farming with Craig. I float happily through my day knowing all will be well again with the world once Mitch and Jeff finally clear the air.

"I'll say it again, Kay," Holly says, emerging from the back room, "how is it fair in any universe that you have those two hot, dreamy men after you and I've been celibate for almost a month?"

I laugh at her. "Trouble in paradise?" I ask.

"Hmmpf," she snorts. "Tom and I haven't been in paradise since he slept with that skank over in the kitchen."

"Since when have you been picky about who he sleeps with? Haven't you two always had some sort of an arrangement?"

"I suppose." She frowns. "But after seeing you with Mitch . . . well, I just . . . I *want* that."

"Did you have that with Carter?" I ask.

"Nah, not really. He was great and we were happy and all. But it wasn't that all-encompassing, fairy-tale love that you seem to have with Mitch." Then a smile creeps up her face. "But the sex was freaking incredible." I giggle with her. "You're lucky, Kay. You got it all in one delicious package."

"Holly Becker, you are one of the most wonderful and caring people I've ever met. If Karma is paying attention, you will get your prince one day, too."

"Can I just order one up from your leftovers and call it even?" she asks, laughing. Then she proceeds to spend the rest of the day telling me exactly what her fairy-tale life will look like. Ad nauseum. I'm so ready to go when my shift is over.

$$\sim \quad \sim \quad \sim$$

After dinner, I run into Austin as he's leaving his apartment for work. He silently laughs when he sees me, like he is enjoying a private joke. He raises a finger to his lips, mouthing, "*Shhh.*"

He pulls me off to the side of his front door that sits ajar and he whispers, "You have impeccable timing, Kay. At this very minute, there are two men in this apartment that both care about you more than you'll ever know. If I didn't have to be at work, I'd stick around and eavesdrop for you, but I can't. So, I'm just going to leave the door the way it is and walk away. What you choose to do with this information is up to you. No judgment here."

"Uh . . ."

"Bye, Kay," he whispers before he kisses my cheek and quietly walks away.

I'm terrified. I literally have no idea what to do. I've been through medical school. I'm trained to deal with all kinds of stressful situations in a calm and cool manner. I'm also the kind of person who always does the right thing. As in, I once found a hundred-dollar bill at a soccer game when I was fifteen and I walked around the soccer field until I identified the rightful owner.

Eavesdropping is wrong. On so many levels. They are having a private conversation. They are entitled to believe they can talk openly and honestly without the topic of said conversation listening in.

I'm going to close the door. Of course I'm going to close the door. I take two steps toward it and slowly reach my hand out to grab the handle.

". . . is an incredible woman," I hear Mitch say.

I stand here. Paralyzed and unable to move.

I'm going to hell.

"She is. Can you believe that she's the one who facilitated this little pow-wow?" Jeff says. "She's been bugging me all week to talk to you. She said you told her everything about our ordeal in Afghanistan and that she wants us to be friends despite the . . . uh, predicament we're in."

"I know. She cornered me last night and said something about reclaiming our friendship." I can practically hear his eyes roll up into his head when he says that. "She said we were jackasses if we didn't try to bury the hatchet."

I smile out here in the hallway. They are doing it. They're communicating. And they aren't using their fists. If I didn't know any better, it almost sounds like they are getting along.

I should leave.

"I know you've heard it all before, but I need you to hear it again," Mitch says. "I came here to fulfill my promise to you. I couldn't help it that I fell in love with her. You have to know I wouldn't have if I'd known who she was. But, even so, I just can't turn my feelings off. I still love her, Jeff."

"Well, she is pretty amazing," Jeff says. "I mean, come on, what's not to love? But, shit, man . . . we have ourselves quite a situation. We both love the same woman."

Oh, my God. Did he actually say that? I inch a little closer to the crack in the door and try to hear what is happening, but all I hear is silence.

Someone say something!

"You're still in love with her?" Mitch asks, incredulously. I can hear his long, drawn-out sigh from outside the door.

"Of course I am," Jeff says. "Why do you think I came back here?"

"For your family? Because you lived here?"

"Well, yes, that's true. But I came for her. I spent every damn day of the last year trying to get back here to her. She's all I've thought about," Jeff says. Then there's more silence. "Hey, you okay?"

"Not really," Mitch responds. "I guess I thought you were kind of getting over her. I knew there were feelings there, but . . ." I can hear something that sounds like his head hitting the wall behind the couch and I can picture him staring up at the ceiling in despair.

"Have you *met* Mikayla Parker?" Jeff asks. "She's not exactly the kind of woman you just 'get over.' I guess I was trying to back off a little; give you guys some time to get used to me being around. But, let's be clear, I'm every bit as much in love with her as I was the day I left for my tour." I hear the distinct sound of a beer can opening and then Jeff says, "So—may the best man win?"

I hear another sigh. Then more silence. And then maybe the sound of someone chugging down a beer.

"That's not how I do things, Jeff," Mitch says. "I made a promise to you. I found her. She's safe. You're back now. And you just told me you never stopped loving her. So I'm going to walk away."

"Walk away? Seriously?" Jeff asks in disbelief. "Just like that?"

"Just like that," Mitch says. "I know you've heard the story of Gina and Dale. That's not me, man. I refuse to do that to a friend. To a brother. So, yes. I'm walking away. I've been thinking about leaving anyway, to go get a piece of land and start my own farm. I guess I'll just go sooner rather than later."

I can no longer hear them speaking through the pounding in my ears. I slide down the wall the same way the tears slide down my cheeks. My breath has left my body and I can't seem to get it back.

He's leaving?

No. He can't leave. This was not supposed to be how this went. They were supposed to make up and shake hands and drink warm, disgusting beer while remembering why they love each other like brothers. Then Jeff was supposed to bow out. Not Mitch. Not the man I love.

No, this is not happening. I won't let him leave. I get up quietly and go to my apartment to settle myself down. I have to figure out a way to get him to stay. He promised me. He promised me he would love me forever.

I try to keep myself busy and let them finish talking across the hall. I seek out anything I can clean. But it's a futile effort trying to find anything messy in here now that Rachel's toys aren't strewn about everywhere.

So I read. I have a new book that I've not read before and I try my best to occupy myself with it even though I have to read the first page four times before I actually absorb it.

The next thing I know, I'm waking up on the couch and it's clearly late—or early, depending on how you look at it. I don't care if it's three o'clock in the morning; I'm going over to talk some sense into him.

I don't even need my flashlight. I've made this walk in the pitch black so many times that I know exactly how many steps it is from my front door to his . . . from his front door through his living room . . . from his bedroom doorway to his bed. When I get to the edge of his bed, I hear him moan out my name, but it's not in delight, it's in desperation, and it becomes clear to me that he's dreaming.

I decide that maybe talking is not the tack I should take right now. I strip down, taking off every stitch of clothing before I crawl into bed next to him. I cuddle into him and his arms instinctively wrap around my body like it's already become a comfortable habit.

I know the second he wakes. His breath hitches. He stiffens up. He draws in all the air he can take into his lungs only to blow it out in a long, agonizing sigh that flows across my hair.

The tension rolling off him is palpable.

"I love you, Mitch," I say in barely more than a whisper.

"I love you, too, Mikayla."

"Don't leave me," I say.

Another long sigh. "I have to. He loves you. He had you first. It's the right thing to do."

Here he is letting me go, yet he's never held me tighter against his body.

"I'll beg you if I have to," I say. "I'll hold onto your leg like a pouting child. I'm not above it. We're meant to be—remember?"

"I've made up my mind," he says.

"And I'm here to change it for you." I turn around and face him. I can barely make out his face in the relative darkness. I trail my fingers around his strong jaw and feel his scratchy stubble.

We stare at each other in the soft light of the full moon. I can see the struggle going on in his eyes. I don't dare look away—he needs to hear my silent pleas. Finally, he lifts a hand and traces my lips with his thumb. "You are so beautiful, Mikayla," he says, and I melt under his now smoldering gaze.

He brings a hand up to push some errant hairs behind my ear right before he presses his lips to mine. He kisses me like he can't get enough. Like if he pulls away, he won't be able to breathe because I'm his air. He kisses me like a man who has made a decision.

I revel in the delight that it wasn't so hard to change his mind after all.

His hands roam my naked body, grabbing, tugging, and caressing every inch of it, sending pleasurable shocks to the center of my being. I moan into his mouth, prompting his even more demanding grasps of my flesh due to his growing carnal needs.

"I want you so much, sweetheart," he says.

A tear slips from my eye at hearing the endearment I've not heard in almost a week. "Yes . . . please," I beg, tugging down his boxer briefs and exposing his throbbing erection.

When I clasp my hand around him, he gasps. When he reaches between my legs, I whimper. We discover each other as if we haven't already done so dozens of times before.

"You are so ready for me," he breathes into my hair. "But, I need to taste you first."

Blushing in the darkness, I arch my back and respond, "Yessss . . ." as he rubs tiny circles on the place that will detonate me. He kisses his way down my body and feasts on me as my fingers weave through and tug on his glorious head of hair. When I get close, my arms stretch out and claw at the sheet beneath me while his tongue brings me to an orgasm so powerful, I swear I can see constellations behind my eyelids.

He crawls up my body—my body that is still having aftershocks, and he holds my stare, looking directly into my soul as he enters me. I let out a cry of pleasure at the thirst-quenching feeling of having him back where he belongs.

"God, Mikayla . . . you feel so good," he moans into me. My caveman does not make an appearance tonight. Mitch is going slow, savoring every thrust as we continue to stare into each other. We move unhurriedly in a sensual dance of pleasure until our bodies demand we give into the lascivious need to push each other over the edge.

"I need you to let go with me, baby," he hisses through clenched teeth.

His words are all I need to send my body tumbling into sweet oblivion as I quiver and buck beneath him while shouting exaltations into the dark night. "Oh, God . . . Mitch . . . yes!" I hear myself cry.

His body joins mine with spasms of his own as he recites declarations of love and promises in my ear.

I trace the scars on his back, that are now slick with perspiration, while we recover from our blissful climaxes.

When he rolls off me and I cuddle into his arms, I say, "See, all proof that you can't go anywhere. We are perfect together." I crane my neck up so I can see him. "Plus, we kind of already built our kids from scratch the other day."

"Perfect . . . yes, you are," I think he whispers.

"You said you'd love me forever, Mitch."

"Yes." He kisses the top of my head.

"You promised me," I remind him.

"Yes." He nods his head and puts my hand over his heart. "I will love you forever, Mikayla," he whispers. Then we fall asleep—two pieces of a puzzle molded together.

~ ~ ~

I wake a few hours later, smiling and feeling wonderfully content. I sneak out of his bed and head over to shower and eat before I go to the clinic. I'm so happy I feel like my body is defying gravity and I'm hovering a few inches off the ground. I know I must have a ridiculous grin on my face. A few patients even comment on it. I'm not about to reveal to them, however, that I've just had amazing sex with the man I'm going to spend the rest of my life with.

Jamie comes in after lunch to start her shift. I roll my eyes thinking that not even working with *her* today is going to spoil my mood.

"Darn, Kay, I could see your stupid grin halfway across the parking lot," she says. "You know, we're all glad that you've finally made a decision and have stopped stringing along those two hotties, but, did you really have to drive the other one out of town?"

"What?" I spin around, dropping a few papers on the floor. "Jeff left? When?" *No, no, no.* This wasn't what I wanted. That was never my intention.

"Jeff?" she asks me, raising a curious eyebrow. "Not Jeff, Mitch. You know, because you chose Jeff."

I shake my head at her. "Uh . . . no, I didn't, Jamie. I chose Mitch. I love Mitch. What are you talking about?"

"The whole town is talking about it, Kay," she says so matter-of-factly. "Apparently Mitch left this morning. He didn't even say goodbye to anyone."

"No. That's ridiculous," I say in disbelief. "I was just with him until I came to work."

"Believe what you want," she says. "But Don said he swung by the PX to get some supplies that the colonel said he could take with him."

What? No! She's wrong. Everyone is wrong.

This must be a huge misunderstanding. I don't even bother to grab my backpack when I head for the door. "You'll have to handle things around here until I get back," I tell Jamie.

"Whatever," she says.

I run the two hundred yards to our apartment building and burst through his front door. "Mitch?" I call out, cautiously walking back to his room. When I get there, I see that it looks just like it appeared after Craig moved out.

Empty.

The sheets have been stripped. There are no clothes in the closet or shoes on the floor. My shaky hands go to the bedside table to open the drawer where he has been keeping the locket.

Gone.

Just like him.

I tear out into the living room, yelling for Austin. But he's not around. I frantically go over to my own apartment thinking that maybe all of this is just a silly prank and he's moved all of his belongings over to my place.

When I get to the door of my room, that's when I see it; and I know—that for the first time in her malicious life—Jamie was telling the truth. There on my bed is a plain white envelope with one word on it.

Mikayla

I fall to my knees and sobs bellow out of me.

He left me.

Last night was goodbye.

My heart stops beating and I'm not entirely sure that I even care.

I crawl over to my bed. I know I have to read it, but I so desperately don't want to. I know it will burn me. Hell, I know it will light me on fucking fire. I stay on the floor and pull it down to my lap and stare at it. Maybe if I don't open the letter, it won't be real. I give myself one more minute before I'm about to be shattered . . . obliterated . . . broken.

Then I open it and try to read it through my tears.

Mikayla,

I know you are upset. Maybe you even hate me, but I had to do what I thought was right. I was going to leave this morning anyway, probably without even seeing you or saying goodbye. Then you came to me last night and at first I thought it was a dream. All I can say is thank you for one last amazing memory. I'm sorry if I used you for that, but I had to take that piece of you with me.

I know you say you love me. You've also said many times that you love Jeff, too. I know you claim to not mean it the same way, but I think maybe you're wrong. The love you have with Jeff has moved out of that initial honeymoon stage that we were in. The love you have with him comes from years of being together, supporting each other and becoming so comfortable with one another that maybe you didn't even realize once you met me that you were still supposed to be with him. He loves you. He is like a brother to me and I owe him everything. Yes, I even owe him you.

I think you're meant to be with him, Mikayla. If it weren't for my accident and memory loss, that's who you would have been with. We would have never even been an option. Jeff is your future, not me. He is your destiny.

My destiny is like that of Orion's. I will love you from afar. I told you I always keep my promises and this isn't any different. I promised to love you forever, Mikayla, and I will.

There are things I need to do now. Eventually, I will find peace knowing I did the right thing. Please don't ever worry about me.

I have zero regrets.

The best thing I've ever done in my life was finding you, Mikayla.

Forever,

Mitch

Chapter Twenty-seven

The past few weeks have gone by in a blur. I eat—sometimes. I sleep—a little. I work—merely to stay busy.

But I'm not living.

When Mitch left, he took my life with him.

I considered going after him. I even packed up a backpack. However, once my friends intervened and talked sense into me, I realized there was little chance of finding him. Even if you set aside the three thousand miles that I'd have to cover to get there and all of the dangers that I could encounter along the way, could I even find him if I made it to Sacramento? I have his name and the names of his family, but in the world today, that may not be enough. Not to mention that he said he wanted to get out of the big city and get a farm in a small town.

There are no cell phones to try to contact him. I can't simply hop on a plane and see if he's out there. I can't even stalk him on Facebook. He's gone. Really gone. As in forever.

Everyone has been trying to engage with me, but I just want to be left alone. Jeff has been treating me as a friend and for that, I'm grateful. He has given me the space to mourn the loss of Mitch in my life. He may be one of the only good things about my days. He makes going into work almost manageable and I vaguely remember what drew me to him so long ago. Everything and everyone else reminds me of Mitch.

This morning I lie awake in bed. Again. In an attempt at further self-destruction, I pull out the letter he wrote me. I've tried to keep myself from reading it, but even seeing his heartbreaking words makes me feel closer to him in some sadistic way. I trace my fingers over each word as I read, imagining what he must have felt like writing them. When I come to the part about him being like Orion, I put the letter down and search for the book he gave me in an attempt to hold something else that he has touched.

I start to panic when I can't find it. I tear my room apart. It takes me back to the day after he left when I tried in vain to find those ridiculous boxer briefs that I was sure were in my possession at the time that he left. My room is in complete disarray when realization strikes me. "Holly!" I yell at the top of my lungs, not caring that it's her day off and she's still sleeping.

I storm into her room and rip the covers off her. I stare at her with my hands on my hips and say, "Where are they?"

"Jesus, Kay," she says, yawning.

I start rifling through her things. "What did you do with them?"

She sits up in bed, stretching. "What the hell are you talking about?"

"You know damn well what I'm talking about. You took them didn't you?" I ask snidely. "Did you think not having them would somehow help me get over him?"

She shakes her head. "Still confused here," she says.

"The book," I tell her. "The one about the constellations that Mitch gave me. And the boxer briefs—the ones with the smiley face. Where are they? I know you have them."

"Oh, man, I think I know what might have happened." She wrinkles her nose at me and says, "Don't get mad. The morning he left, he came to our apartment and said he was looking for something. I had no idea he was leaving. He didn't tell me. He didn't tell anyone. He was in your room for a few minutes so he must have taken them." She frowns and her eyes reflect my sadness. "I'm so sorry, Kay."

He took them?

I suppose it should make me feel better, knowing that he wanted them to remember me by, but I don't. I'm pissed that *I* don't have them. I'm pissed that he loved me so much that he wanted to take a piece of us with him. I'm pissed that he loved me that much but he left anyway.

God, I miss him.

I must have something of his besides that damn letter.

"Sorry," I mutter to Holly, feeling badly that I woke her up and so blatantly accused her.

"It's okay," she says, getting up to hug me. "I know it's been hard for you. And I don't mean to sound like a total bitch, Kay, but you need to re-join the living at some point. We miss you. *I* miss you."

"I know. I'm sorry." I release her from our embrace. "You're not a bitch. I know I need to get over myself and move on. I just don't know how to do that. How did he come into my life and turn it upside down in a matter of weeks? I will never be the same after him. Nothing and nobody will ever be enough for me now."

Suddenly, I think of something that has me racing from the room. I tell Holly I'll see her later and throw on a pair of shorts and an old t-shirt before I run over to the clinic. I'm not scheduled to work today, but I can't wait. I have to see him.

I enter the front doors of the clinic and announce to Nancy and Jeff, "I'm not really here. I just have to do something real quick." I go into the back room, grateful that nobody follows me. I fish the phone out of its hiding place. And for only the second time ever, I use it for my own benefit. I know there are dozens of pictures of Mitch on here. Jeff would send them to me almost weekly. Yes, Mitch's hair was shorter and he wore fatigues instead of civilian clothes, but at least I will see his gorgeous face. It seems to take forever for my phone to boot up as I sit in a chair, legs shaking in anticipation of seeing him again. Finally, it's up and I go into my picture gallery. My heart jumps into my throat when I see what the very first picture is.

A new picture—the only picture taken since before the blackout—comes up on my screen. It's of Mitch. He has a smile on his face and I don't miss that he's wearing the locket along with a seductively raised eyebrow. Oh, God, he took this long ago. Before Jeff came back. Before he knew he was leaving me. He took it so that I would find it and laugh at the surprise he left me.

Little did he know that he's just given me a gift I will treasure forever.

I almost leap out of my chair when a hand touches my shoulder. My attempt to cover up the phone is futile. Jeff has already seen it.

I take a few minutes to explain how I came to be in possession of a working phone. Then I show him the picture Mitch left for me.

"I'm sorry, Kay," he says. He looks sad for me and I can tell he understands how much I'm hurting. "I know you loved him. I loved him too."

I shake my head at him. "Not loved, Jeff," I whisper. "Love. I *love* him."

"I know, I'm sorry," he says again.

I put the phone back and swear him to secrecy. I promise myself that I'll not be so selfish again and use it to look at Mitch's picture.

It's a promise I know I'll never keep.

"You know I'm here for you, right?" he asks. "You may not be ready to move on, but I'm here when and if you want to try again. I love you, Kay. I'm even willing to accept the fact that you don't love me anymore. Well, not in the way I want you to. But, we were great together before. We were a good team. I think we could be again." He kisses the top of my head and gives my shoulders a squeeze. He turns to walk away saying, "I'm not going to give up on you, babe."

He walks through the door, leaving me alone. His endearment echoes in my head.

I can't think about his offer. It's preposterous. He wants me to try to be with him, knowing that I love another man?

I go out the back door of the clinic, not wanting to have any more confrontations today. I decide to go to the place I've avoided for three weeks. The place I know will slay me over and over again when I visit it, but I have to do it. Maybe it will help me get past this deep despair, this unimaginable anguish, this sense of brokenness . . . and somehow allow me to move on. I have to go to the meadow.

When I arrive at the stables, a surprised Brad hurries over to greet me. "Dr. Parker, it's so nice to see you again. Sassy has missed you, the poor girl. Shall I saddle her up?"

"Yes, please, Brad," I say. While he is occupied with that, I walk over to try to get past hurdle number one. But when I get to Rose's stall, she's not there. I take a peek in the other stalls.

Perhaps she's been moved for some reason. When I can't find her anywhere, I ask Brad, "Is someone out on Rose right now?"

"Rose?" he repeats. "No, she's been gone for weeks." He gives me a sad look. "Um . . . the colonel allowed Mitch to take her." He looks at the ground. He knows how this must devastate me. Yet, unlike the book and the underwear, I feel oddly comforted knowing that he has a living breathing being that he loves so dearly with him.

I can't get myself to go directly to the meadow. I need a minute. So I take the long way around the perimeter. It's here, by the fields that I run into Craig.

"Hi, Kay," he yells, waving me over to him. "Nice to see you out and about again."

I chide myself. I really have been a recluse, haven't I?

"Thanks, Craig. I'm trying," I say. "What's new with you?"

"Well, if you don't know then I guess you haven't seen Pam in the last few days." A smile brightens his face. "We are going to be leaving soon. I signed a contract for a farm not far from here." He shakes his head like he can't believe what he's saying. "It's actually happening," he says. "We're going to lead normal lives again soon. It's amazing, isn't it?"

I put my hand to my chest and sigh. "Wow, that's wonderful! I'm so happy for you guys. I know you love little Connor like he's your own. He will adore living on a farm."

He nods his head emphatically. "Yes, and once we're—" he stops talking and bites his lip, cursing to himself.

"Once you're what?" I ask.

"Shit," he says. "Listen, you need to talk to Pam. She's got stuff to tell you, but she's been afraid to talk to you in your current state."

I think about what a terrible friend I've been to Pam these past few weeks. She found out she lost her husband, after all, and I'm whining about Mitch leaving when he is alive and well. What could she possible be afraid to talk to me about?

Then it hits me and I gasp. "Oh, my God!" I scream. "You're getting married, aren't you?"

He smiles from ear to ear. "You didn't hear it from me, got it?"

"Oh, my God," I repeat. "I'm so happy for you." I mentally hit myself. "I've been such a crappy friend, caring only about my own problems. I promise to be better."

There's just some stuff I have to do first.

I turn Sassy around to leave and he shouts after me, "Don't worry, you'll get your happy ending one day, Kay."

But what he doesn't know—what nobody knows—is that I'm no longer looking for blissfully happy, that reality left along with a horse named Rose. Now I'm willing to settle for compatible mediocrity.

I take a deep breath. I'm ready now. I point Sassy towards the spot in the trees that line the meadow.

When we get there, I tie Sassy to a tree. But not our tree. Then I walk over and find a spot to sit. But not our spot. I just sit and stare at our spot. I look longingly at it and think about all the endless conversations we had. We may have only known each other for eight weeks before he left, but we crammed a lot of talking into those fifty-six days. I feel like I know him better than I've ever known anyone in my life.

It's been three weeks since he left. I wonder where he is now. Taking a horse across the country must be difficult and slow. He's resourceful. I wonder why he didn't try to find a truck. But, I already know the answer to that question. It is the same reason I plan on asking Colonel Andrews for Sassy when I leave.

Leave. It sounds so final. Once I leave here, Mitch won't be able to find me. What if he changes his mind and comes looking for me after I've gone? I would never know he was even searching for me.

Don't be stupid, Kay. I shake my head at myself. He isn't coming back. He would have changed his mind by now. I have to accept it.

I sit here for hours, wasting away the day trying to figure out my life . . . my future.

The hair on the nape of my neck stands up and suddenly I don't feel so alone. I quickly spin around and look over to where Sassy stands. But my hopes are dashed when I see that she is still alone and that my thoughts have not, in fact, conjured up Mitch.

Then, out of the corner of my eye, I see movement. I stiffen as I see a shadow far off in the tree line on the other side of the prairie. Alarms clang in my head and my body goes on high alert as I'm taken back to my traumatic experience in the pool hall. I feel very vulnerable all the way out here, and so completely alone. I run over to Sassy and fumble my way up on her before racing her back to camp.

I immediately find Colonel Andrews. "I think John is still stalking me," I say. "I saw him in the forest line in the north meadow. He scared me to death, just standing there, lurking behind a tree."

It takes the colonel all of about five minutes to find someone who will train me with a firearm. He tells me to carry it whenever I'll be alone and to not take unnecessary chances. Then he sends a few guys out to do a search of the area.

After a few hours of gun safety and target practice, I'm exhausted and all I want to do is sleep. Once in bed, however, my brain has an agenda of its own so I lie here awake. Again. There is so much I wish I could have told Mitch. So I get out my lamp and decide to.

Mitch,

The irony of this letter is not lost on me. It wasn't too long ago I was writing to Jeff, thinking I'd never see **him** again. But, he came back against all odds. Does that mean there is hope that you will, too? I've waited for you every day. And every day I think you will come back simply from the sheer power of my love for you.

I know you'll never read this. I know you'll never answer the one question I wish I could ask you. What the hell were you thinking? Love like this doesn't happen more than once. It's the kind of forever-love you read about in books. Yes—even **those** books.

So now that you are gone and there is literally no way I can find you, I'm destined for what—a life of mediocre love? Can I even settle for that, having experienced so much more? Can you?

I think every day, every minute, about the promise you made to me. Will you keep it? Can you keep it? Maybe some promises are meant to be broken. Like the one you made Jeff. But, then again, when you really think about it, you didn't let him down at all. In fact, you did quite the opposite. You found me, you took care of me, you loved me. You made me happier than I'd ever been. Ever. How is that breaking your promise?

But you left me no choice, Mitch. So, now I'll go tuck this letter in a shoebox among countless others, right alongside the one you wrote to me. I'll get into bed and if I sleep, I'll dream of you like I do every night. Then, I'll wake up tomorrow and try to start living again.

Forever,

Mikayla

Chapter Twenty-eight

I laugh as Jeff strikes out for the second time tonight. It's kind of sweet how he's trying so hard to fit into my new life. It's been two weeks since he made the proposition to me. He hasn't brought it up since, but I see what he's doing. The softball games, the flirty banter at work, the longing gazes. But, I have to give him credit for not pushing me.

Even though he's technically Army, Jeff is playing on my team tonight. Participation has been dwindling with so many people leaving Camp Brady. Our community that once approached a thousand people is down by almost half now. The colonel has agreed to stay on here until every last person has a place to go—a daunting task considering we have residents such as Timmy and his alcoholic mother.

Most people are headed to Jacksonville. Some have gone to Miami or Tampa; places we heard are also growing areas. Some, like Pam and Craig, are getting farmland. They moved out a few days ago. I'm sad that I won't get to see her on a daily basis, but I'm happy that she's found her future. They are only ten miles from here, but even being that close it still takes a while on a bike or a horse to get there. We may technically be neighbors, but it's not like we'll be setting up weekly coffee dates at Starbucks anytime soon. Pam said they will come back often, and of course, they will be making a big appearance in a few weeks when the colonel marries them.

Jeff and Holly still talk of leaving for Jacksonville. However, the colonel asked that we stay on until more people leave. It's a relief really, because I'm still torn. On one hand, I don't want to go to Jacksonville, but on the other hand, almost everyone I know will be going. Except for Pam, there will be nobody here for me.

I shake off my thoughts and take a few practice swings before going up to bat. As I step up to the plate, I'm picturing that big yellow softball as Mitch's face. The face that ruined my plans for the future.

Smack! I make solid contact and the ball flies past Tom, who is covering first base. It's a near-perfect hit, right down the base line. The runner on second base easily makes it home. Then, thanks to a bad throw by the outfielder, I make it all the way home, narrowly escaping a tag at home plate.

My entire team comes out to cheer for me and I get caught up in the celebration. All of a sudden, I'm being picked up and by the time I realize that it's Jeff's arms around me, it's too late to stop his lips from finding mine. His kiss is somewhat familiar and oddly comforting. Still, I pull away because I feel the guilt creep into my head. I don't miss the disappointment in his eyes.

When we're done celebrating my walk-off home run, Jeff grabs my hand and pulls me to the side. "Was it really that bad?" he asks. "Being with me?"

I shake my head and look to the ground. No, it wasn't that bad. In fact, it was pretty great at times. But, it wasn't like it was with Mitch. It wasn't heart-stoppingly, breath-takingly wonderful.

"Kay, I know you love the guy, but he's gone. It's been over a month now. I don't think he's coming back and I think you know that, too." He lifts my chin so our eyes meet. "We were good for each other once. We loved each other. Out of respect for that, don't you think you at least owe us a chance?"

I close my eyes and think about what he has said. I know he's right. Mitch isn't coming back. People who leave here don't come back. The world is a different place now. We have to make difficult decisions—decisions that we may not have made a year ago.

I go over the options in my head for the millionth time. Jeff is a nice guy, a gorgeous and skilled surgeon. He's good to me and he seems to want this so badly. Hell, even *Mitch* wanted this. What choice do I have? I take a deep breath and resign myself to settling for, what was it . . . compatible mediocrity?

I let out a sigh and whisper, "Okay."

His eyes go wide and his face lights up. "Okay?" he asks.

I nod my head.

He pulls me into his arms. He rubs his hands down my back in that familiar way that he used to. "Thank you, babe," he whispers in my ear.

We grab our things and head over to the bonfire. Jeff and I hold hands the entire way. I try to enjoy the feel of my fingers entwined with his. I want to be happy. I can make myself be happy, right? So, then why is my subconscious wagging her finger at me and calling me a traitor?

"Damn, Kay," Holly says, looking all dreamy-eyed at Jeff. "How do you get so freaking lucky in the boyfriend department?"

I look over at Jeff. Yes, he's hot. My boyfriend is hot.

My boyfriend.

My boyfriend, Jeff.

I've had to keep reminding myself for the past week that's who he is again. I've made the decision to be happy. Whether my heart likes it or not, my brain is now in control. Jeff catches us staring and winks over at us. Holly giggles and I swear she even blushes. I realize I never do that anymore. Blush. I don't think I've blushed in weeks. I shake my head to rid the thought.

"Go get your own, Hol," I joke.

"Awww, come on Kay. I'm your best friend. Don't best friends share?" We laugh as we file away the paperwork of more residents that have left the camp.

"Aren't I sharing him with you enough as it is?" I ask. "I mean, good Lord, how many procedures did he teach you this week?"

"Only five or six," she says. "It's been a slow week." She gives me a wink. "That man's brain is almost as sexy as his body."

Well, she's got that right. His brain is what initially attracted me to him. He has so much knowledge to offer. He was a wonderful mentor in medical school. Is it possible to simply be in love with someone's skill and make that be enough on which to build a relationship?

When Jeff passes by my chair, he squeezes my arm when he leans down to plant a quick kiss on my head. I smile up at him sweetly. Because that's what girlfriends do, right? They smile sweetly at their boyfriends that are trying seriously hard to please them.

"It won't be long, now," Holly says. "I hear there is another group of fifty that's leaving for Tampa tomorrow. There already isn't a need for two doctors and three nurses here. You make up your mind yet?"

I shake my head.

"You know that's why he hasn't left yet, don't you? He's waiting for you to decide."

"I know," I say. "I don't want to be away from you guys, but I'm still not sure about going back to a big city. I know I need to decide soon and I will."

"Did you hear that Amanda and Denny are going, too?" she asks.

"Yes." I nod. "I guess that's just all the more reason for me to go. I think Claire and the colonel will go there, too, once everyone else has left."

"God, I can't wait to get there. I here that they have shipped in huge generators for apartment buildings and that people get a few hours a day of electricity. Can you imagine, Kay? We will be able to take warm showers and flat-iron our hair!"

I laugh at Holly that after fifteen months of being without electricity, she is excited about a flat iron. It makes me feel guilty, however, for keeping them from leaving. I know that like Jeff, she is waiting on me, hoping I'll decide to join them.

The front door opens and in walks Kelly holding three-month-old Toby. They've come for his checkup. I get them settled into an exam room and go in search of his chart.

"Thank God," Jeff says when he sees me gathering supplies for a patient. "Finally, an actual patient today." He takes the chart from me and I giggle at how he must always be in motion. We walk back out front where he opens the chart and frowns. He looks in the exam room. "Baby?" he groans.

"Not just any baby," I say. "The most adorable baby I've ever seen. I delivered him, you know."

Jeff rolls his eyes, not looking very happy over the fact that there isn't carnage to deal with. "You can do it." He hands me the chart. "Babies aren't really my thing," he says, walking away leaving me stunned.

I turn and go into the exam room. When I pick up little Toby I could swear my ovaries spontaneously release a few eggs.

Babies aren't really my thing. I hear Jeff's words play over and over in my head.

~ ~ ~

"Ready, babe?" Jeff holds his hand out to me and I give the rest of the charts to Holly. It's only noon, but there are so few patients left here that we all pretty much work half days now.

"Yup," I say. "See you later, Hol."

"Where to?" he asks, escorting me through the door.

"I was hoping we could take a ride. I haven't been on Sassy in a few days. What do you think?"

He rolls his eyes. "If we have to," he pouts. "My ass always chafes when I ride," he murmurs to himself.

"Fine," I acquiesce. "We can just walk if you want. There's a good trail over by the housing development."

He smiles over at me. "That sounds perfect," he says. He reaches out to grab my hand and holds it firmly in his. We walk in silence for a few minutes. Then he asks, "Do you think my mom will marry Colonel Andrews?"

"I don't know," I say. "She appears to be very happy with him. Would it bother you if she did?"

"No, I think I'd be okay with it," he says. "I had a long talk with her. She said it took her a long time to move on, but that she's as happy now as she was with my dad. That says a lot because she was pretty happy before. Maybe it goes to show that you can find happiness more than once in life."

I know we are no longer talking about Claire and the colonel.

"Was it like that for you?" He stops walking and locks eyes with me. "Did you have to accept me as dead in order to move on?"

Oh, crap. What a loaded question. "Jeff, I—"

"Don't answer that," he interrupts. "I shouldn't have asked you. I'm sorry." He pulls me close to him and wraps his arms around me. "I know we live in a different world now and that people do what they need to do to get by."

He runs his fingers through my hair and I close my eyes, trying my hardest to savor the feeling. It was always his favorite thing to do. He'd play with my hair when my head was in his lap as we watched TV. He would even reach over and twist my hair with his hand while he was driving. Anything to touch my hair. I never called him on it, but it was almost like a fetish. I can see that's one thing that hasn't changed about him.

"I've missed this, babe," he says. He leans down to kiss me and I let him. We've kissed a few times over the past few days, but nothing like this. He's been taking it slow and I've appreciated that. But this kiss—it's obvious he's ready for more. He nibbles on my lips and plays with my tongue. He kisses me long and hard and pulls me up against his body. I belatedly realize that my hands are still by my side, so I wrap them around him. I tell myself that this is okay, that I'm doing nothing wrong. I almost have myself convinced of it.

Then I feel it through his shirt. The long, raised scar that spans from hip to hip and is just above the waistband of his jeans. The scar that will forever tie Jeff and Mitch together. It's the one thing about Jeff that'll never stop reminding me of Mitch. He must feel me stiffen. "It's okay, it doesn't hurt," he says through our kisses. "God, please don't stop touching me."

My hands continue to run shakily up and down his back, along the smaller, thinner scars that they sustained together. For one ridiculous second I think maybe I can pretend he is Mitch, but my fingers can't be fooled, they can tell the difference. The pattern of Jeff's scars are not the same as those I studied, traced, kissed and memorized night after night.

I hope he doesn't stop kissing me because then I would have to explain the tears that threaten to fall from my eyes. Maybe if I avoid his back altogether, I can get past this. I have to get past this. I reach my hands up to his neck and run them through his hair. I focus on this task to keep me from feeling like a loser, a failure . . . a traitor of my own heart.

"Babe, will you go to Jacksonville with me?" he asks amidst our kisses.

I pull back and look into his questioning eyes. "Maybe," I say. "But I'd like a little more time. Pam's wedding is in two weeks and I'd like to get through that before making any decisions."

He picks me up and swings me around with a grin on his face. "I'll take it. Maybe is better than I hoped for. And that gives me two weeks to work my magic on you," he teases.

"Can I ask you something, Jeff?"

"Anything." He puts his arm around my shoulders and we start walking again. "You can ask me anything, Kay."

"If I decide not to go to Jacksonville, will you still go?"

The pregnant pause that oozes tension is all the answer I need.

He sighs. "Babe . . . I *have* to go. I'm needed there. *All* surgeons are needed there," he explains. "How the hell will I improve my skills staying here in the sticks treating injured farmers and snotty-nosed kids?" He gives my shoulder a squeeze. "I still don't quite understand why you wouldn't want to go. You are so gifted and you're just beginning your career. You'd be wasting your talent staying here."

"I don't think of it that way, Jeff," I say. "Doctors are needed everywhere. Even here. I guess my priorities have changed." I turn away and mumble to myself, "I like the sticks."

"Well, maybe you should change them back. Even Holly is determined to go. Hell, she's more eager to learn than you are and she's only a nurse," he says.

～　～　～

I lie here under the stars on this mild spring night tracing Orion with my fingers. I don't come out here as much as I used to because it makes me sad. I try to concentrate on Pam's upcoming nuptials and how happy she is. I again think of how I've decided to be happy. Can I decide to be happy in Jacksonville?

Mitch said Jeff and I were meant to be together. But Jeff doesn't want to stay here for me and I don't want to go there for him. Jeff doesn't seem too eager to have kids, yet I long for them. Jeff hates horses—*who hates horses?* In what world does that make us right for each other?

Yet, we share the commonality of medicine. We've always had that. We were even happy once. If we try hard enough we could be again, right? Or at least we could be compatibly mediocre. That will be enough. It will have to be enough for me.

Won't it?

Chapter Twenty-nine

"I know it's not the first wedding here," Claire says, as we set up the folding chairs that line the aisle up to the altar. "But I believe it's the most significant."

"What do you mean?" I ask, shielding my eyes from the morning sun as I look over at her.

"Well, some of our residents have gotten married out of need, out of fear, even out of obligation." She shoots a raised eyebrow my way before continuing to set up the chair in her hands. "Pam and Craig seem to have found their soulmates in each other. That's so rare, especially after losing a first love. Believe me, I know." She smiles brightly and I know she's thinking about Colonel Andrews.

Claire concentrates on tying a large white bow around the chair she just placed on the grass. "How wonderful that they found each other in all this. How incredibly special they must feel that they didn't simply settle for each other; that they didn't resolve to be anyone's second best." She finally looks up at me with a sorrowful face. "Don't you think so, Kay?"

All I can do is nod and fumble with the bow I'm trying unsuccessfully to tie. If I try to speak, my voice will crack and the tears welling up in my eyes might fall. Claire is truly amazing. I understand what she's doing and I love her for it, but it doesn't change things. How can she not see that I don't have a choice? This has become my life by default and I'm just going to have to make the best of it.

$$\sim \quad \sim \quad \sim$$

When Pam walks down the aisle, our collective breaths hitch and the world goes silent with the exception of a few birds playing chase in the mid-afternoon sky and the soft strumming of the guitar near the altar. We stare at her in awe. She is breathtaking in a lovely designer dress procured from a warehouse in Gainesville that most likely none of us would have been able to afford before the blackout.

Waiting for Pam at the altar are Craig and her fidgety three-year-old son, Connor, who are wearing matching tuxes. There are no bridesmaids. No groomsmen. No pomp and circumstance. Just a simple handmade wooden altar adorned with those beautiful purple petunias from the meadow that Holly and I picked this morning.

Jeff grabs my hand, squeezing it once before placing our joined hands to rest on his thigh. I look at his freshly shaven face that compliments the suit he borrowed from one of the houses on base. He is stunning. He whispers in my ear that I look beautiful and then we both face forward to watch one of my best friends marry the man of her dreams.

Before the ceremony starts, Pam quickly looks behind us and smiles for a moment, prompting me to turn and see what caught her attention. I'm surprised to see a small group of strangers standing over by the community center. I recall hearing of a group staying here for a few days as they pass through on their way across the state. I guess they were curious about the wedding and stopped for a look. I'm glad they keep their distance, however, since some are pretty scruffy, especially the man with the ball cap pulled low over his forehead.

Then the hair on my neck rises when I remember that the gates are now open and the perimeter watches have ceased. Seeing these strangers reminds me that John could very well be among them. I should probably start carrying my gun with me.

I put John out of my mind for now and turn my attention back to the bride and groom as the colonel walks over behind them and starts the ceremony.

When they recite their heartfelt vows to each other, tears fall from my eyes. Not happy tears. These tears are not joyful at all. They are sad tears. Sad tears because I know that if Jeff and I ever stand up on an altar and exchange vows, I would be a fraud. I love Jeff. Of course I do, and I always will in some way. That's why I thought maybe we could make this work. But I realize now, watching Pam marry the love of her life, that no matter how hard I've tried to force it, I can't deceive myself this way. Like Claire alluded to earlier, I shouldn't have to settle for second best and Jeff shouldn't have to settle on *being* second best.

I now know what I have to do. I have to break Jeff's heart.

My hand goes limp in his.

I look over at Jeff, who has obviously been studying me this entire time. Can he see through me? Am I that transparent? We stare at each other. Then my silent questions are answered when he pensively nods at the ground and places my hand back in my lap. He gives me a sad smile and gets up to sneak away as the ceremony comes to an end.

I look over at Claire, who is watching me intently with narrow eyes. She gives me an understanding nod as if she's been privy to the telepathic conversation held between Jeff and me.

Clapping startles me and I shift my gaze back to Pam and Craig as they blissfully make their way back up the aisle. Craig is holding Connor and they are the epitome of the perfect family. Happy tears finally flow down my face as I pull Pam into a hug moments later.

"You will always have a place at our house," she whispers in my ear. "For as long as you need, Kay."

I'm stunned that even being decidedly otherwise engaged, she noticed that Jeff left and assumed I would need a friend.

We all walk over to The Oasis where Claire's kitchen staff has set up an incredible buffet for their reception. We dance, eat and drink late into the night. Pam and Craig are spending their honeymoon in one of the remote houses on base that some helpers set up with candles and wine. Amanda graciously offered to take Connor for a few days while they settle into married life.

Making my way back to my apartment, I look up at the stars. I smile when I spot Orion and I wonder if the constellation looks the same from California. Is he thinking of me at this very moment? I contemplate lying down and stargazing all night, but then I remember the strangers in town and decide it's safer to head home.

When I open my apartment door, Holly stands up and comes over to hug me. "Everything will be alright, Kay," she says on her way out the front door.

I'm confused, but only for a second. Because then I see Jeff sitting on the couch, still wearing his dress clothes. However he's shed his coat and tie and his dress shirt is unbuttoned at the top and looks slightly disheveled. He's a mess. He looks broken. And I'm about to shatter him.

He holds my stare and gives me an understanding smile. "You don't love me," he says.

My eyes close as guilt overcomes me. He knows I'm going to break up with him. That's why he left the wedding. I guess it really was that obvious, the moment I realized we couldn't be together. I take a few steps into the dimly-lit living room and sit down next to him on the couch. "I'm sorry, no," I say softly. "Not in that way."

He nods his head. "I feel incredibly guilty," he says, closing his eyes briefly.

"Why do *you* feel guilty?" I ask, snapping my eyes up to look at him.

"I've tried so hard to get back what we had, Kay." He takes my hand in his and I let him. It's not a romantic gesture on his part. It is a friendly gesture, a sign of support even. "Maybe I feel guilty because I spent so long trying to get back to you that I felt we had to at least try to be together. Maybe I feel bad about Mitch leaving and my ruining that opportunity for you." He sighs. "Maybe it's because I felt like I had to win some kind of twisted competition with Mitch." He shakes his head and looks at the ground. "Most likely, it's a little of all those things."

I attempt to gather my thoughts. I cock my head to the side and stare at him, trying to absorb exactly what he is saying. "Let me get this straight," I say, incredulously. "This entire time, you've been trying to be with me because you thought it was the right thing to do, not because you love me?"

"Not exactly," he says. "I mean, I love you. I'll always love you, Kay. And when I returned, I did think we should be together at first. I was sure of it. Then after a while it became clear to me how different we've become. Not different, bad—just different from how we used to be together. And once I realized what Mitch gave up for me, I felt guilty as hell and thought I needed to make it work so his leaving wouldn't have been in vain."

My brow is crinkled and I'm shaking my head, still not quite believing that all these weeks, we've both been pretending to be happy together.

"You don't know how incredibly sorry I am for that, Kay. I would give anything to be able to find him and get him back to you. You have to know that I truly did want us back when I found you again. I would have never allowed him to leave if I had thought for even a minute that we shouldn't have been together."

Tears of relief cascade down my cheeks. Jeff wipes them for me with his finger.

"Kay, I hope we will always be friends. You still mean the world to me and I'm glad I found you. I just wish there was something I could do about Mitch. You deserve to be happy. We both deserve to have that great love that we just can't be for each other anymore." He laughs sadly. "I knew the minute you felt it at the wedding. I could see it in your eyes. I could feel it in your hand. I knew you had come to the same conclusion. I knew you were going to break it off with me. And I knew I needed to let you."

"What do we do now?" I ask through my tears.

"I go to Jacksonville with the others. And you figure out how to get your happiness." He rubs a soothing hand across my back. "I hope someday you will find him. Promise me you'll try."

I nod, almost unable to speak through the knot in my throat. "I promise," I say. "Someday I will go to the ends of the earth to find him. Just like you did for me."

For the first time ever, I see a tear roll down his face. "Good," he says, choking on his words. "Because he is the best man I've ever had the pleasure of knowing."

We hold each other in a long embrace, mourning the relationship that will never again be. Celebrating the friendship that will always remain.

We talk until after the candle burns down and the moonlight is our only source of illumination. Jeff tells me stories about Mitch and the good times they had in Afghanistan. I've heard similar stories from Mitch, but I learn even more about him hearing them from Jeff's perspective. I'm not sure how I ever got so lucky to have these two amazing men come into my life. And it becomes even more evident to me how they truly became brothers over there. By morning, we have solidified our forever friendship and unwavering support of each other.

After Jeff leaves, I finally change out of my wedding clothes and get comfortable in my bed. I pull out some paper to write a letter by the brightening light of the sunrise.

Mitch,

Tonight I let go of Jeff for the second time. I've now had to let go two of the most important men in my life. One a dear friend, the other, the love of my life—my soulmate.

I get it now after the long talk that Jeff and I had last night. I get why you left. When I felt Jeff's scar that first time; when I felt that terrible reminder of what the two of you endured together, I think I finally realized the bond that you share. You are more than brothers. You are soulmates. Just as you and I are soulmates.

So, I understand why you felt like you owed him your happiness. Maybe in some small way you did us a favor. We will never have any doubts now about what could have been between him and me. We simply have a friendship that is stronger than I could have imagined. I will never regret a thing.

I, too, made a promise to Jeff last night. One I intend to keep no matter how long it takes me.

Forever,

Mikayla

Chapter Thirty

I'm helping to load supplies into the pickup truck that will take Jeff and the others to Jacksonville. Almost everyone who is important to me is leaving. The colonel has graciously provided them one of the few trucks on base and we are loading it with food and clothing for their journey. It will only take them a few short hours to reach their destination, but they didn't want to show up empty-handed.

Colonel Andrews has allotted me many provisions as well. When I leave tomorrow, he will send me off with most of the remaining medical supplies. There is no need to keep them here with most everyone leaving. I thought about staying a while longer, until I figure out exactly what I want to do, but there are just too many memories here. It's time for me to move on like everyone else.

I will be taking Sassy with me as well, for which I'm eternally grateful. Craig will be loading up my supplies in his truck—also a gift from the colonel—when he moves me in with him and Pam.

The colonel comes up behind me. "I'd give you a vehicle as well, Kay, but I'm afraid you'll do something crazy like high-tail it across the country to find Sgt. Matheson." He winks at me.

"Oh, no," I reply. "You've done quite enough for me as it is. There are others that need your remaining few jeeps far more than I do." I sling another large suitcase into the back of the pickup truck. "I won't go running off to California, you know. At least not until it's safe. I'm not stupid."

He laughs at me. "No, you're definitely not stupid, Kay. I'm not sure what we would have done this past year without you here. You are one fine doctor." He pulls me in for a hug and then he helps load the rest of their gear into the truck.

I'm already crying. Even before the goodbyes, I'm crying. What am I going to do without my very best friend, my touchstone, my person?

"Awww . . . come on, Kay, none of that," Holly says. "We are both going to get exactly what we want one day, you'll see. And as soon as cell phones get back on-line, we'll talk every day. It'll be like I never left."

We don't have a long drawn-out goodbye. We did that last night when we spent the night together, all four of us—Holly, Pam, Amanda and me. It was a regular teenage slumber party. But with booze.

We embrace each other in one final hug. "I love you, Kay. We are both going to be alright."

Jeff helps her up into the truck and I'm amused when I see a certain look pass between them.

Yes, I think Holly Becker is going to be just fine.

"I'll miss you like crazy, you know," Jeff says. "These past few days with us doing the friend thing, it's been great. It feels so right. You'll always be my friend, Kay, and I'll always love you."

"Right backatcha," I choke out as I look up at his gorgeous face once more through my tear-blurred eyes. "I love you too, Jeff Taylor."

"You'll find him," he says. "That's something that didn't change about you, Kay. You'll always be stubborn and driven and it's going to get you to Mitch one day."

I nod at him as we share one more hug.

Amanda and I say our goodbyes then I pick up Rachel one last time and give her one of the hair bands from around my wrist for the ride.

"Bye-bye, Kaykay," she says, her little hands waving at me as her dad secures her in the middle of the back seat.

All I can do is stand and watch as the truck gets further away from me, eventually turning into nothing but a cloud of dust that is taking so many important people out of my life.

Claire comes up behind me and, just like a mom, puts a comforting arm around my shoulder and walks me back home. On the way, I take in the reality of the past few weeks when I look around our little community. When we pass by The Oasis, it is empty. Not a single soul sits at one of the numerous tables on the deck that surrounds the grey, sooty remnants of the last bonfire. I glance over at the softball field that hasn't seen a game in over two weeks. Even the clinic is just a place to get an Aspirin and a Band-Aid now that everyone with medical issues has moved on to Jacksonville.

Camp Brady finally resembles the ghost town from the Wild West that Mitch joked about when he first came here.

Austin and I are among the few residents that remain in the apartments. He is helping Craig move me to the farm today and then he will leave for Tampa. His wife's family used to live there before the blackout so he figures it will be his best chance to find her if she comes back.

Craig's truck is packed with the medical equipment that the colonel has given me. It may just be enough to start a small practice wherever I end up. Craig will store it all in his barn for now. He and Austin have gone on ahead while I say goodbye to what has been my home for the past fifteen months.

The last thing I get before I leave is the cell phone that stayed hidden at the clinic. I turn it on and pull up the picture of Mitch that I've stared at so many times I'm beginning to think it will fade like an old photograph. But I'm no longer sad when I look at it. It gives me hope for the future. I know that no matter how long it takes for me to find him, he will be waiting for me. He said he'd love me forever.

He promised.

He never breaks his promises.

I stow away the phone and charger in my pack and walk Sassy through the middle of the almost-abandoned camp. I can't help but think of how being here changed my life. Yes, the blackout changed everything for everyone, but for me, it somehow made me a better person, a better doctor, a better friend. It reminded me that there is more to life than a job. I think the blackout was the best thing that ever happened to me. I laugh thinking how my mom would be so proud.

After saying my goodbyes to Claire, the colonel and a few stragglers that are left, I make my way outside the gates for only the second time in fifteen months.

I don't want to tire out Sassy, so we take our time and walk the entire ten miles. Along the way, I marvel at how the dream I had as a little girl finally came true. I feel like Laura Ingalls Wilder. I pass other people riding on horses, all of whom stop to strike up a friendly conversation. Some have horse-drawn wagons taking huge piles of fruits and vegetables to a Farmer's Market that has been set up on the other side of Ocala where people barter and trade for what they need.

It's almost humorous how out of place the three cars that pass me on the road look, but even those people stop to say hello. The world has transformed while we've been stuck in our little cocoon at Camp Brady. I'm passed twice by an old police car patrolling up and down the road, making sure everyone is safe. I'm amazed by everything I encounter along the way. It's absolutely wonderful. I look up to the clear blue sky and tell my mom she finally got her wish.

I arrive at Pam and Craig's farmhouse just in time to eat. Pam has put together a fresh salad, made with everything they've either grown here or traded for. Craig, Austin, Pam and I eat a delicious lunch while little Connor takes a nap.

"So, where's my room?" I ask. Pam and Craig share a look and I already feel guilty that I'm imposing on them. "Or, I can just sleep on the couch," I quickly add.

Pam says, "There'll be time for that later. I was hoping to take you on a tour of the area so you can see what a great town this is. It's kind of like back at camp, only way more spread out. Everyone helps each other. I'd like to introduce you around. If you're not too tired from the trip, that is."

"No, I'm not tired. I'd love to take a tour," I say.

Pam checks on Connor and gives the men instructions on what to do when he wakes. Then we head outside and get on a pair of old bikes. We are barely a half mile from her farm when she turns us down a winding dirt road. "Town is that way." She points in the opposite direction. "But I wanted you to see this place first."

The dirt road leads up to a small farmhouse. Smaller than Pam's, but it still boasts a barn and stables and looks like it weathered the blackout fairly well. "I was thinking you might want to check this place out. Maybe you could live here."

I raise a questioning eyebrow. "Live here?" I ask. "Pam, I don't plan on being here all that long. Plus, what would I do with a farm? I don't know anything about raising crops. I couldn't possibly run it myself."

"People around here help each other. We even pitch in to help new people start up their crops," she says. "Listen, I know you're not a farmer. But just give it a look. You know, for the future maybe."

I sigh. I get it now. I already feel like a third wheel and I've not even spent my first night in their house. I guess she doesn't want me getting too comfortable over there. I shouldn't blame her. They are newlyweds, after all. "Fine, I'll take a look," I say.

We ride up to the front and I park my bike. I walk around the side of the house and do a double take because I see laundry hanging from a clothesline, blowing softly in the mid-afternoon breeze. The sheets look clean so I doubt they've been hanging here very long. Anyway, it's ridiculous to think that after more than a year, laundry would even remain hanging like this.

"Pam, it looks like someone lives here already," I say, turning back to her. But she's gone. Maybe she went around to the other side of the house already. I continue on by the laundry and go around back. There is a lovely wrap-around porch on the back of the house and I climb the three steps to get up on it, still trying to find Pam. I look out over the fields that look newly planted. Darn, I guess that means this place is out of the question.

My eyes catch movement over by the stable and I see a horse walking around in the enclosed pen. My eyes bug out.

I know that horse.

My heart rate increases exponentially as I once again look around at my surroundings. I stare over at the drying laundry to see what I'd missed the first time. There, hanging among the linens in the breeze, is the pair of boxer briefs with that stupid smiley face.

My heart slams into my chest and before my brain fully has a chance to comprehend what is happening, I hear, "See something you like?"

I spin around and see him.

Mitch.

I close my eyes, squeezing them tightly shut, thinking this must be a dream. When I open them and focus on what is before me, I think . . . no, I'm *sure* . . . that seeing my Florida cowboy sitting on the porch railing, complete with his three-day stubble and wide-brimmed hat, holding a single rose, is without a doubt the sexiest thing I've ever seen in my entire life.

He stands and I run over to him, launching myself into his waiting arms. He kisses me like I'm his long-lost love. I kiss him like he's the sun and moon all rolled into one.

Then I think better of it and pull back, hitting him over and over in the chest as tears wet my face. "Why did you leave me? How could you do that? Do you know how hard it's been without you? Do you even know what I've been through? I thought you were gone . . ." As I go on and on, he puts me down and pulls my hair out of my ponytail and then tucks some strands behind my ear. He just stares at me like he's not sure I'm actually here. Like I might also be a dream.

Then I remember the last letter I wrote to him and my anger suddenly disappears. There is only one thing left to say. "Thank you." I lean in and feather kisses along his jaw. "Thank you for not going to California without me. Thank you for loving me enough to let me go. Thank you for letting me come back to you with no regrets."

The biggest smile I've ever seen takes over his face. "Can I talk now, sweetheart?"

"No," I say, right before I kiss him with all the passion, all the hope, all the want and need that's been percolating for the past few months without him.

He breaks our kiss, laughing as he puts an arm under my knees and another behind my back, picking me up as if my weight is of no consequence. He carries me through the back door and into the house that I don't bother to look at. Looking at his gorgeous face is all I want to do. I could live in a cardboard box and it wouldn't matter as long as he was with me. "I never left," he finally says. "It never even crossed my mind to leave you, Mikayla. But I didn't know any other way to give you and Jeff the chance to figure things out without me getting in the way. I owed him that much."

He places a kiss on my hair as he carries me up the stairs. "I made you a promise," he says. "I never stopped loving you. I never stopped being with you. I was always there. You just didn't know it."

I absorb what he is saying and suddenly, everything makes sense. "Oh, my God! It was *you* in the meadow that day, wasn't it?"

He nods his head.

"The colonel gave me a gun after that, you know."

He laughs. "Yeah, I know. His guys found me leaving the area and I swore them all to secrecy. I was a little more careful after that. I didn't want you to go shooting me. That would have ruined everything." He winks.

"He knew? The colonel knew you didn't leave?"

"After that, yes. But just him and the guys that found me. And of course Pam and Craig knew all along."

Another thought occurs to me. "Was it you at Pam's wedding; in the back with the ball cap on?"

He smiles his answer.

"Where else?" I ask, curious as to how he pulled it off without me knowing.

"I saw your home run," he says.

I look guiltily at the ground.

"No, it's okay," he says. "I'll admit it sucked having to watch him kiss you, but it was a necessary evil. I knew it had to happen."

My eyes snap to his. "I didn't sleep with him. I swear."

He laughs. "I know you didn't," he assures me. "I knew if you loved me even half as much as I loved you, you wouldn't be able to go through with it."

"That was an awfully big risk you took, Mitch. I had almost resigned myself to being with him."

His eyes burn deeply into mine. "It was worth the risk, Mikayla. Anything worth having this much is worth the risk."

At the top of the stairs, my caveman kicks the bedroom door open and I look in the room to see the bed embellished with red rose petals. It looks beautiful. It smells beautiful. I wonder how one man can be so perfect. I giggle. "Bit of a foregone conclusion, wasn't I," I say.

"Sweetheart, there was never going to be any other conclusion for us," he says, as we both study the bed and then each other, our carnal needs seeping from every pore.

I reach a hand up to weave it into his magnificent hair. My fingers then trail down to his neck, enjoying the feel of his rapidly increasing pulse before moving on to his strong shoulders. My hands on him have the desired effect and he looks at me with hooded eyes. His smoldering stare tells me just what's in store for me.

Oh, yes, please!

He lays me on the bed and the fragrant scent of the roses further heightens my senses as I watch him quickly remove his clothing. He then takes his time with mine, starting at my feet, taking off each shoe and working his way seductively up to the button on my jeans. He hasn't even rid me of my clothing yet, but fire shoots through my body as heat and desire pool within me.

When he finally has me stripped naked, he assesses me appreciatively and says, "I love your body." His lips feather kisses down my neck. "I love your mind," he whispers in my ear. He gets closer to my chest, licking into my cleavage as he murmurs, "I love your soul." He purposefully avoids the place I need him to touch so I nudge his head over to my breast and feel him smile against my skin before taking it into his mouth.

My head falls back against the pillow as his hypnotic mouth draws out tiny darts of pleasurable pain when he nips at me. He stops briefly, saying, "I need to *see* you when I do this to you, sweetheart."

I lift my head and look down at him. He resumes the teasing flutters of his tongue and I gulp at the intoxicating sensation of watching him watch me as he does it. "I need to *hear* you when I do this to you," he says. A slave to his command, I moan out his name over and over as my fingers weave and tug at his hair.

He works his way down my body silently claiming me with every touch. Just before his mouth finds the most sensitive part of me, he demands, "Tell me you want me, Mikayla. I need to hear you say it."

"God, yes!" I nearly scream with carnal anticipation. "I want you, Mitch . . . please!"

Moments later, I cry out again under the lashing of his tongue that is coaxing my body to the brink of orgasm. I can tell from the sexy sounds coming from his throat that he is just as happy giving me pleasure as I am to be receiving it. I reach my peak with a violent shudder while my hands tear at the sheets and I shout out praises of his masterful skills.

When he has finished milking every last quiver out of me, he crawls up my body. He takes my hands and pins them to the mattress along the sides of my head, holding me captive and controlling me completely. He speaks declarations of my beauty and tells me how perfect I feel under him. "I will never make love to anyone else. Only you. You own me," he says.

And as he enters me and we consummate our forever, he looks deep into my eyes, into my very soul and says, "Marry me, Mikayla Parker."

Unsure if the tears I feel on my face are my own, I answer, "Yes, of course, yes!"

He smiles, filling me with unencumbered love and passion when he says, "Promise?"

Epilogue

Dear Jeff,

I know, I know—call me old fashioned, but sometimes I just like to feel the way a pen rolls across a piece of paper. You know better than anyone how that year changed me. I mean, I still run my practice out of the converted barn out back. But it works for me. It works for us. Just as the fast-paced life of Atlanta works for you and Holly.

Mitch can't stop talking about your upcoming guys' outing and how excited he is to be flying up to the mountains to go hiking this year. Thanks for including his brother. It means a lot to him.

I cannot wait to see Holly in all her pregnant glory when she and Parker get here to spend the week with us. You could have knocked me over with a feather when she told me that you'd decided on a second baby. Parker is sure to have a gorgeous little sibling.

How's my godson doing, by the way? I can't believe he's going to middle school soon. It seems like just yesterday that Taylor was teaching him how to ride a bike during our summer vacations together.

Speaking of your goddaughter, Taylor has her first boyfriend and it's about sending Mitch to the looney bin. He is so protective of her. She is most definitely a daddy's girl, just as M.J. is my little mama's boy.

Taylor asked me again the other day to tell her the story of how she got her name. One day, when she's older, I'll give her the full, unabridged version, but at age 14 she's still too young to understand how one woman could love two men. When she's ready to hear it, I'll tell her that her dad and her godfather are the two great loves of my life. I'll tell her how grateful I will always be that you sent Mitch to find me. But, most importantly, she'll learn to never give up; never settle; and always keep fighting for her forever-love.

I'm not sure our children will ever be able to fully understand the bond that we all share—you, me, Mitch and Holly. I can only hope that they are so fortunate to have relationships like ours when they grow up.

All I know is that I'm the luckiest girl in the world to have such incredible people in my life.

See you soon and love you always,

Mikayla Matheson

Samantha Christy

Acknowledgments

There are so many people to thank as I wrap up the writing of this, my third novel. As always, I have to first and foremost thank my family. The life of a writer is an interesting existence. I once read that writers never go on vacation because they are either writing about something or thinking of writing about something. It's true. I had every intention of taking a nice long break over the holidays. Then inspiration struck. When that happens, there is no turning back. My family has gotten used to me disappearing for hours and sometimes days at a time until I get out on paper all of the ideas that constantly float around in my head.

So, thanks to my husband, Bruce, who is also my best friend and biggest cheerleader when it comes to my writing and every other dream I've dared to chase. To my youngest children, Kaitlyn and Ryan, who have learned to master homework without Mom's help; something I may have felt guilty about early on, but now realize is one of the best gifts I could have given them—self-sufficiency. And to my two oldest, Dylan and Austin, who both left the nest this year to pursue the world of advanced education, I couldn't be any more proud of them if they had left to explore the moon.

To my editors Jeannie Hinkle and Ann Peters who have been with me for all three novels and still haven't complained about getting bored. Your eagle eyes are invaluable and forever appreciated.

To my beta readers, Tammy Dixon, Sarina Wiechens and Debbie Doran, without your commitment to reading, re-reading and re-re-reading, this novel wouldn't be anything more than mere words on pages. You helped me organize, rearrange, reword, and rethink to the point of sheer insanity. Thank you just doesn't seem enough.

Lastly, to my readers, some of whom are now starting to follow me and ask when my next book is coming out. My answer will always be—soon. Because, as I already mentioned, I don't take vacations from writing.

About the Author

Samantha Christy's passion for writing started long before her first novel was published. Graduating from the University of Nebraska with a degree in Criminal Justice, she held the title of Computer Systems Analyst for The Supreme Court of Wisconsin and several major universities around the United States. Raised mainly in Indianapolis, she holds the Midwest and its homegrown values dear to her heart and upon the birth of her third child devoted herself to raising her family full time. While it took time to get from there to here, writing has remained her utmost passion and being a stay-at-home mom facilitated her ability to follow that dream.

When she is not writing, she keeps busy cruising to every Caribbean island where ships sail. Samantha Christy currently resides in St. Augustine, Florida with her husband and four children.

You can reach Samantha Christy at any of these wonderful places:

Website: www.samanthachristy.com
Facebook: https://www.facebook.com/SamanthaChristyAuthor
Twitter: @SamLoves2Write
E-mail: samanthachristy@comcast.net

Made in the USA
San Bernardino, CA
21 July 2017